C   ng

ASHLEY LISTER

Raven and Skull

Fiction to die for

Published by Caffeine Nights Publishing 2016

Copyright © Ashley Lister 2016

Ashley Lister has asserted his rights under the Copyright, Designs and
Patents Act 1998 to be identified as the author of this work

Published in Great Britain by
Caffeine Nights Publishing
4 Eton Close
Walderslade
Chatham
Kent
ME5 9AT

www.caffeinenights.com

British Library Cataloguing in Publication Data.
A CIP catalogue record for this book is available from the British Library
ISBN: 978-1-910720-53-0

Cover design by
Mark (Wills) Williams

Everything else by
Default, Luck and Accident

To Tracy, love always

Acknowledgement:

I couldn't have written this book without support from a lot of friends and family: too many to name individually. It would also have been impossible to write this story without the inspiration of so many writing students who've taken the time to share their work with me. Thank you all.

Raven and Skull

'Tell us about a time you nearly died, Tony.'

Heather's suggestion was greeted by a barrage of laughter.

There were half a dozen of them sitting around the table – the last souls left in an otherwise empty bar. Drained beer bottles and lipstick-smudged glasses stood between them like abstract monuments to the memories of good times gone. The darkness outside the bar window was fading to the apocalyptic grey of another dawn.

Tony glanced at his five colleagues and flashed an automatic grin. He hadn't yet drunk enough beer to be light-headed, but he could feel the mood around the table was shifting. The evening had started as an early weekend escape from the offices of Raven and Skull; a two fingered salute to the workplace in the time-honoured tradition of every godforsaken Friday. After a grim week working nine-to-five – a grimmer week than any of them were used to suffering – Geoff's idea that they should get pissed and have a laugh together had seemed like a stroke of pure genius. But now, whilst the maudlin veil of melancholy felt like it was finally lifting, Tony thought it was revealing something strange, unpleasant and potentially dangerous.

It was no surprise that they were talking about death.

Given the events of the previous week it would have been more surprising if that topic hadn't come up. But the fact that they were laughing about the subject seemed somehow unnatural, twisted and grisly.

'Go on,' Becky encouraged.

Out of all of them, Becky looked the worst for wear after a night on the sauce. Geoff had nudged a glass of red down her white blouse, leaving a bloody stain over her right breast. Her usual pristine office composure had been destroyed as the night dragged her downwards. She now wore snagged tights and a snapped heel. With her hair awry and her eye make-up smeared, she looked like she had fought her way off a mortician's slab. Smiling blearily, and clearly unaware of how wrecked her appearance was, Becky slurred her words when she repeated her request. 'Go on, Tony. Tell us a story.'

'Someone get the next round,' Tony decided. 'And I'll tell you a story.' He raised a warning finger as Geoff disappeared in the direction of the bar. Glancing purposefully at Heather, he said, 'But I won't tell you about a time I nearly died. I'll tell you about a time when I thought I was going to die…'

Wednesday night I worked late. Ordinarily I'm the first person out of the office come five thirty. The idea of staying on to catch up with work is unheard of. But, with us being hit by three deaths in that one week, I was trying to clear a backlog of my own work and struggling to organise interviews, redistribute accounts, deal with client apology letters and get on top of all the rest of that miserable nonsense. I'd locked myself in the boardroom on the fourteenth floor and I was working with four laptops and the active paper files for Chloe, Nicola and Shaun.'

Geoff had brought a tray with fresh drinks. When those three names were mentioned all six of the colleagues raised their glasses in silent toast to the memories of Chloe, Nicola and Shaun.

Tony took a deep breath before continuing. 'I'd got my iPod playing,' he admitted. 'I don't normally use the thing whilst I'm supposed to be working but I figured it was late, I was alone in the building, and there was no chance I was going to miss a call or not hear someone talking to me. And I think it was helping me to get through the work more effectively. I'd got it tuned into my classical tracks, I was listening to Saint-Saëns' Danse Macabre, and the job was moving along with surprising speed. I was lost in my own little world of file allocations, schedules and prioritising.' He drew a deep breath and said, 'I looked up from my paperwork and almost shit my pants. Moira was standing over me.'

Heather laughed.

Becky sprayed a mouthful of red onto her skirt. The droplets looked like something from the blood spatter analysis of an inner city's forensic laboratory.

Geoff sat back in his seat, chuckling.

Cindy and Richard pressed close together in their single seat. They smiled approval and nodded for Tony to continue.

'I hadn't realised Moira was in the building,' Tony went on. 'I hadn't thought there was anyone in the building. The iPod, and my involvement in the files had created a vacuum where nothing else existed. And so, when I looked up and saw that stone-faced old hag from accounts glowering down at me, I came close to having a heart attack. I pulled the earphones out of my ear and tried not to look like I'd just soiled myself…'

'Mr Wade,' Moira began.

She had the sort of raspy voice that suggested a lifetime of smoking and lungs the colour of a tramp's underpants. Tony could hear every syllable struggling to make its way through layers of yellowing phlegm and tar-blackened bronchioles as Moira gasped his name in her gravel-strewn death rattle.

'I'm glad I found you here alone, Mr Wade. I've been wanting to talk to someone from management.'

Tony pointed to a seat and waited for Moira to sit down. His heart pounded from the surprise of discovering he wasn't alone in the building. He didn't particularly want to talk with Moira – ideally he would have been happier finishing his work and going home – but there was no polite way to dismiss her from the office without causing offence. Telling himself that a break from the workload might not be such a bad idea, he stretched his neck until it cracked and then he settled back in his chair.

'What's the problem, Moira?'

Silence.

He could hear the sounds of the office around him as the building breathed. The heavy sigh of an expectant printer, the constant whisper of fluorescents above, and the tinny faraway crackle of Saint-Saëns' *Danse Macabre* building to its distant conclusion from his iPod speakers. He studied her eyes – the whites turned rheumy yellow and the pupils a black that was unnervingly deep – and waited for a response. Although Moira had been with the office since he began working there, it was the first time he had sat in the same room with the woman and studied her at such close proximity. Her hair was a tangle of grey barbs. Her face was a relief map of porous flesh and ravine-deep wrinkles. There was a wart on her jawline, a gnarled lump of discoloured flesh sprouting a dozen short black hairs. Tony thought the hairs looked like insect legs wriggling from beneath her skin. Previously, he had thought Moira was another of the forgotten office drones; a dinosaur from accounts plodding towards extinction. But staring into her eyes, he got the impression that she might be far more than he had ever imagined. The thought trailed an icy finger down his spine.

'What's the problem, Moira? What did you want to talk about?'

'I think I might have killed them.'

In her raspy, cancerous voice, Moira's admission sounded gruesome. Tony's smile faltered and he fumbled with the iPod for a moment to silence the nuisance of the whispered music.

'Killed them? Killed who?'

'Chloe. Nicola. Shaun. I think I killed them.'

'They weren't murdered,' Tony reminded her. He wasn't sure what he had expected when Moira appeared in his office but this confession was so far removed from his expectations he found himself doing mental gymnastics as he tried to understand what she was saying. 'Chloe had that unfortunate encounter with her boyfriend, Nicola had–'

'I know *how* they died, Mr Wade,' Moira rasped. She didn't bother to hide her impatience. She sat close enough so Tony could smell the foetid scent of her breath when she spat the words. The pungent fragrance reminded him of sweat-stained sickbeds.

'I know that they died of *supposedly* natural causes,' Moira assured him. 'But I still think I might have killed them. I think I might have killed all of them. And more besides. I think that's what I do for Raven and Skull.'

'Why do you think that?'

'I've been knitting.'

This time Tony knew he was responsible for the protracted silence. He tried to work out if Moira's comment was as absurd as it initially sounded, or if he could possibly be overlooking something obvious.

'You've been knitting?' The conversation had the surreal headiness of something from an art movie or a badly translated foreign language sitcom. He understood the words but the meaning behind those words was just a little bit beyond his grasp. Tony closed his eyes and rubbed the heel of one hand against his forehead. For a brief instant he expected Moira to have disappeared when he opened his eyes. To his disappointment, he found her still sitting there and facing him. Drawing a deep breath, he said, 'You've been knitting. And you think that killed Chloe, Nicola and Shaun?'

Moira nodded.

Forcing himself to appear patient, Tony asked, 'Why would you think that, Moira? You'll have to explain it to me because I can't quite see the connection.'

She graced him with a look of contempt that he had seen before. It was the same belligerent question he had seen in the eyes of too many lesser ranking employees who were either disgruntled or disappointed. It was a silent expression that asked, '*How did you get to be in such a responsible position when you know so little?*' Since moving up to management level Tony had become used to receiving the expression. It was most often shot at him during disciplinary hearings and assessment reviews.

'I knitted for each of them,' Moira began. She lowered her gaze to the file-cluttered surface of the boardroom table. Her creased and time-rumpled features looked painfully heavy. 'I knitted for Chloe, Nicola and Shaun,' she murmured. 'And now they're all dead. It's my fault.' She hitched a breath – the sound of an ugly animal in pain – and then raised her gaze to meet Tony's. 'Have you ever heard of the Fates?'

She was making no sense and was jumping sporadically from one topic to another. Tony wondered if she was always like this or if this evening's irrationality might be symptomatic of some condition. If he had known her a little better he would have felt qualified to judge. Because this was proving to be the longest conversation he'd ever had with Moira, he felt cruel deciding she was a headcase just because her way of speaking didn't perfectly match his expectations.

'The Fates?' he repeated. He wondered if it might be a brand of knitting wool or maybe some pop group from a bygone era with which she was more familiar. Either seemed likely and promised to make as much sense as anything else in this abstract conversation. Glancing slyly at one of the open laptops on his desk, noting that the time was getting late, he fixed his smile into a rictus of forced politeness and said, 'No, Moira. I don't think I have heard of the Fates. What are they?'

'The Greeks called them the Fates. Clotho. Lachesis. Atropos.'

Tony said nothing. He was trying to think of a way to get Moira to leave the office so that he could finish the remainder of his work and then puzzle about the new problem of the woman from accounts and her questionable sanity.

'The Fates controlled every destiny. Clotho span the thread of life. Lachesis measured the length of each thread. Atropos cut the thread with her abhorrèd shears.'

'*One of us is fucking crazy, Moira,*' Tony thought. He wondered if the crazy person in the room was the one spouting rubbish about Greek mythology or the one sat listening to her instead of getting on with a demanding workload of unpaid overtime.

'Clotho, Lachesis and Atropos,' Moira repeated.

Tony didn't know why but those names conjured up images of three haggard crones bent over with age and the weight of their onerous tasks. It was easy to see them as the witches from Macbeth with their plotting, cursing and general doom prophecies. A rash of goosebumps tickled down his forearms.

'Greek gods,' he said, nodding. 'Is that who they were, yes?'

'No.' She regarded him with another sneer of contempt. 'The Fates weren't *mere gods.*' She spat the final two words with a disgust that was palpable. 'The Fates were so powerful that even the gods feared them.'

'And what does this have to do with–'

'The Fates had the perfect system,' Moira broke in. 'Clotho span the thread of life. Clotho was responsible for the quality and colour of each person's life. Lachesis used her measuring rod to decide how long each person's allotted time would be. And Atropos ended each of those lives with her abhorrèd shears.'

'*Abhorrèd shears,*' Tony thought. '*That's twice she's said that now.*' He didn't like the phrase – it made him want to shiver and shift in his seat. 'I still don't see what these three–'

'They were like the Holy Trinity,' she exclaimed. 'The Father, the Son and the Holy Spirit: one in essence.' Her low, raspy voice had increased in pitch and volume.

Listening to her, Tony had the lunatic idea that he was hearing something older than time. There was the mad thought at the back of his mind that, if he concentrated just a little harder, all her words would begin to make sense and he might stumble on truths he had never really wished to uncover. He rubbed his forehead again.

'It's been a long day,' he began, wearily. 'And you must think I'm a real idiot for not getting this straight away. But I don't know how your knitting and these three gods–'

'Fates!'

'–Fates,' he amended, 'all tie together with Chloe, Nicola and Shaun's deaths.' He flexed a grin that was meant to inspire sympathy and maybe some understanding.

Moira stared at him with dead black eyes.

'What am I missing?'

'I think I'm the Fates,' Moira told him. Her voice had returned to its previous tone. She spoke in a low, coarse whisper. 'I'm the essence of Clotho, Lachesis and Atropos.'

Tony nodded and tried to present a facade that was solemn with sympathy and sage understanding. *'Nutty as a fucking fruitcake,'* he decided. First thing in the morning he was going to send a memo to human resources and have them arrange a leave of absence for Moira. If there was any way of insisting on a psychiatric evaluation before she was allowed to return to the office then he was going to make that recommendation too.

'Last week I took it upon myself to knit Chloe a woolly jumper,' Moira said, earnestly.

Tony glanced at the open laptops and realised his overtime was now a lost cause. It would take the best part of an hour after he was rid of Moira to get his thoughts back to the zone where they had been when he was reorganising schedules and remembering the technicalities of all the clients being dealt with by Chloe, Nicola and Shaun. The thought was disheartening and he had to make a physical effort not to show his anger to Moira.

'I'd thought she looked cold,' Moira continued. 'I know it's fashionable for young girls to wear short skirts and next to nothing in the way of clothes, but Chloe always looked chilly because of it.'

'Chloe died of extensive head trauma,' Tony said, softly.

Moira wasn't listening. 'I remember cutting the final thread for her jumper at ten o'clock on Sunday night. Last Sunday night. The news had just come on the telly. When I close my eyes I can still hear the theme tune to the news. That and the rusty snipping sound of those abhorrèd shears.'

Tony studied her, warily.

'When I came into the office on Monday, I had the jumper wrapped up in a parcel for her. Nicola was crying and she told me that Chloe had died the previous night. She told me that Chloe had died at ten o'clock – just when I was cutting her thread.' Moira stayed silent for a moment, allowing Tony to digest what she had said.

He shook his head. 'No. That's just coincidence.' The acoustics in the boardroom stopped his words from carrying any real conviction.

'Nicola asked me what was in the parcel,' Moira continued. Her low and raspy voice was now a flat monotone. There was no inflection of remorse or upset in the way she spoke. She was either mechanically reiterating facts or she had simply stopped caring. 'Nicola thought the wool I'd used on Chloe's jumper was lovely. It was a lilac cashmere. She asked if I had any left and, when I said I had a little, she asked if I could knit a beret for her.'

Tony shifted uneasily in his chair.

Moira's level gaze remained fixed on him. 'I finished knitting that beret on the Monday night. Do you know what time I finished?'

'I really think you're making–'

'Do you know what time I finished? Do you know what time I cut her thread with my abhorrèd shears?'

Tony thought, '*Stop saying those words!*'

Aloud he said, 'Nicola died at six o'clock. She was hit by a train and died instantly.'

'That's when I finished her beret.'

Her lips parted and the corners twisted upwards. Tony saw that she was attempting a hideous parody of a smile. The result made him nauseous.

'Are you starting to believe me, Mr Wade?'

He coughed and cleared his throat. 'This is foolishness, Moira.' He tried to inject an appropriate note of authority into his voice but it refused to ring with any real conviction. 'This is nothing more than coincidence and, if you sat down and thought about it, you'd realise that I'm right. You're not these Greek gods–'

16

'Fates!'

'–Fates. You're not these Greek Fates. You're just Moira from accounts who enjoys knitting in her spare time. You've obviously been upset by the death of your colleagues. We've all been upset and we're all grieving. But I think you could use the help of a counsellor. I'm going to recommend to human resources that they arrange for–'

'I figured it out with Nicola,' Moira told him.

Her words killed everything Tony had been about to say.

'When Nicola died at six o'clock, the same time I was cutting her thread, I knew my knitting was responsible for her death. I found out about it on the Tuesday. I was sick to the stomach thinking that I'd done that to her and I wondered how I could prove it and how I could try to make amends. That was when I started to knit a scarf for Shaun.'

Tony simply stared at her.

'You can write a reprimand for me if you like,' Moira went on. 'But I didn't bother doing any work for the office that morning. I simply picked up my needles and pulled out some black wool I'd brought with me. I thought about Shaun because – well...' Her level gaze skewered Tony to his seat. '...I'm sure you can understand why I chose Shaun.'

The smile had disappeared from her face. She now wore an expression of cold intensity. 'I saw him smirking at the water cooler. He'd just made a crass remark about Nicola catching the train. He was talking to that nice girl Heather and she looked appalled by his insensitivity. That's why I picked on him. I told him I was going to knit him a scarf to keep himself warm now winter was approaching. He said he wanted one as long as his cock, so he suggested I should go out and get some more wool. Then he laughed in that cruel and nasty way of his. It made me more anxious to knit the scarf for him. I've never done any knitting as industrious as that. If I had any sense for the fanciful I'd be telling you that sparks were flying from the tips of my needles as they clashed together. I really was working at a blistering speed but I think, if anyone had seen me, they would have just noticed an old woman with her knitting, making a rather formal scarf. I cut his thread exactly at noon. Do you remember what time Shaun died, Mr Wade? I think you do remember because you were the one who spoke to the police about the incident, weren't you?'

'The lift malfunctioned at noon,' Tony said, quietly.

'Noon,' Moira repeated. 'I cut his thread at noon and I killed him.'

'No.' Tony shook his head. 'I refuse to accept that this is anything more than coincidence. You're just–'

'Would you like me to knit you something, Mr Wade?'

'Oh-mi-God!' Becky said. 'What did you do?'

Tony took a swig from his pint and grimaced at the bitter taste. The light outside the pub windows hadn't changed since he began his story. The world still seemed to be painted with the prospect of a terrible dawn.

'What else could I do?' he asked. 'If I'd told her not to knit anything for me, that would have been as good as admitting she was right. That would have been like saying I believed her stupid story about Clotho, Lachesis and—'

'What did you do?' Heather asked.

'I told her to go ahead.' He stared at his friend defiantly. 'I told her to knit me a woolly hat, or a scarf or a jumper or whatever it would take to prove to her that I didn't believe she was the Fates.'

The silence around the table was stifling.

Even Cindy and Richard — usually so absorbed in each other, constantly passing whispered confidences back and forth — sat silent. They watched Tony expectantly.

'She knitted you one?'

'Is that the one?' Becky asked, pointing to the black scarf draped over his jacket in an empty seat. 'Is that the scarf she knitted for you?'

'She's knitting me one,' Tony corrected. He stared at the scarf, puzzled, and wondered how it had found its way there. 'I told her there was no rush.' He raised his wrist and glanced at his watch. 'She agreed to have it ready for Friday night or Saturday morning, so that means…' He shook his wrist and then slapped the heel of his palm against the watch. 'Damned thing's stopped working,' he muttered. 'Batteries must have gone. Or—'

'Which one is Moira?' asked Geoff.

'Yeah,' Becky agreed. 'I don't remember any Moira in accounts. I thought the only woman there was that Muslim woman.'

'No,' Geoff argued. 'There's no Muslim woman in accounts. It's all men—'

'Except for Moira,' Tony interjected. 'She's the one who…' His voice trailed off. He had been about to point out that they all knew who Moira was. She had knitted the black scarf for him and the gloves for Geoff and the matching cardigans for Becky and Cindy. He wanted to say those things

because he felt sure they were true but something stopped him. Voicing those thoughts would be tantamount to heresy and would destroy an illusion.

'I don't even think—'

'Another story,' Heather said. 'I want another story.'

Cindy and Richard groaned.

'Go on, Becky,' Heather said. 'Tell us about a time when you nearly died...'

Becky raised her freshly replenished glass into the air. 'I need to dedicate this story to the memory of Shaun,' she announced.

'To Shaun,' they muttered, in mildly drunken unison. Heather's wine glass connected with Geoff's bottle of Löwenbräu. The sound was as shrill as a smashing windscreen. Cindy and Richard giggled instead of repeating the toast. Everyone took a sip of their drinks before coaxing Becky to continue.

'I need to dedicate this story to his memory,' Becky explained, 'because I think it's important we all remember what a despicable and loathsome piece of shit the bastard was. I know it's not the done thing to speak ill of the dead, but Shaun was one of those bastards who deserved his death and should have had it come a lot sooner.'

'Let's get that engraved on his tombstone,' Geoff suggested.

'I was planning to use the same phrase in his obituary,' Tony grinned.

Becky said, 'I'm only sorry he didn't suffer more. It was Shaun who was supposed to be looking after me when I started doing overtime...'

As soon as the clock shifted past five-thirty, Becky's stomach clenched and her bowels grew tight. It was hard to explain why, but being in the office after normal hours seemed somehow strange, different and wrong. In the minute between the clock creeping from five thirty to five thirty-one, Becky could feel the shadows lengthening and the room's light changing to a more sinister hue. She thought the effect was like being in an empty house without the owner's permission, or being in a cemetery when there wasn't a funeral.

'This is the biggest and best skive going,' Shaun said cheerfully. He was a broad-shouldered office boor. With a shock of dark hair contrasting with his pale complexion, and sharp dark eyes appraising her in an overly familiar fashion, he managed to appear both attractive and repulsive in equal measures. 'We get to sit around doing fuck all and we get paid time and a half. What could be better than that? Apart from sex?'

Becky tried to match his enthusiasm but the knot of unease tightened in her belly. The effort of smiling was an arduous strain and the urge to grab her coat and bolt from the offices of Raven and Skull was almost irresistible. It didn't help that Shaun's language was offensively colourful – richer than she cared to hear. It also added to her discomfort that he was blatantly leering at her breasts whilst he spoke. She was a cuddly size sixteen, blessed with a chest size that was not disproportionate for her large frame, and Shaun was staring at her cleavage as though her breasts were tattooed with next week's winning lottery numbers.

'The only thing you've got to watch out for is Harry Shaw,' Shaun told her breasts. 'He's got a habit of trying to get his hands on every new recruit to the overtime gravy-train and you'll probably be prime pickings for him during this first month.'

Becky nodded and said nothing. She didn't consider herself worldly but she had heard enough stories in her time to be aware that Shaun was building up to some sort of fib. She also wasn't sure that either of her breasts wanted to hear about Harry Shaw, whoever Harry Shaw might be.

'Right,' she agreed. 'Harry Shaw. I'll watch out for him.'

With that, said she took off from Shaun's desk and joined Nicola and Chloe by the water cooler. She knew the two girls as casual acquaintances from her days in the office and from the occasional girls' night out with the rest of the office staff.

Nicola looked to be the taller of the two women but that was only because she was so anorexically thin. Outside the office, Becky had seen Nicola wearing a pair of hipster jeans that were no larger than a size two and cut low enough to reveal a stomach that was so childishly flat it was almost concave. In the office, she wore the traditional uniform of a black skirt and white blouse but she made the clothes look as though they had been tailored to fit her stick-like figure. Chloe, big breasted and blessed with the sort of curves that made Nicola look like a boy, wore identical clothes. Despite their Laurel and Hardy size difference, Becky knew the two women were inseparable friends. Outside the office, seeing them together was more common than seeing them apart. Inside the office, it was unheard of for them to be away from each other.

Chloe and Nicola welcomed Becky with obvious sympathy when they saw she was trying to escape from Shaun. Nicola made a hospitable gesture whilst Chloe snatched a fresh plastic carton from the water cooler's dispenser and began to pour Becky a drink. They chatted easily for a moment; Chloe explaining that they had to drink water during overtime because the use of a kettle wasn't allowed; Nicola saying that the only unlocked lavatories in the building during overtime were those situated in the basement. Becky took all this in and grimly accepted that the world of overtime was drastically different to the normality of the office life that she had grown to know and understand.

'What's Captain Creepy up to this time?' Chloe asked. 'I saw him getting an eyeful of your rack.'

Nicola threw a disdainful glance in Shaun's direction and said, 'He's not trying to show you his cock again, is he?' She shivered theatrically and said, 'How any man can be proud of three inches of spotted dick is beyond me.'

Chloe handed Becky a carton of water. 'I've spoken to Tony about that arsehole. I swear, if he doesn't do something soon, I'm going to put in an official report to human resources about sexual harassment. I might even go to Roger Black about the situation.'

'He wasn't trying to show me his… his… anything,' Becky whispered. Although she didn't like Shaun she didn't want him to know she was talking about him. 'He was just telling me to watch out for someone called Harry Shaw.'

Chloe rolled her eyes.

Nicola cast another disparaging glance in Shaun's direction.

'I swear,' Chloe began, 'if that cock-focused pillock isn't taken off this overtime rota I'm going to get my boyfriend to sort him out properly.'

'You'd do that?' Nicola sounded surprised and enthusiastic.

Becky watched the exchange with growing bewilderment.

'Your Kevin is pretty tough,' Nicola went on. 'He'd snap Shaun into small pieces.' She lowered her voice to a conspiratorial whisper and said, 'I'm serious, Chloe. Your Kevin could genuinely kill someone like Shaun.

Genuinely.'

'And wouldn't that be a great loss,' Chloe muttered.

'Who is Harry Shaw?'

Chloe and Nicola exchanged a glance. 'Get sorted with your work for the night,' Chloe said. 'Let Captain Creepy go through the process of telling you what you're supposed to be doing. Me and Nicky have a water break every hour or so and one of us will come and find you. Then we'll fill you in on Harry Shaw.'

Becky thanked them both.

'Go on,' Nicola said, nodding in Shaun's direction. 'Go and give him his fifteen minutes of glory as he explains that overtime is just playing catch-up for the constant backlog of paperwork that comes from customer services.'

'And,' Chloe broke in, 'if he starts off with his Harry Shaw bullshit, tell him you're not arsed about his fucking ghost stories and you just want to know what you're supposed to be doing.' She said the words in such a loud voice Becky knew they would be carrying across the office towards Shaun.

Glancing at him, poring over a ream of paperwork, she saw his smile tighten to an unpleasant grimace. His eyes were small, dark and mean. His fat fingers clutched tight around a thick pen.

'I'm so fucking serious,' Chloe told Nicola. 'I'm so tempted to get Kevin to meet him in a dark alley one night.'

'If Kevin wants an alibi,' Nicola said, 'I can always get Don to say he was round at The House of Usher.'

Becky remembered that Don was the head chef at a restaurant called The House of Usher. She smiled at the way Nicola always managed to slip the name of her boyfriend's restaurant into every conversation.

'All we'd need to do is get his credit card there and, with Don and his waiters backing up the story, it would look like he'd spent the night at the restaurant.'

Becky stepped away from them. She couldn't decide whether their planning was serious, or whether it was just typical overtime bravado and banter. Sauntering back to Shaun, sipping at her carton of water, she asked, 'What am I supposed to be working on?'

'You want to be careful hanging round with those two bitches,' Shaun sniffed. 'They're a pair of poisonous cunts.'

Becky swallowed. She couldn't think of how to respond to such a vitriolic exclamation. 'What am I supposed to be working on?'

Shaun pointed at her desk. 'There's a night's work in your in-tray. Geoff Arnold wants us to do some work getting his department's books ready for the year-end but he can suck my big fat cock. The stuff in your in-tray comes from a Customer Services backlog. Get started on that. If there's anything you don't understand go and ask one of those whores.' He flicked his head towards the water cooler where Chloe and Nicola still stood. Raising his gaze from the work on his desk he glared at Becky and said, 'If you end up getting caught by Harry Shaw, don't bother asking why I didn't warn you about him.'

Who the hell is Harry Shaw?

Becky didn't ask the question. Instead, realising Shaun had dismissed her, she started towards her desk. It was only as an afterthought that she made the grim discovery that the strangeness of working overtime was now a minor consideration. The shadows had stretched to breaking point. The office windows were darkened to a deathly pall that overlooked the grey remnants of the world's end. And, with other considerations to worry about, the environment now seemed terribly normal.

7

'Here,' Chloe said, handing Becky a carton of water.

Nicola pulled a chair from the neighbouring cubicle and the two women settled themselves on either side of Becky.

'How's the work?' Nicola asked.

Becky shrugged. 'Mind-numbing.'

Chloe laughed. 'Has that arsehole been troubling you?' She glanced towards Shaun's desk as she spoke. She made no attempt to lower her voice or disguise the fact that she was talking about him.

Becky shook her head. 'He just pointed at the workload and told me to get on with it.' As she said the words, Shaun glanced up and glowered at the three of them. Becky lowered her voice and said, 'You two don't like him much do you?'

'And you do?' Chloe challenged.

'He's a bit abrasive,' Becky allowed. 'But that's probably just his way.' She tried to toss a sympathetic smile in Shaun's direction but he wasn't looking. She became aware that Nicola and Chloe were staring at her with wide-eyed disbelief.

'Are you serious?'

'Do you know what he did to Chloe?'

Chloe made shushing sounds but Nicola seemed determined to make her point. Her cheeks were flushed with angry colour. 'I'm surprised Shaun didn't get sacked for that. I'm mightily pissed that Tony never pressed charges. That was genuine harassment.'

'I don't want you talking about this,' Chloe warned Nicola.

'What did he do?' Becky asked.

'Don't,' Chloe insisted.

Nicola ignored her. 'Shaun set up a webcam in the ladies' loo.'

Becky placed a horrified hand over her mouth. Now Chloe was blushing and glaring at Nicola with unconcealed venom. 'I'm trying to put that behind me.'

'Yeah,' Nicola agreed. 'And he was putting your behind on the internet, wasn't he? Chloe takes a dump on pervs-dot-com and

Shaun gets a big chuckle from the lads in this place for being so bold as to capture it on camera.'

'You're not serious,' Becky gasped.

'I don't want to talk about this,' Chloe decided.

'Aside from that,' Nicola went on. 'Shaun's taken a shot at feeling up every girl on overtime. He's spread rumours about every one that's knocked him back—'

'Which is most of them,' Chloe interrupted.

'—and the rumours are all pretty sick and twisted.'

'This is terrible,' Becky said.

'But he's not tried anything with you yet?'

Becky shook her head. 'He seemed pretty angry that I was talking with you two. Maybe that's killed his appetite for doing anything?'

'I doubt that very much,' Nicola said, bitterly. 'Only a serious beating could kill that bastard's appetite.'

Becky went cold. She didn't like the overtime atmosphere and she was determined this would be her last night working late at the office. Nicola obviously had no qualms about having Shaun beaten by Chloe's boyfriend. If what she had been told was true, Becky could feel herself beginning to believe that the action might be justified. The idea that a part of her found violence acceptable was a horrific discovery and she wanted to get away from the environment that had allowed her to think such unthinkable thoughts.

A frown furrowed Nicola's brow and she studied Becky with sudden concern. 'Did you check your seat before you sat down to work?'

'Why on earth would I do that?'

Nicola and Chloe exchanged a glance.

Chloe touched Becky's thigh and motioned her to move her chair backwards. Puzzled, Becky did as she was told. Nicola slid out of her chair and squatted on her haunches. With one arm she reached into the kneehole beneath the desk.

'Bastard,' she muttered.

Becky frowned.

'He hasn't has he?' Chloe hissed.

Nicola nodded. She reached deeper into the kneehole and pulled her hand down hard. There was a ripping sound that was almost muffled by Chloe's gasp of shock. Becky watched, intrigued, as Nicola pulled out a webcam from beneath the desk.

'What the–?'

'A fucking webcam?' Chloe marvelled. 'Another fucking webcam?'

Becky felt ill. She didn't know much about webcams but she could guess that its single eye had been staring up her skirt and between her thighs. Her stomach folded with disgust as she thought about the sight of her crotch being viewed by Shaun's camera.

'The dirty–'

'I'm going to deal with this,' Chloe snapped. She was reaching into her handbag and removing her mobile. As she flipped it open, Shaun glanced across at the three of them.

'No mobiles during overtime!'

'Pervert,' hissed Nicola. She kept her voice lowered so he couldn't hear what she said.

'We're on a break,' Chloe called. She raised the phone to her ear. 'We should be allowed to make calls on our break if we want.'

'No mobiles during overtime,' Shaun repeated. 'You know the rules.'

'Bastard,' Chloe grunted. She snapped the phone closed, thrust it into her bag, and stood up. 'I'm going for a pee,' she said loudly. Glaring meaningfully at Nicola she said, 'D'you want to come with?'

Nicola responded with a whisper that Becky could barely hear. 'You want me to get Don to be Kevin's alibi?'

Chloe nodded.

Becky's stomach folded again. She watched Nicola wrench the webcam from beneath the desk, and then drop it into the waste bin by Becky's side. Nicola checked her purse and briefly pulled out a mobile phone before slipping it back out of sight. Placing a reassuring hand on Becky's shoulder she said, 'We're going to go and sort this out.'

'Damn right,' Chloe agreed.

Nicola asked, 'Are you OK to cover for us?'

'Cover?'

Nicola cast a meaningful glance in Shaun's direction. 'Keep him *occupied*,' she said softly. 'Keep him distracted so he doesn't realise we've gone.'

Becky wanted to protest and say that she couldn't stomach the idea of looking at Shaun, let alone consider the prospect of talking to him. Nevertheless, because events seemed to be moving at a furious pace, she realised she had little choice except to do as Nicola asked. In a last ditch attempt to save herself from the ordeal of talking with Shaun she asked, 'How the hell am I supposed to keep him distracted?'

Nicola and Chloe answered in unison: 'Ask him about Harry Shaw.'

8

'Where the fuck have those two sluts gone?'

'Chloe and Nicola said they were going to the loo.'

'Lezzing off in there, I expect,' Shaun grunted. His sneer of contempt was briefly replaced by an expression of dreamy approval, as though he was mentally picturing Chloe and Nicola lezzing off. And then he was leering again as he addressed Becky's breasts. 'So what do you want?' His eyes shone with lewd hunger as he asked, 'Are you trying to find out if it's true why they call me the donkey?'

Is it because the ass is too obvious a nickname?

She wanted to say the words; she knew that neither Nicola nor Chloe would have hesitated with the put-down. But she couldn't bring herself to be so confrontationally rude. Taking a deep breath, glancing towards the door where Chloe and Nicola had disappeared, she gave her most politic smile and asked, 'Who's Harry Shaw?'

He cocked his head to one side. For an instant his gaze shifted from the front of her blouse and moved up to her eyes. Then he was looking back at her breasts again. 'What have those bitches said?'

'Nicola and Chloe said I had to ask you about him.'

He raised his eyebrows. 'That's a surprise. Normally they go round telling everyone that the Harry Shaw story is a sack of shit, and that I'm making it all up and only telling folk about him because I want to put the wind up them.'

'Well, you've not told me anything about him, yet.'

He raised his gaze again, as though trying to judge whether or not she was teasing. She watched him glance towards the door where Nicola and Chloe had disappeared, then slide his attention back to her.

'How long have you been with Raven and Skull?'

'Six months.' She shrugged. 'Maybe longer. It feels longer.'

He nodded as though he wasn't interested. 'I take it you've not been down to janitorial in that time.'

The question was unexpected. Becky thought for a moment, trying to work out if she'd ever visited the janitorial department since she started working for Raven and Skull, or if it was simply one of those locations she'd heard people mention as she went through her daily routine. Whenever anything got spilt, or that time Geoff had walked into the office oblivious to the fact he was treading dog poo into the carpet, or when anything spoilt the otherwise sanitised perfection of the office environment, someone always mentioned janitorial. But, now she thought about Shaun's question, Becky realised that she had never visited the basement offices. The phrase made her think of a cold, dank cellar. She could almost hear the drip of water and envision the suffocating darkness.

'No. Never.'

'Who did your initial interview? Was it Raven or Black?'

'Black. Why?'

'It figures it wasn't Raven. He doesn't do much nowadays, except sit in his chair and dribble.'

Becky said nothing. She didn't like talking about her employers – especially Raven. She had seen the man on a couple of occasions when he visited the offices. Confined to a wheelchair, breathing wheezily through a respirator that hissed like a coiled snake, he had been rolled past her as she cowered inside her cubicle. A plastic mask – supposedly transparent but made opaque with spittle – had hidden most of his face. His leering, frantic eyes had met hers for a moment and then – thankfully, mercifully – he had been snatched away and pushed into a boardroom. The moment had only lasted for a fraction of a second. But turning her thoughts back to that instant never failed to send a shiver tickling down her spine.

'Raven's one of the original family members that set up this company,' Shaun explained. He laughed and added, 'Judging by the age of the old bastard, I'd say he was *the* original family member. Some say that Black's a relative, but I think that's just rumours. I've not seen a family resemblance, although I've never seen Black sitting in a wheelchair with a respirator over his mouth, so I'm in no position to judge.'

Becky wanted to ask a dozen questions. In all the time she had worked for the company, no one had ever explained why it was called Raven and Skull, but owned by two men called Raven and Black. Had there been someone called Skull? And, if so, what had happened to him? And why hadn't the name been changed to Raven and Black?

'What does any of this have to do with Harry Shaw?'

Shaun's smile was sly. 'Back in his day, Raven was a bit of a naughty lad. He did business in a way that was...' He paused and licked his lips before saying, 'He did business that was underhand. He dabbled with the black arts.'

'Black arts?' Becky frowned. 'You mean, like African paintings?'

Shaun thought about this for a moment, and then shook his head. 'No. Not black arts like paintings done by coons. These were the black arts like witchcraft, black magic and voodoo.'

Understanding began to wash over Becky. She tried to suppress her shock when she realised Shaun had just been offensively racist. Without thinking, she glanced towards the door and silently wished for Nicola and Chloe to return.

'What does this have to do with Harry Shaw?'

'Raven liked all the kinky ceremonies,' Shaun explained. 'Bondage, buggery, blood, virgins and sacrifice.'

'Jesus!' Becky gasped. The mild blasphemy was the closest she had ever come to profanity. 'Surely there's no truth in those rumours?'

Shaun's laughter was a harsh cackle. 'They weren't just rumours. He was famous for his depraved appetites. Infamous.'

'What does this have to do with Harry Shaw?'

Shaun chuckled. 'Raven had a lot of money back then and a lot of influence, both in this world and the other world. He was a very powerful man on the night he had Harry Shaw hauled into his office...'

9

Charles Raven kept a gold-plated skull on his desk. Most visitors believed it was an innocuous paperweight: a characteristic combination of the glamorous and gruesome, befitting Charlie's distinctive tastes. Most visitors believed it was designed to impress and unsettle in equal measures. Whenever Charlie patted the skull, his palm resting on the parietal bone, his slender fingers stroking at the frontal section, he would say this was the original skull from Raven and Skull.

And then he would laugh.

And most visitors smiled as though he was joking.

Harry Shaw didn't smile when Charlie made the remark. Instead, Harry Shaw continued to watch Raven warily.

Harry Shaw was a gangly man, his Van Dyke beard giving his face a long and ferret-like appearance. His teeth were nicotine-yellow and there were too many of them for his mouth. When he watched Charlie Raven stroke the cap of the skull, distracted affection fluttering across his sharp eyes, Harry Shaw nodded as though Raven was speaking the absolute truth.

'This is the original skull from Raven and Skull,' Raven explained.

'You killed him,' Harvey noted. The words were spoken as a statement. Not a question. Harry Shaw said, 'You killed John Skull and claimed ownership of all the company rather than the forty-eight per cent you did hold. Roger Black assisted you with disposal of the body and you rewarded Black with a senior management position here. The gold-plating on the skull was done by a friend of yours – a friend who owed you a favour for staying quiet about a dark deed.'

He paused, glanced towards the ceiling, and frowned as though he was able to see this specific dark deed being performed. Anyone watching him closely would have noticed a small tremor of distaste rack his body. When he lowered his gaze, to study Raven again, he was still frowning.

'The rest of Skull's body is decomposing in landfill somewhere two hundred miles north of here but, if it ever was discovered, no one would be able to identify it as the remains of John Skull. No one would be able to link his murder to you.'

He considered Charlie Raven warily and said, 'You did something to the corpse to make sure it could never be identified, didn't you?'

Charlie smiled. He looked relaxed, leaning back in his chair. His tone was courteous and cheerful, as though this was a meeting of old friends.

'This is a very impressive demonstration from a chef, Mr Shaw. What else do your psychic powers reveal about my best-kept secrets?'

Harry Shaw took a deep breath and stood up. His suit was five years out of fashion and looked like it had been tailored for a man twice his build. The fabric hung from him as though he was a badly dressed scarecrow. With forced confidence he walked over to the desk where Raven kept a decanter of port and a cabinet of balloon-shaped glasses. Pouring himself a generous measure of blood red port, Harry Shaw sipped at his drink before speaking.

'Help yourself to the contents of my cabinet,' Charlie murmured.

'I'm detecting an aura–'

'How exciting for you!'

'–something to do with shamanism or voodoo?'

Charlie Raven raised an eyebrow. 'Which?' he asked, earnestly. 'Anyone can pull those names out of the air. I'm not giving you any clues, Mr Shaw. Is it shamanism or voodoo?'

'Voodoo,' Shaw decided. His nostrils tightened as he added, 'I'm getting the scent of chicken's blood, human blood and cayenne. I keep getting images of feathers and I hear the sound of drumbeats.' Nodding to himself he said, 'Definitely voodoo.'

'Good grief,' Charlie Raven smiled. 'You really are impressive, aren't you?' He opened the cigarette box on the top of his desk and retrieved an unfiltered Woodbine. Tucking it into the corner of his mouth, lighting it with a match, he blew a plume of smoke into the air before saying, 'I really didn't think psychics – genuine psychics – existed. You've just proven me wrong. Congratulations Mr Shaw.'

Shaw sipped another mouthful of port.

He stared out of the office window without responding.

Charlie was sufficiently familiar with the view to know what the man would be seeing. A rain of biblical proportions fell past the window. Charlie knew the view would show a busy city road slick with rain, murky with twilight, and crammed with the scuttling black beetles of taxicabs. The pavements would be hidden beneath a slithering snake of oily black umbrellas. It wasn't a view Charlie ever enjoyed. He suspected Harry Shaw wasn't getting much pleasure from the sight. 'You do know, this knowledge of yours means I'll have to have you killed?'

Shaw's grin, reflected in the window, remained firmly in place. He continued to study the view of the approaching night and miserable weather, seeming confident of his invulnerability. 'You won't have me killed,' he declared. 'I'm psychic. I know that I don't die from your hand or your instruction.'

Charlie Raven drew on his cigarette and thought for a moment.

There was a revolver in his desk drawer. He could pull it out, point it at Shaw and prove the smug bastard wrong by simply pulling the trigger. Over such a short range a kill would be almost inevitable. It would be a certainty if he got to fire off two or three shots. Roger Black was on his way up to the office and he would have no qualms about helping Charlie resolve his difference with Shaw through whatever means were necessary. There was no one else in the office building to overhear or make a report to local authorities.

Charlie knew the clean-up would be easy to organise. Roger Black had proved himself more than competent at arranging such necessities in the past. Charlie's secretary, Fiona, would be the first person to visit the office in the morning and Charlie knew that Fiona would tell him or Roger if any incriminating detail had been overlooked.

But natural caution told Charlie not to act with imprudent haste.

Harry Shaw appeared to know too much and Charlie Raven was determined to find out how he had gathered his information before he progressed any further. He placed his hand on the gold-plated skull and patted it gently.

'Pour me a port would you, Shaw? I prefer the vintage.'

Shaw did not respond.

Harry Shaw was not the first blackmailer Charlie Raven had encountered but he seemed to know more than any of the others. His claim to be psychic was an interesting one and Charlie suspected the detail was important. He pulled his hand away from the skull. Instead of reaching for the gun, as he wanted, his slender fingers found the gorilla's paw ashtray on his desk. Without shifting his gaze from Harry Shaw, Charlie tapped ash from the Woodbine into the ashtray.

Shaw had mentioned Charlie's original forty-eight per cent stake in Raven and Skull. That detail alone was enough to convince Charlie that the man was a genuine psychic. He and John Skull had settled on that specific division of investment a decade earlier in a very private meeting that had involved the pleasing ritual sacrifice of a rather obliging virgin. Charlie grinned tightly to himself as he remembered the satisfaction of that particular evening. The flesh at his loins tingled as though he was revisiting some of that ceremony's more salacious highlights.

Skull's liquid assets had been vastly superior at the time. Charlie had offered to find half the start-up stake needed but John Skull had wanted a controlling interest and suggested a fifty-one/forty-nine split. Because Charlie had a superstitious aversion to the number forty-nine, he and John had decided to make the division fifty-two/forty-eight. The figures were not a closely guarded secret but, aside from the corporate accountant, Charlie Raven didn't think those specific numbers were known by many living souls in this world.

Yet Harry Shaw had stated those precise figures as though they were common knowledge. Just as he had been absolutely sure that John Skull had been murdered. And that it was John Skull's skull on the desk. And that the gold-plating had been done by a nefarious little jeweller who owed Charlie Raven a favour. And that the remainder of John Skull's corpse, rendered unidentifiable, was rotting in a Midlands' landfill. And that a voodoo protection spell was safeguarding the corporate interests of Raven and Skull.

'You have me at a disadvantage,' Charlie decided. 'You know too many things about my business that you're not supposed to know. I know nothing about you, aside from your name and the fact that you're a chef-turned-psychic. Take a cigarette and please tell me about yourself, Mr Shaw.'

Harry Shaw stroked his Van Dyke and turned away from the window. 'My knowledge is going to benefit you by keeping you out of prison.'

Charlie nodded.

He had expected this much.

This was a typical blackmailer's device that Charlie had often used in the past. Negotiations were best started by telling the victim how much they would benefit from the looming transaction. Mentioning such a detail early on in the conversation meant the blackmailer could keep referring back to that advantage, as though the negotiations were civilised and genuinely being set up to benefit both parties. Even though this was a technique Charlie had used on more than one occasion he had never before realised that it could be extremely irritating.

'How laudable,' Charlie exclaimed. 'Thank you, Mr Shaw.'

'In return for my keeping you out of prison,' Shaw continued, 'you're going to give me—'

Charlie raised a finger. 'I've always been curious about psychic abilities,' he interrupted. 'May I ask a couple of questions whilst we're still being civilised? In a moment, I know, you're going to make a list of demands, I'm going to refuse to give into them, and all attempts at pleasantness will be over. So, now, before we get to that stage of animosity, may I ask a couple of questions about your mystical powers?'

Shaw's frown of impatience would have withered a lesser man. As Charlie continued to regard him with cheery expectation, Shaw eventually sighed. 'Go on then,' he snapped. 'What are your questions?'

Charlie doffed his cigarette into the gorilla's paw ashtray. Leaning forward in his seat, resting his elbows on the desk he said, 'Have you been communing with the dead? Have they been giving up their secrets? Have the dead been giving up *my* secrets?'

Shaw grinned. 'I've spoken with John Skull. He's told me everything.'

Charlie stood up and went to the decanter. After pouring himself a large glass of port, Charlie returned to his desk and got himself another Woodbine. His hand shook ever so slightly when he touched the tip of a match to its end. Absently, he reached for the gold-plated skull on his desk and stroked the parietal bone.

'You always did enjoy talking didn't you, Johnny?' he muttered.

'That's how I found out all those secrets you'd like to keep quiet.' Shaw's ferret-like grin was wide and vicious. 'That's how I found out about the murder you've committed. That's how I found out about—'

'Why did you talk to this chef, Johnny?' Charlie rapped his knuckles against the top of the skull. The sound was hollow and flat. 'What was going on inside that empty head of yours?'

Harry Shaw frowned at the interruption.

Charlie turned the skull on his desk so it faced him. An outsider would have thought he was rehearsing a contemporary performance of Hamlet's graveyard scene. His hand rested on the top of the skull and his gaze was set on the empty dark circles of the orbital sockets.

'What made you chat with this pissant pastry-chef?'

Harry Shaw rounded on Charlie. His mouth was open in an expression of outrage. Colour flushed his cheeks and his fist gripped tight around the balloon-like base of his port glass. The liquid in the glass sloshed up the sides and threatened to spill.

Charlie silenced Shaw before he could splutter his first syllable of indignation. Raising his hand, glancing briefly away from John Skull's skull, he smiled at Harry Shaw and said, 'Johnny's spoken with you at great length. It's only right that you let him chat with me for a moment before you lay down your demands.'

Before Harry Shaw could raise an argument, Charlie Raven had returned his attention back to the skull.

'Are you telling me you're psychic?' Harry whispered.

Charlie laughed. 'Not at all,' he said. 'I just chat with Johnny occasionally. He was always a garrulous bastard. Death hasn't stopped that habit.' Waving a hand to dismiss Harry Shaw, he turned his attention back to the skull.

Harry Shaw watched as Charlie nodded and continued to mumble through his conversation with the inanimate skull. The chef-cum-psychic scowled and worked away at his glass of port until there were only the musty dregs in the base of the bowl. His shoulders stiffened and he flinched unhappily when Roger Black burst through the office doorway.

Short and squat, Roger Black's massive breadth made up for his lack of height. He had dark, curly hair and the swarthy skin of a

Heathcliff. Under his left arm he held a manila envelope. His expressionless face flashed briefly in Harry Shaw's direction. Stepping into the room he turned and locked the door before glancing again at Harry Shaw and then taking the seat in front of Charlie's desk.

'Roger, Harry. Harry, Roger.'

Charlie made the introductions with cheery civility. He was no longer locked in studious contemplation with the skull on his desk. His mood now seemed incorrigibly bright.

'I'm sorry for that delay,' Charlie told Shaw. 'I wanted to hear Johnny's side of this arrangement, just so I had a fuller picture of what was happening.' He exercised a genial smile – as though the nuisance of conversing with a dead man's skull was an unavoidable inconvenience in the day-to-day running of a modern office. 'You were going to list your demands,' he prompted. 'Do you want to tell me what those were?'

Harry swallowed.

His composure began to slowly dissipate. He cast an apprehensive glance in Roger Black's direction and, catching the man's eye, his jaw worked soundlessly for a second or two. The remaining port in his glass trembled as though the building was on the periphery of an earthquake tremor. A single bloody droplet of the drink splashed over the side and onto the carpet.

Roger Black noticed the accident. Frowned. Shook his head.

'Go on,' Charlie encouraged. 'Tell me your demands, exactly the way that Johnny told you to make them. It seems, contrary to my earlier reservations, Raven and Skull will be willing to accede.'

'You can't kill me,' Harry Shaw said, defiantly.

Roger Black passed a large envelope across Charlie's desk. Charlie accepted it without a word of thanks. He poured the contents onto his desk and leafed through foolscap pages and black and white photographs.

Harry could see his own image in some of the pictures. He swigged at his empty glass, realised there was no drink left, and then slammed it down too heavily. He stared anxiously from Black to Raven and then towards the office's locked door.

'Just tell me your demands, Mr Shaw,' Charlie Raven repeated. He continued to idly leaf through the paperwork on his desk. 'Let's get this over and done with. It's getting wearisome now.'

'You're going to provide me with financial security for the rest of my life,' Shaw stammered.

Charlie pushed a notepad and pen to Roger Black. 'Write this down,' he said, crisply. 'Make sure you get it all verbatim.' His genial smile slipped into something predatory as he added, 'Old Johnny has been very clever here. We have to meet this chef's demands to the letter. But I'm adamant it will be to *my* letter.'

Black picked up the pen and pad and then hesitated. 'I could just deal with this problem now, Mr Raven.' He patted his breast pocket. No one in the room needed to be psychic to understand what he meant. 'It won't take a minute.'

Harry Shaw turned pale.

Charlie Raven shook his head. 'There is no problem,' he assured Black. 'Johnny has just been recruiting for the company. Harry Shaw will soon work for us and we're agreeing the terms of his employment. Johnny has brought him here with promises of financial security and a permanent place working with Raven and Skull. Harry's going to state his demands and I'm going to give them to him.'

Black shook his head. 'The door's locked, Mr Raven. The building's empty. I can snap his neck if you're worried about the noise of a gunshot. The clean-up will be minimal.'

Charlie Raven's smile was sympathetic. He took another Woodbine from the box on his desk and lit it before responding. 'Johnny's thought this one through,' he said. He patted the gold-plated skull affectionately. 'And this negotiation can't work that way. There are forces at work here that are beyond our control. If we don't meet Mr Shaw's demands he will expose us to ruin. If we kill him, it's predestined that we'll make some mistake that results in our downfall. Johnny assures me that we have to give Harry Shaw everything he believes he wants.' Glancing at Harry, nodding for him to continue, he told Black, 'Just write down everything he says he wants. Nothing more and nothing less.'

As Harry resumed his list of demands, Roger Black wrote and Charlie Raven leafed through the papers on his desk. Harry's voice trembled over the words, as though he was no longer so sure of his ground, but he made his way through the items. It took him ten minutes and another glass of port.

Charlie Raven smoked two further cigarettes whilst Shaw dictated.

'Is that everything?' Raven asked, eventually.

'Erm... I think so.'

'Read the list back to him,' Charlie told Roger.

Black cleared his throat. 'Financial security for the rest of Shaw's life. This is to include luxurious accommodation and coverage of all expenses.'

Charlie nodded. He savoured a mouthful of vintage port.

Shaw swallowed twice. His head was now shaking so much it was impossible to tell if the movement was meant as a nod of consent or a nervous palpitation.

'A salaried position working for Raven and Skull,' Black went on. 'This is to be a position of vital importance within the company, honestly acknowledged by Mr Raven.'

Roger Black drew an exasperated sigh before continuing. His fingers patted absently at his breast pocket. Charlie Raven, again, shook his head.

'The absolute assurance that no harm will befall Mr Shaw. The absolute assurance that no harm will befall any of Mr Shaw's relatives.' He slammed the notepad down and glared at Charlie Raven. 'Just let me kill him.'

Harry Shaw trembled.

'No.' Raven's voice was sharp with authority. 'There's a bigger picture, here. Shaw's destiny is intertwined with ours. I don't know how and I don't know why. But that's an inescapable fact. If we kill Shaw there will be investigations and ramifications and the results will prove disastrous.'

Shaw flexed a smile and began to relax.

'Shaw was destined to encounter Raven and Skull,' Charlie explained. 'The thread of his life was intertwined with mine. The fates had put him in a position where he could have brought the company down, although I'll be fucked if I know how a mere chef could have done that. But because Johnny is now working on the other side, he discovered there was a way to use Shaw's destiny to our advantage.'

Roger Black did not look convinced but he made no further attempt to argue his case.

Raven glanced at Shaw and said, 'Initial Mr Black's notepad, please. Acknowledge that you agree with the terms and conditions you've laid out. I'll have my secretary type this into our usual contract in the morning and then forward a copy for your records.'

Roger Black offered his pen and the pad.

Harry Shaw hesitated.

'Sign it, Shaw,' Raven hissed.

The echo of the sibilants lingered long in the room whilst Harry nervously scratched his signature against the bottom of the pad. Outside, from the depths of the rainstorm, a grumble of thunder rattled against the windows. When Harry Shaw had finished writing he looked up and saw Charlie Raven was offering a hand.

'There we go,' Charlie grinned.

The handshake lasted too long.

Shaw removed his fingers from the grip and then wiped them on his hip. He leant slightly towards Black, as though trying to snatch another glance at the notepad.

'You're now employed here as the head of our janitorial services,' Raven proclaimed. 'Welcome to the team, Mr Shaw.'

Shaw shook his head. 'That's not an executive position. I don't think—'

Raven's smile disappeared. 'Refuse the job offer and Roger here will dispose of you immediately.'

As if to confirm Charlie's threat, Roger Black put his hand inside the breast pocket of his jacket. His merciless smile made it look like he was more than pleased to make the unspoken threat. His fingers remained out of view.

'The position has executive status and will be salaried. It comes with luxurious staff accommodation located just behind the janitorial offices in the basement. I'm sure you'll be very comfortable there. I'm sure you'll also be delighted to hear that your only duty is to help Mr Black here with some of his disposal problems—'

'You bastard,' Harry Shaw hissed.

Raven tapped the papers on his desk. 'You have a lovely family,' he said, easily. 'You'll never see them again. One of the terms of your employment is that you must remain on these premises at all times. Break that condition and Mr Black will terminate your employment, your family and then you.'

Roger Black fixed Harry with a hungry leer.

'But I don't see any need for us to be making threats and spoiling the mood of this pleasant occasion,' Raven continued. 'Congratulations, Mr Shaw. You are no longer working as a chef in a backstreet restaurant. You've used your psychic abilities to blackmail me into giving you an invaluable position here at Raven and Skull. There aren't many men who get the better of me.'

Harry Shaw reached for the decanter. He held it by the neck as though he was wielding a club.

'Attempt any retaliatory action, Mr Shaw, and the consequences will be severe.' Charlie Raven tapped at the pages on his desk again. 'Attempts of violence towards me will nullify our agreement. And it's not just Roger here who can make your existence miserable. Johnny continues to work for Raven and Skull on a different plane and he will happily make your move to the afterlife an unpleasant experience. It wouldn't be the first time he's done that.'

Reluctantly, Shaw replaced the decanter. His jaw was clenched tight. Barely moving his lips he asked, 'What am I expected to do now I'm your janitor?'

Charlie laughed. 'This is wonderful really. I'm sure you're going to love this part, especially since it's going to capitalise on your culinary skills…'

He exchanged a knowing glance with Roger Black.

As Harry Shaw stood and watched, the two men guffawed loudly together. If Shaw had bothered to look at Raven's desk, he might have noticed the gold-plated skull was grinning along with Raven and Black.

'You spoke with Johnny for a long time, didn't you?'

Shaw nodded. Because Raven and Black were both sitting, occupying the only chairs in the room, he had to stand like an errant child summoned to the headmaster's office.

'He told you that we'd disposed of his body and made it impossible to identify?'

Shaw nodded again.

'Did Johnny tell you what lengths we go to, to render a body unidentifiable?' Laughing softly, shaking his head, he said, 'No. I'm sure he didn't. Perhaps it will be easier if Roger tells you this part.'

Roger Black seemed to relish the opportunity. Standing up, squaring himself confidently in front of Harry Shaw, he said, 'The first process is killing.' He smiled when he said the final word of the sentence.

Harry Shaw said nothing.

'Once we have a dead body we then begin the process of dismemberment. Mr Skull was an exception to this process. Mr Raven needed Mr Skull's head for part of a voodoo protection spell. Ordinarily we don't remove the head. It's easier just to smash in all the teeth so the victim can't be identified through dental records.' Black grinned at Shaw and added, 'You don't need to worry about that part. It's something of a speciality of mine.'

Harry Shaw took a step away from Black's menacing grin. He raised a faltering hand at chest level, as though he was trying to urge Black back. Watching with amusement, Charlie Raven thought it was like someone trying to fend off a hungry lion with a catnip treat.

'But our main problem comes from disposing of remains,' Black continued. 'Bodies begin to smell if they're just left to rot. You can't keep them refrigerated forever without running the risk of someone discovering your frozen assets.'

He chuckled quietly and with obvious personal amusement.

No one else in the room bothered to smile.

Continuing, untroubled that no one had shared his mirth, Black said, 'You can't burn corpses without facing the danger that some concerned citizen will see the smoke, or some smart-arse forensic scientist will be able to identify something from the ashes. So Mr Raven and the late Mr Skull came up with a secure way of getting rid of human remains.'

Harry swallowed.

'We tried feeding the corpses to animals,' Charlie Raven sighed. 'But animals are so unreliable. They don't always eat everything you give them. That meant there was evidence lying around.'

Understanding struck Harry Shaw like a slap across the face.

'Consuming a corpse renders it completely unidentifiable,' Roger Black assured Harry. 'The chewing, the digestion, even the elimination: they make it possible for a body to disappear without a trace.'

'You can't seriously expect me to—'

Charlie Raven tapped the notepad. His long, slender index finger pressed against Harry Shaw's initials. 'You work for Raven and Skull now, Shaw,' he said, crisply. 'I expect you to adhere to your side of the bargain.' With a sniff that suggested he had dismissed the matter, Raven gestured towards the door and said, 'Mr Black will take you down to your new accommodation in the basement. I trust you'll be very comfortable there. He'll show you where everything is and I expect you'll be pleasantly surprised to discover that the kitchen is of a gourmet standard.' Laughing, he added, 'The freezer is already well-stocked with a good supply of meat.'

10

'I don't believe it,' Becky muttered. One of the ceiling lights fluttered. It spat a series of shadows into the corner of the room before settling back to its dull, forgotten glow. Becky wrapped her arms tight around her ample chest. 'That's just a story. That's just a silly, scary, made-up story.'

'It drove poor Harry insane,' Shaun said, softly. 'Raven kept him living in the basement of this building. He was trapped. He was away from his family and sunlight. He was eating corpses. Of course, it didn't take him long to get an appetite for his work. He got so passionate about eating human flesh they say he filed his teeth so that they were sharper, pointier, more easily able to tear through skin and muscle.'

Becky shook her head.

'And they say,' Shaun continued, 'now that Raven is no longer keeping him supplied with all the meat he wants, Harry has to prowl the corridors of the basement and grab what he can, when he can—'

'Stop it!' Becky insisted. 'You're making this up!'

She flinched – startled – when the door burst open. It was only a mild relief to see Nicola and Chloe returning to the office. The earnest expressions on their faces looked contrived. Dancing behind their serious frowns Becky could see grins of the wickedest malice.

'There's a rat in the ladies loo,' Nicola told Shaun.

'We thought it might be one of your relatives,' Chloe added. 'But it didn't have a weight problem.'

Nicola giggled.

Shaun glared at them both. 'A rat?' he repeated. 'Why didn't you just hit it with one of your broomsticks?'

'Fuck you,' said Nicola.

'Why didn't you just go straight to janitorial and tell them about it?' Shaun pressed. 'Why come all the way up here to tell me?'

Chloe shook her head. 'We didn't want to be late back. We know how important it is to you that we don't spend too long away from our desks whilst working your overtime shift.'

Wearily, Shaun dragged himself from his chair. 'Are you serious? A fucking rat in the ladies' bogs? Couldn't you have done something about it?'

'Not our responsibility,' Nicola said, airily. Glancing at Chloe she added, 'Plus, when we saw a rat in there, we both thought of you straight away.'

'We were going to name it after you,' Chloe told him. 'But then we thought that would be cruel to the rat.'

Shaun glowered. Reaching for the jacket from the back of his chair, he rolled his eyes and said, 'I'm going to have to go and deal with this, aren't I?'

'Ladies loos in the basement lavatory,' Nicola said. 'You know where they are, don't you?'

Shaun had the good grace to blush.

'Be careful,' Chloe said. 'It had really big teeth.'

'Rats don't scare me,' he grunted. Not bothering to discuss the matter further, he pushed out of the office doors and disappeared from their view.

'Oh-mi-God,' Becky whispered. 'That must have been so scary. You really saw a rat in the ladies' loos?'

Chloe laughed.

Nicola shook her head. 'That was just a story to get Shaun to go down there,' she explained. 'Chloe's boyfriend is waiting there to kick seven shades of shit out of him.' She smiled darkly and said, 'With any luck, Kevin might finally teach that little fucker a lesson.'

11

Becky went back to her desk. Coils of nausea, like fat, slimy worms, writhed and untangled in her belly. She didn't like Shaun. She felt uncomfortable with his prurient interest in her breasts. She disliked the nasty story he had told her about Charlie Raven, Roger Black and Harry Shaw. Most of all, she was still furious that he had put a webcam beneath her desk.

But she didn't like the idea of him receiving a beating for his faults. The whole idea seemed cruel and barbaric. Chloe and Nicola's decision to have Shaun punished seemed almost as though they were appointing themselves judge, jury and executioner. Remembering Nicola's concerns about how severely Kevin might punish Shaun (*I'm serious, Chloe. Your Kevin could genuinely kill someone like Shaun. Genuinely.*) Becky was suddenly swathed in a clammy cold sweat. She glanced towards the door where Shaun had disappeared. Less than two minutes had gone since he left. He was probably still hurrying to the basement's toilets to deal with a fictitious rat. Becky wondered if there was a chance she could get there ahead of him and warn him that he was in danger.

'You look freaked out,' Nicola observed.

Becky glanced up, startled that the two women had crept up on her so quietly. She was suddenly aware of the darkness of the office. There was now no light outside the windows. The fluorescents cast a disconcerting hue over the office that made the landscape strange and alien. Shadows fluttered in the wrong direction. The darkness of open doorways seemed to stretch forever. The overhead lights, always too bright, now seemed to be edged with encroaching darkness.

Chloe extended a carton of water for Becky.

Nicola studied Becky with sisterly concern.

'You look sickly,' Chloe said. 'D'you need an aspirin or something?'

Becky reached up for the water. She didn't know whether to be grateful for the sympathy the two women were showing, or disquieted by the fact that they could behave so normally after arranging to have Shaun beaten. Torn between responses, and still wondering if there was time for her to warn Shaun before he met with his fate, she missed her grip on the water and watched it fall to her desk. The carton upended, splashing its contents across the keyboard.

Nicola and Chloe blinked with surprise.

'Shit!'

'Fuck!'

Chloe acted swiftly. Dropping to the floor, she slipped into the kneehole of Becky's desk and snatched the keyboard's USB connector from the back of the PC.

'Quick thinking,' Nicola marvelled. She and Chloe turned. As one, they stared expectantly at Becky.

'Sorry,' Becky mumbled. She didn't feel particularly apologetic. Chloe had dropped the water, not her. But she could see an apology was needed. Because both women were staring at her, she figured it had been her fault. 'I mustn't have been concentrating,' she said weakly.

'Don't worry about it,' Chloe said. 'It'll be easy enough for someone to clean up the spill if you go down to janitorial and tell them what's happened.'

12

The corridors of the basement were like something from a forgotten catacomb. Too narrow, and badly lit, they stretched endlessly into the distance. Hollow acoustics reverberated each of Becky's footsteps into an ominous echo. There was a lingering mustiness in the air, the vague scent of something damp, forgotten and rotten.

It was subtle.

The smell was only slightly more powerful than the faraway perfume of pine-fresh toilet chemicals. Becky didn't know whether those lavatory smells were coming from the basement's loos or the janitorial department. In an ideal world, she knew she would never have had to find out.

Becky had argued against Chloe's decision. She had said she didn't want to go down to the basement. She had no desire to visit janitorial after hearing Shaun's tales about Harry Shaw. She had even offered to use her own supply of tissues and hankies to clean up the mess but Chloe and Nicola had insisted that she had to go, especially as electrical equipment had been damaged in the incident.

Apparently, it was part of the health and safety policy.

In hushed tones they also said, if Becky didn't go down to janitorial, it would look *suspicious*. Becky knew they were talking about the plan to have Shaun beaten by Kevin. She felt ill when she saw that her actions were now a part of that diabolical scheme. Raising every protest she could think of – she had never been to janitorial, she didn't know where it was, she was feeling a little sickly, she needed to get her blouse wiped clean – Becky eventually relented and took the lift down to the bowels of the building.

She had been painfully aware of the ancient machinery clattering and clunking as it lowered her slowly downwards. She could hear the grinding of something rusty and something that sounded like metal shearing against metal.

Her heart had been racing before.

Now it thundered. Her stomach folded with unexpected pangs of nausea. It felt as though a large, cruel fist clutched her intestines.

When the lift came to a shivering halt the carriage rocked and trembled so violently she thought it was going to fall apart or send her plummeting to some deeper floor below. The idea made beads of nervous sweat break across her brow. The lift door drew slowly open to reveal the basement's long, narrowing corridor. Summoning all the courage she could muster, inhaling the unpleasant fragrance of the basement, Becky stepped out of the lift and walked into the corridor.

'I'm never doing overtime again,' she muttered, softly. 'Never again.'

The words were whispered back to her as a mocking echo.

never again… never again… never again…

Common sense told her she should be shouting for assistance, calling someone from janitorial to rush to her aid. But the idea of boldly breaking the basement's stillness made the muscles of her anus clench tightly.

The walls were a drab olive. The carpet was worn and the colour of rain-starved grass. It was barely thick enough to muffle the clip of her sensible heels with each step she took. She walked steadily towards a sharp bend at the end of the corridor and then paused.

Her mind was playing tricks, telling her that the route was getting darker and more oppressive. Another mile-long corridor stretched out before her. It was broken by doors labelled NO ADMITTANCE, OUT OF SERVICE and MAINTENANCE STAFF ONLY. As she crept hesitantly along the corridor, Becky felt sure there would be a sinister figure lurking around the corner – ready to pounce as soon as she stepped into view.

Her heartbeat pounded at a deafening roar.

Her throat closed tight as she tried to swallow down her nervousness.

'Hello?' she murmured.

lo… lo… lo…

Aside from the dwindling echo of her own cry, there was only silence.

Bravely, she stepped around the corner. Seeing another length of empty corridor should have allowed a wave of relief to wash over her. Instead, because this seemed like another mile-long stretch that diminished into faraway gloom and darkness, she groaned.

'No way!'

way… way… way…

The echo of her sigh came back to her.

Becky flinched from the sound.

Who's there?

She strained her ears, not sure if she had heard the words. Standing as still as a brittle ice sculpture, not daring to tremble, she clasped a hand against her breast and called again, 'Hello?'

'BECKY!'

The cry came from behind her.

She glanced back over her shoulder and screamed. A bloody figure lurched towards her. She briefly recognised Shaun. His familiar bulk was the canvas to a painting of battered brutality. Although she only looked at him for an instant, the image of his torment was immediately imprinted on her retina.

One eye was closed and circled with dripping crimson. A spray of blood had been slashed across his chest. The colour was so dark it shifted from meaty red to slick black in the basement's dim lights. Shaun lurched towards her, dragging behind a leg that was obscenely twisted. Through his head, a long and bloody knife entered the left side of his skull and came out through the right.

'Oh-mi-God!'

'BECKY!'

Her shriek was deafening in the confines of the corridor. Becky tried to run, but for one heart-stopping moment, her legs refused to move. Groaning miserably, dimly aware that a hot gush of piss had rushed through her panties, she started to fall away from Shaun.

Only then did she find herself running.

It took a moment to work out what she was doing. Her need to distance herself from Shaun had her banging into the corridor wall. Almost falling. The impact was so hard she thought she heard the crack of breaking bone when she slammed into the wall. And then she was able to run and run and run.

'BECKY!'

Shaun's final cry was followed by a cackle of girlish giggles. Becky was rushing into the darkening gloom of the corridor by the time her mind had told her there was someone with Shaun. She half turned, still terrified that Shaun would be lurching after her.

Behind him, she saw Chloe and Nicola were standing and laughing.

Shaun had removed the comedy knife-through-the-head gag. He held the prop in one hand. He was laughing as helplessly as Chloe and Nicola. All three of them were bent double as the mirth racked through their bodies.

Becky mentally replayed the events as she continued to stumble down the corridor away from him. Shaun had told her his ghost story of a nefarious janitor. Chloe and Nicola had told her their own contemporary horror story of boyfriend brutality. Becky had stupidly believed them all. And now they had jumped out and scared her.

They had scared the piss out of her, she thought miserably as the liquid at the tops of her thighs began to cool. She was suddenly so conscious of the damp garment at her crotch that she wasn't sure if she had yet managed to stop peeing.

A sob lurched from her chest as she saw they were enjoying a cruel laugh at the expense of the new girl on overtime.

Her legs continued to run down the corridor even though she now just wanted to stop, collapse and weep at the way they had embarrassed her. She had been made to look foolish. She had believed their stupid stories. And she had pissed her knickers in fright.

She continued stumbling down the corridor away from them.

'Come back,' Shaun called.

'Yeah,' Nicola shouted. 'We were just ragging on you.'

Chloe called, 'We do this to all the newbies.'

She reached the end of the corridor. Another blind bend. She stared incredulously back at the trio. Hate, anger and relief were all vying for control of her emotions. She didn't want to face them. She couldn't bring herself to talk to the wretches that had induced such a terror. The idea of just running away from them, even if she was only running down a darkening corridor, was far more appealing.

She turned to stare down the new stretch of corridor.

From the shadows, there was a glimpse of a face. A tall man. Gangly. He wore a suit that was too big for him. His face was made ferret-like by an old-fashioned beard and moustache.

When he smiled, she saw his yellow teeth had been filed to points.

'Do we have to talk about the office all the time?' Cindy demanded.

Becky fell silent.

The air round the table turned chilly as everyone glanced at Cindy. She remained on Richard's lap, one hand behind his head, the other stroking his chest. Fixing the group with an expression of cold contempt she said, 'It's bad enough spending forty hours a week in that shithole, as well as ten hours a week travelling to the place and another ten travelling away from it. That office dictates the clothes I have to wear, the price of the house I have to live in, the cost of the food I have to eat and the way I end up living my shitty little life.'

Her voice was in danger of rising to a strident shriek.

Richard placed a soothing hand on her arm but she shrugged it away with a vicious jerk.

'Can't one of you think of something to talk about that doesn't revolve around that godforsaken office? Don't any of you think that going there, existing for that place, and talking about it incessantly, is like a living hell? Why can't someone talk about something that has nothing to do with Raven and fucking Skull?'

'What did you want to talk about, Cindy?'

Tony spoke in his diplomatic voice. This was the voice they had all heard him use to calm the angriest outbursts. 'What would you prefer we talk about this evening?' he urged. 'The floor's all yours, Cindy. What do you want to talk about?'

Cindy hesitated for a moment before opening her mouth.

Cindy always thought of Melissa as the woman who had everything. Melissa lived in a huge and magnificent manor house. It had been bought using her über-rich parents' resources. Melissa had good looks that would not have been out of place in the celebrity pages of *Heat* magazine. Melissa had horses and free time and hobbies. And, most maddening of all, she had Richard.

It was an idyllic summer's evening. A lazy sun nudged its way towards the horizon, taking the time to illuminate Melissa Mansion in all its ostentatious splendour and glory. A snow-white bastion, set in its own grounds, surrounded by landscaped greenery and looking like a stately home, Melissa Mansion was a huge and imposing reminder to Cindy that the hateful bitch had everything. High walls circumnavigated the grounds of Melissa Mansion, securing the property and keeping the real world well away. The driveway was paved and polished. A snake of glossy Yorkshire stone that sat well against the manicured greenery of the lawns. The driveway was long enough to make a car drive a necessity to get from the front door to the wrought iron gates. The entire estate gave an impression of enviable excess that was gratuitous enough to make Cindy seethe.

Seeing Melissa saunter towards the car, dressed in jeans, wellies and a shapeless blouse, Cindy loathed the way the woman was able to glide like a fashion model on a catwalk while wearing clothes that would have made any other woman look like a plodding bloke from a council estate.

'Cindy,' Melissa said sweetly, as she approached the open window of Cindy's Ford Focus. Melissa tilted her head in polite greeting, forming a perfect pout with her lips as she kissed the air.

Twice.

Cindy could have happily raked the woman's eyeballs from their sockets. 'Hi Melissa,' she said. 'How are you today?'

'Busier than you could imagine,' Melissa sighed. 'You have no idea what hard work this last week has been.'

Cindy kept her mouth deliberately shut.

Melissa didn't work for a living. She relied on money that came from her parents. Melissa didn't know how hard it was to try and manage a CNS department, negotiate the demands of a workforce against the restraints of tough employers and try to deal with her own burgeoning workload. Melissa's idea of hard work was having a manicure and hairdressing appointment booked on the same day.

Beside her, in the passenger seat, Richard sighed softly beneath his breath. 'Poor little rich girl,' he whispered.

Cindy felt a moment's twinge of sympathy for him, and then that emotion was drowned in a rush of hatred and frustration as she realised Richard was climbing from the car to be with Melissa instead of her. He would have an evening alone with Melissa in the luxury of Melissa Mansion. The evening would lead to a weekend where the pair of them had every amenity they desired. They would have every need satisfied throughout the day and their nights would be shared in Melissa's bed beneath silk soft satin sheets.

There was a taste of acrid disgust at the back of Cindy's throat.

'I'll see you on Monday morning?' Richard asked.

He was leaning into the car from the passenger side.

The urge to lean towards him, to touch him and kiss him and drag him back into the car, was almost irresistible. Cindy tightened her grip on the steering wheel and forced herself to ignore Richard and stare at Melissa. With a supreme effort, Cindy twisted her lips into a smile.

'What have you been working on this week?'

'Jolly good idea,' Melissa agreed.

Cindy blinked and wondered if she had missed part of the conversation. It was automatic to glance in Richard's direction, with the hope that he could interpret or offer assurance that the *non sequitur* was of Melissa's making and not a side-effect of too many drinks from the office coffee machine. Remembering the role she had to play when they were in Melissa's presence, she kept her gaze locked on Melissa and repeated politely, 'A jolly good idea?'

'You're just the person I need,' Melissa explained. 'Come inside and have a drink. I simply must talk with you.'

This time Cindy couldn't stop herself from glancing at Richard.

He shrugged. His expression was puzzled.

Melissa didn't notice the exchange because she was walking back to the house with her despicable catwalk glide. 'Join me in the kitchen,' she called over her shoulder. 'Richard. You'd best make yourself scarce for half an hour. This is girls' talk.'

Cindy watched Melissa slip between the double doors of Melissa Mansion. She finally turned to Richard and hissed, 'What's going on? Does she suspect something?' Panic made her pulse accelerate. She tried to mentally brace herself for a conversation where Melissa irately demanded: *What the hell have you been doing with my husband?*

He shook his head. 'She doesn't suspect a thing.'

From the expression in his eyes, Cindy thought Richard might be hiding something.

15

'So, what's been keeping you busy this week?' Cindy asked.

The kitchen of Melissa Mansion was obscenely impressive. Cindy felt as though she was walking onto the photo-shoot of a catalogue for an overpriced furniture store. The blend of polished silver splash-backs and black and white tiles looked classically elegant. It was early enough in the evening so there was no need for the mood lighting to be switched on, but Cindy imagined, when it was needed, it would transform the kitchen into a room that looked like a kitchen from paradise.

The entire journey through Melissa Mansion had been an exercise in reminding Cindy that Melissa possessed everything that she would never own. The hallway was a huge and splendid reception area, with double stairways rising up to a broad minstrels' gallery. White tiles on the floor gave the space a Spanish charm, although the steel banisters and glass fittings modernised that first impression. The smooth, cool lines of the corridor that led from the hall to the kitchen were equally stylish. The uniformity of the walls was broken only by samples of abstract art in bright, primary colours.

'I've had an horrendous week,' Melissa confided.

Cindy was appalled to hear Melissa enunciate the letter 'h' in horrendous. Her speech implied a childhood of privilege, ponies and private education. She wondered if there was a moment of Melissa's life that had not passed in pampered, over-indulged bliss.

'I don't think I've worked so hard since I was swotting back at Cambridge.'

Her voice came from inside the open double doors of a huge, silver refrigerator. Cindy could hear the clink of glasses, bottles and ice cubes. Air conditioning in the kitchen meant, for the first time that day, her body was allowed to cool a little. Perspiration from the long day at Raven and Skull and the arduous drive home started to chill against her flesh. She shivered slightly but decided the coolness was not unpleasant.

'Would bourbon suit you?'

'I can't drink,' Cindy said dully. 'I'm driving.'

'Just one? A small one?'

Cindy opened her mouth to refuse. She knew it was not a good idea to mix alcohol with driving. She was certain it was not a good idea to mix alcohol with talking to Melissa.

'It's Friday night,' Melissa urged. 'And we can't have a girls' talk without bourbon.' She appeared from behind the fridge doors and placed a fat highball in Cindy's hand. A large measure of golden liquid sat in the bottom of the glass beneath a tumult of clattering ice cubes. Cindy noted that the highball Melissa had poured for herself contained more bourbon and less ice cubes.

'Go on then,' she agreed.

'If you get too drunk to drive I can either call you a cab or you can bunk up in one of the guest rooms,' Melissa said. 'I'm sure Richard won't mind if we have an overnight houseguest.'

Cindy refused to let herself think about that idea. Spending the night so close to Richard, perhaps having him slip into the guest room so they could fuck together under the roof of Melissa Mansion, was too thrilling a concept to consider. She sipped at her bourbon and tried not to gasp in surprise as the liquid fire burnt her throat.

'Dicky says you're one of the most organised women he knows. He says your nickname in the office is FED-EX, because you always deliver. Is that true? Is that really what they call you? Is Dicky right?'

Cindy had to think for a moment before she realised who 'Dicky' was. She stopped herself from appearing shocked at the hurtful contraction Melissa had given to Richard's name. 'That's very kind of... of Dicky.' It was hard to say the word without wanting to smirk. But it somehow seemed easier to talk about Richard using an unfamiliar name.

'He says you run your *thingy* section–'

'CNS,' Cindy offered, obligingly. Realising the acronym would mean nothing to Melissa she added, 'Communication Network Systems.'

'Yes,' Melissa agreed. 'He says you run your section with the utmost efficiency.'

'I have a good team,' Cindy admitted. 'And it's easy to run any IT department because the programmers are used to a disciplined regime and they prefer a working environment that is as orderly as—'

'Fascinating.'

Cindy fell silent. She did not feel particularly passionate about her career and she knew enough to hear the hollow clang of a patronising exclamation.

'Yes,' she said, sipping more bourbon. 'It can be fascinating.'

'You know it's Dicky's birthday next weekend, don't you?'

'Yeah.'

'That's why I wanted to chat with you. You give him a lift home from work each evening. He must talk to you. Has he said anything about what he'd like for his birthday?'

Cindy turned pale. The ice cubes in her glass began to rattle. She had already planned Richard's birthday present. After listening to some of the things he had spoken of fondly during the past few months, she had bought a red and black basque with a matching thong, a pair of opaque stockings and some patent black heels. She intended to wear the ensemble under her office suit on Richard's birthday. The idea was to sneak into his office during lunch on that day, show him what she was wearing, and then get down on her knees and make him feel like a god in the horniest fashion possible. The plan was so perfectly laid out in her mind's eye she could already envision the scene as though it was a memory. She knew how he was going to respond, how deliciously pungent his perspiration would taste, and how fulfilling it be to have his manly body spasming against hers through his throes of orgasm.

'A watch? A wristwatch?'

The idea only popped into her thoughts because she saw Melissa glancing at the slender, feminine Rolex on her slender, feminine wrist.

Melissa shook her head. Going back to the fridge, taking her empty highball with her, she said, 'Not this year. I want to give him something really special. I'm trying to decide if he would want a month in Africa or a Caribbean cruise. Which do you think he'd prefer?' As she spoke her words were almost drowned by the glug of Jack Daniel's splashing into her glass. She appeared briefly from behind the discretion of the fridge doors and waved the bottle in Cindy's direction. 'You need a refill?'

Cindy glanced at her own barely sipped drink and then shook her head. 'I'm OK, thanks.' Her thoughts were busy going over the idea of Richard spending a month in multi-star luxury with super-rich Melissa. It didn't matter if they were ensconced beneath the canopy of an African nightscape, or enveloped in the pampered luxury of a Caribbean cruise liner: either idea was enough to make her feel ill.

A trill series of beeps spiked from her hip.

The sound was loud and unexpected in the kitchen. Even though her mobile received two dozen or more texts on a regular basis, the noise was surprising enough to make her start. Her drink jolted so violently an ice cube flew out of the glass and onto the floor. A splash of bourbon followed it.

'Shit,' she spat.

'Not to worry,' Melissa said, easily. She glided towards a gleaming sink and retrieved a dishcloth. The dishcloth looked like it had only just been removed from a fresh pack. Cindy suspected it had been placed there by a diligent housekeeper, and guessed that it would ordinarily be discarded without being used, to be replaced by another sterile dishcloth by the same overworked and under-appreciated servant. Melissa held the item as though she was unfamiliar with handling such utilitarian artefacts.

Cindy shook her fingers dry and grabbed the mobile from its place on her hip pocket. Flicking it open with practised ease, she saw the message had come from Richard. After flashing a guarded glance in Cindy's direction she opened the message and read it before snapping the phone shut.

'I need to borrow your bathroom,' she explained, hoping Melissa wouldn't hear the subterfuge in her voice. 'Whereabouts is it?'

Melissa pointed towards the kitchen doors. 'Through there,' she began. 'Up the stairs, and it's the fourth door on your right.'

'I'll be back in a couple of minutes.'

'I'll top your drink up.'

16

Richard met her in the bathroom, as his text message had promised he would. Before either of them spoke he had taken her in his arms, pressed his powerful body against her and stolen a deep, passionate, penetrating kiss. His tongue slipped easily into her mouth. She wrestled playfully against it with her own whilst enjoying the hungry, greedy taste of his desire. The weight of his thinly concealed erection pressed hard against her thigh. She rolled the weight of her own needy sex against him. The urge to stroke Richard's erection through his pants, release him and pleasure him and do so much more, bordered on being irresistible.

It didn't matter that they were in a lavatory.

It didn't even matter that the lavatory was hatefully stylish and reeked of Melissa's expensive tastes and ability to finance luxuriant fixtures and fittings. Gold-plated taps sat over an onyx-black sink. The onyx-black lavatory was fitted with a gold-plated handle. Every surface gleamed as though the same overworked housekeeper who kept the kitchen so pristine had put an extra effort into glossing each glistening tile that morning.

When their mouths finally separated Cindy realised she was hungry with fresh desire for Richard. 'You make me horny.'

'I guess that's why we're so well suited,' he grinned. He stepped out of her embrace and glanced towards the lavatory's closed doorway. Cindy knew him well enough to know that his gaze was going through the door, down the ostentatious double stairway, and along the long corridor that led to the kitchen. Following his gaze she could imagine that they were both staring at a lonely Melissa sitting small and ignored behind the huge breakfast bar in the magnificent glamour of her fantastic and fashionable kitchen.

'What did the money want with you?'

Cindy's smile was thin. 'Melissa can't decide which you'd like most for your birthday,' she explained. 'A month in Africa or three weeks on a Caribbean cruise.'

His upper lip curled into a sneer of contempt. It made his otherwise handsome face seem momentarily ugly. 'We've been married seven years,' he grunted. 'And still she hasn't noticed I've got ginger hair and a complexion that goes as red as a baboon's arse with the first flash of summer in this ice-cold country.' He rolled his eyes in dismay and said, 'Why would the evil bitch want to torture me like that?'

Cindy made a sympathetic sound. She whispered her reply in case there was a risk that Melissa could overhear their conversation. 'You could wear sunblock.'

'Fan-fucking-tastic,' he grunted. 'A month lathered in grease, baking like a fucking potato beneath the African sun, and only that vacuous bitch for company. I could have sworn the Geneva Convention made legislation against shit like that.'

'You wouldn't be able to get so long away from work, would you?'

This time Richard's sneer of contempt was directed at Cindy. 'I could get a year's paid sabbatical if she wanted it,' he scowled. 'All she'd have to do is go running to her uncle Roger, telling him that her precious husband needed some time away from the office, and it would be sorted.'

'Roger Black? She's Roger Black's niece?'

Richard nodded.

Cindy shivered. 'I need to pee.'

He raised an eyebrow. His smirk was the perfect combination between boyish innocence and lewd suggestiveness. 'Go on,' he said, glancing towards the luxuriant onyx loo. 'The show should brighten my whole weekend.'

She considered refusing but couldn't think of one good reason.

Stepping out of his embrace, releasing the button and zip on the hip of her skirt, she allowed the garment to puddle at her feet.

Richard released a breath of raw enthusiasm.

Cindy stepped away from the skirt, poised over the toilet seat, and then slowly slipped her thong downwards. It was not the first time she had undressed in front of Richard. It was not the first time she had shown him her smoothly waxed sex. But the appreciative glint in his green eyes always made her feel as though she was giving him his first glimpse of naked female flesh.

He dropped to his knees as she sat on the toilet's seat. Uninvited, he stroked a hand against one stocking-clad thigh.

Cindy trembled. She knew they didn't have the time to play properly, but she kept her legs spread so, if he wanted to watch, he could enjoy seeing the golden stream of pee cascading beneath her.

'I want you,' he murmured.

The fingers on her thighs slid higher. His caress was a velvet massage against her skin, inspiring a need that was sudden and made her hot and wet. The idea of refusing him was unthinkable but Cindy knew it would be madness to give in to that urge under these circumstances.

His fingers continued to slide upwards, stroking her thigh, passing the black band of her stocking tops, and finally touching bare flesh. The gush of Cindy's pee, splashing into the bowl beneath her, tapered to a trickle. She barely heard the sound over the throbbing pulse of arousal that beat behind her temples.

'I really, really want you,' Richard murmured.

'No,' Cindy told him. Remembering she only had a few moments to spare, she snatched a couple of sheets of toilet paper from the nearby dispenser and patted herself dry. Urging Richard's hands away, wrestling her thong back into place, putting her skirt back on with practised swiftness, she said, 'Melissa's wanting to know if you'd prefer *The Heart of Darkness* or *The Love Boat*. Which should I tell her?'

Richard looked sick with frustration and disappointment. He shook his head. 'Don't tell her either. Let's just kill the bitch so you and I can have her money and live happily ever after.'

17

Back in the kitchen, Cindy hugged her highball with white-knuckled ferocity. Melissa sat on the opposite side of the breakfast bar, sipping on another bourbon, her smile growing broader and more mellow as the light began to fade from the sky.

'I've always had a soft spot for Africa,' Melissa declared.

Listening carefully, Cindy noted that the woman had managed to articulate the 'h' in had, but the sibilants in 'soft' and 'spot' sounded a little slurred. It was more interesting to listen to the way she pronounced her words rather than the content. Everything Melissa said just came out like another boastful exclamation of her wealth and affluence.

'Have you ever visited?'

'I've never been,' Cindy murmured. 'I thought Africa was all famine and jungles and people starving to death and getting eaten by flies.'

Melissa shrugged. 'It probably is,' she admitted. 'But you don't see a lot of that from the traveller's bar at the Nairobi Hilton.' She continued talking, saying many more things about the Nairobi Hilton, its swimming pool and other amenities, and how she had spent a glorious summer lounging there and working on her tan during a gap year.

Cindy wasn't listening. She wasn't even paying attention to the slurs in the woman's speech anymore. Richard's macabre suggestion still rang in her thoughts. It was more darkly exciting than any other proposition she had ever heard from him, and that list included quite a few deviant proposals that had thrilled her to the centre of her sex. She deliberately shut those salacious memories from her mind, not wanting to think about having kinky sex with Richard whilst she was sat facing his hateful wife.

It was easier and more comforting to think about practical matters, such as murder. The idea of removing Melissa from their lives would have been exciting on its own. Melissa was the one thing that stopped Cindy and Richard from openly showing their affection for each other in the office. Melissa stood between them living together and starting a family and being a normal couple. Removing Melissa would mean that their lives could be absolutely perfect. The prospect was so tempting Cindy couldn't understand why they'd never discussed the idea before.

And, as Melissa continued to sip at her bourbon and talk about a five-star hotel on the other side of the world, and how wonderful it had been ten years ago, Cindy's gaze fell on a block of knives by the side of the kitchen sink.

The kitchen itself was hatefully free of clutter.

Cindy couldn't imagine living in a kitchen that didn't have a jar of instant coffee permanently sat beside the kettle, or stains on one worktop or another, or takeaway packages sitting near the fridge, or empty wine bottles waiting beside the sink for her to remember to dump them in the recycling bin.

But Melissa's kitchen was meticulous. The only clutter on the worktops came from items that were supposed to be in a kitchen or, at least, those items that were shown in the kitchens of the rich and fashionable. There was an espresso machine beside the hob, a rack of dark green wine bottles beside the fridge, and a block of chef-standard knives sitting like bold temptation by the side of the sink.

Cindy wrenched her gaze from the knives before her interest aroused suspicion. She couldn't bring herself to stare at Melissa's perfect face. The woman's sultry pouting lips and sculpted cheekbones were another reminder that Melissa had more than any person deserved. Instead, Cindy found herself studying the glossy tiled walls, the easily wiped-down kitchen surfaces, and the shiny kitchen floor that would undoubtedly be so simple to mop clean of every last red stain.

'What are you thinking?' Melissa asked.

Cindy started.

'You're thinking he'd prefer Africa, right?'

Cindy swallowed and agreed. She guardedly supposed that Africa would be preferable for Richard. Melissa clearly intended to condense the entire continent of Africa into a month-long hibernation inside a luxury hotel with a traveller's bar and a swimming pool. She supposed Richard was bound to find that more pleasing than the threat of seasickness, shuffleboard and drowning. But she also thought, if Richard was serious in his earlier proposition, the choice between Africa and a Caribbean cruise might become moot.

Melissa took the empty highball from Cindy's hand. Their fingers touched briefly and Cindy was stung by an electric sliver of excitement. She glanced into Melissa's face, saw the woman's eyes grow momentarily wider, and then Melissa was turning away and returning to the fridge and her hidden bottle of Jack Daniel's.

Cindy considered refusing another drink and then changed her mind. Melissa clearly drank like alcohol was a necessity. Cindy wondered if she was being foolish for thinking of killing Melissa when common sense told her that the woman's drinking habits were undoubtedly going to put her in an early grave. Pragmatically, she reasoned that Melissa's drinking habits were unlikely to put her in a grave by the end of the evening.

Thinking about it rationally she figured, if Cindy's alcohol abuse continued, someone from her wealthy family would either force an intervention and spirit her off to a five-star detox clinic, or simply buy her a new liver and kidneys for Christmas and then have the organs slipped into her body the next time Melissa was visiting her regular cosmetic surgeon.

'You can bunk up in the spare room,' Melissa declared. She returned holding two freshly replenished glasses. Cindy could see that Melissa's glass was almost full to the brim. The woman was no longer diluting her drink with ice cubes. Cindy was surprised the woman had bothered to transfer the drink from the bottle.

'I'll tell Dicky to make the bed up for you.'

'If it's no trouble,' Cindy murmured.

Melissa put a hand on her arm. Again there was that sliver of electric excitement that made the light dusting of hairs on Cindy's forearms bristle and stand erect.

'It's no trouble,' Cindy promised. 'It's fun having you round here to chat with at last. Dicky talks so much about you that I've been longing to meet you and talk with the legendary Cindy myself. And it's been fun too.'

Cindy smiled and said nothing.

There had been no conversation. It had just been Melissa talking and Cindy pretending to listen. She doubted Richard had said that much about her. He was a careful man and Cindy believed he would do nothing to raise his wealthy wife's suspicions about the woman with whom he was car-sharing and having a clandestine affair. Sipping at her bourbon, and nodding a polite thank you in Melissa's direction, she watched the woman glide smoothly towards the kitchen door.

'DICKY!' Melissa called. Her voice echoed shrilly from the kitchen tiles. 'Dicky! Do you have a moment? We need you in here!'

Cindy's gaze returned to the block of knives.

The uppermost one was clearly a cleaver and, although she could only see the handle, Cindy could imagine the blade was a highly-polished square of lethal, razor-edged steel. She had a brief mental picture of the cleaver in her hand, Melissa's mouth open in a scream of protest, and then the shiny silver blade would be glossed with thick red liquid.

Melissa was shrieking in agonised bewilderment.

The blade was slicing down for a second time. It was whistling through the air, slapping wetly as it buried itself into the split flesh of Melissa's throat. A third swipe silenced her screams of protest. A fourth cut through the remaining skin and allowed Melissa's head to roll free of its body. There was an unspectacular scarlet fountain spurting from the stump of Melissa's neck.

Then the body fell heavily to the floor.

Cindy trembled in her seat. She had thought the arousal Richard inspired in the bathroom had been powerful when he encouraged her to pee whilst he watched. But the aphrodisiac qualities of plotting Melissa's demise were even more powerful. Cindy shifted on her seat, pointedly aware that there was a growing warmth and wetness in her loins.

'I shouted him,' Melissa said as she returned to the breakfast bar.

She took three attempts before finally managing to balance herself on her stool. There was a flutter of embarrassment on her face, as though she realised her lack of grace was a dead giveaway that she was drunk, but the embarrassed blushes had disappeared before they could become a fixed feature of her expression.

'He'll be down in a minute.'

Cindy continued to stare at the block of knives. The murder would be easy. She could be mopping and cleaning the kitchen whilst Richard dug a hole in the substantial grounds of Melissa

Mansion. It was getting close to nine o'clock. The sun was finally sliding behind the horizon. Cindy figured, if she killed Melissa now, she and Richard would be able to share a shower to clean themselves up and be fucking gratuitously by midnight. She could have a screaming orgasm and the cries of her satisfaction would resound freely from the palatial walls of the house.

The idea made her squeeze her thighs tight together.

She looked up at Melissa with sudden, predatory interest. Not thinking about what she was doing, not allowing herself to question her actions or fret that there might be consequences she hadn't considered, Cindy reached out for the fat, stubby handle of the meat cleaver.

18

'Cindy!' Richard exclaimed. 'You're still here. Has Melissa kept you talking this long?'

'Cindy's staying the night,' Melissa told him. 'I wanted you to make up the bed in the spare room for her.'

Cindy carefully slid her fingers away from the tempting handle of the meat cleaver. She was sure that Melissa had not seen what she was doing. A part of her suspected that Richard might have noticed.

'Make up the spare bed?' Richard's voice sounded plaintive. 'Can't Jack do that?'

'*Jacinta*,' Melissa corrected, absently, 'is off this evening. You know she doesn't work Friday nights.'

From Melissa's tone of her voice, Cindy guessed that Jacinta was the overworked and underpaid Polish housemaid who clearly did all those chores that were beyond the abilities of Melissa. Cindy had never met Jacinta, and suspected she never would, but she felt a rush of sympathy for the poor woman who had to endure Melissa's demanding worthlessness. She guessed if Jacinta had been in the kitchen and privy to her thoughts, the housemaid would probably have been encouraging Cindy to take the meat cleaver and put it to good use.

'The lazy Polack bitch doesn't work most nights,' Richard grunted. 'Why isn't she here? And why doesn't she keep a bed made up in the spare room? What's the point of having a spare bed in there if it's never made up when needed?'

Cindy's gaze was drawn back to the block of knives. If she reached for one now, she wondered if Richard would hold his wife down so they could get rid of her in the most efficient fashion. With Richard holding her there would be no hope of Melissa running or fighting back or raising the alarm.

Melissa pouted at her husband from behind her glass of bourbon. 'Come on, Dicky,' she coaxed. 'Be a good boy and make up the spare bed for Cindy here. We're having a really good girls' talk together. This is the best fun I've had in simply ages and I've already decided that Cindy is definitely coming to your birthday party next weekend.'

Cindy acknowledged this new information with a blink.

'Are you still hiding the bourbon in the fridge?' Richard sounded tired.

'It's not hidden,' Melissa protested. 'It just tastes better when it's cold.'

'Tastes irresistible,' he muttered, trudging past her. Opening the door, snatching the bottle and pouring himself a generous drink, he took a desperate swig from his glass and said, 'Yeah. I'll go and get a bed made up for Cindy. Anything else you want me to do before I finally get a moment to wind down after putting in a full week's work?'

Cindy glanced expectantly at Melissa. She could see the woman was seriously contemplating her answer to his question, as though trying to remember if there were any further chores she need him to perform before he was finally allowed to put the working week behind him. Cindy had only known Richard for six blissfully short months but already she believed she understood him and his sarcasm far better than this woman who had been married to him for seven years. She marvelled that Melissa could be so indifferent and insensitive to the man with whom she shared her life.

'Get yourself another drink when you've finished,' Melissa grinned. 'I think you've earned it, Dicky.'

Richard stormed out of the room without another word.

Melissa laughed musically. The sound was a surreal contrast against the murderous anger that seemed apparent in Richard's indignant egress.

'Dicky tells me you're divorced.'

'Yes.'

'What happened?'

Cindy hesitated for a moment, and then decided there was no reason to keep the truth from Melissa. She didn't like the woman, but the causes of her divorce were not something she held as a precious secret. 'I caught him screwing around,' she said. She sipped at her bourbon to show that was the end of the story. The silence in the kitchen grew ominous and thick and Cindy deliberately kept her gaze from returning to the block of kitchen knives.

The mobile phone on her hip emitted its familiar trill beep.

As though the sound was a prompt for her to speak, Melissa said, 'What a bastard. Tell me you got some revenge on him.'

Cindy shook her head. 'There didn't seem a lot of point.'

Melissa downed her drink with one gulp and then slammed the glass against the kitchen worktop. Cindy flinched from the thump of the heavy impact. Her senses were dulled by drink but she could feel a rising disquiet in the pit of her stomach. The idea that Melissa could be something of a threat made her ready to retaliate should the need arise.

'Of course there's a point to having revenge,' Melissa insisted. 'If I discovered Dicky was… if I discovered he was doing something he shouldn't I'd… I'd have my revenge. I'd… I'd… I'd…' She glanced desperately around the kitchen. Her gaze fell on the block of knives. Her eyes grew wide with childish excitement. She snatched a large cook's knife from the middle of the block. With a drunken lunge she pushed it towards Cindy's face.

Cindy was momentarily dazzled by a flash of the setting sunlight darting from the polished blade. She remained perfectly still in her chair, not sure this was how the evening was supposed to progress, and certain that she would do nothing to rouse Melissa's suspicions about her relationship with Richard. The tip of the knife's blade was mere millimetres from the end of her nose. Cindy could smell the lemony fresh tang of the washing-up liquid that had been last used to clean its steel edge. It occurred to her that, if she had been sober at that moment, she would have run screaming from the kitchen, demanding that Richard save her from the crazy bitch with the knife.

'I'd cut his bollocks off if I caught… if I caught him doing something.' Melissa spat the words with drunken glee. The confusion on her face vanished when she glanced at the knife in her hand. A clarity of purpose made her eyes shine and she said, 'I'd cut them both off.' She prodded the knife into the air with a couple of vicious thrusts that were somewhere close to chest height. Cindy thought if that was the woman's idea of cutting a man's bollocks off, she had clearly forgotten where those parts were usually located on a man's body.

'I'd cut his bollocks off,' Melissa said again. 'And then I'd make him eat them.'

'Innovative,' Cindy conceded.

'And as for her…' Melissa growled. She turned on Cindy. Because the large cook's knife was still gripped tight in her fist, the tip of the blade was pointed at Cindy's face. Orange daggers of the fading sunset bounced from its silver length. In the kitchen's muted light the colour was like diluted blood. 'As for her…' Melissa began again.

'You'd get her too?' Cindy asked.

Melissa shook her head and put the knife on the counter. Retrieving her highball she stumbled towards the refrigerator and disappeared inside the familiar sanctuary of its large double doors. 'I wouldn't do anything to her. Nothing that the bitch doesn't have coming.'

'What does that mean?'

Melissa laughed. It was a surprisingly bitter sound that rang hollowly from the tiled acoustics of the kitchen. 'I know exactly how I'd deal with any woman who tried to take Dicky from me,' she said. 'I come from a family who have a lot of experience in meting out appropriate revenge. No woman in her right mind would cross me or my family.'

Cindy suppressed a shudder. She swallowed the remnants of her drink and, when her mobile emitted another sullen beep, she remembered there was a text message waiting for her. Flipping open her mobile she was not surprised to see the message came from Richard. Confident that Melissa was busy pouring herself another large bourbon, Cindy pressed the button to open the message.

LET HR FINISH THAT BOTTLE OF JD N THN GET HR TO GO 4 A P. I'LL W8 HERE N PUSH HR DOWN THE STAIRS. IT WL LOOK LIKE N ACCIDENT.

Cindy snapped the phone shut and smiled broadly for Melissa. 'Is there any chance of another drink?'

19

As Cindy had suspected it would be, the kitchen's lighting at night was spectacular. Spotlights, concealed within the suspended ceiling, created stark overlapping circles around the room. The over-polished surfaces glistened wetly beneath the bright beams. The spacious stylishness of the room gleamed like a showcase of desirable perfection. Slightly awed by the spectacle, and wishing she possessed something as functionally glamorous, Cindy suddenly realised that this kitchen would be part of her prize if she helped Richard to kill Melissa.

'May I have another drink?'

'You went through that one quickly,' Melissa remarked.

Cindy bit back an acerbic response. Considering the amount the woman had drunk this evening, Melissa had no right to comment on Cindy's drinking.

'I'm just getting a taste for the stuff,' Cindy explained. 'I don't normally drink bourbon and it's got a nice vanilla flavour, don't you think?'

Melissa shrugged as she took Cindy's glass. 'It never stays in my mouth long enough for me to taste the flavour.' She was starting to obviously slur her words and Cindy could see a definite sway in Melissa's gait as the woman lurched to and from the fridge. Reappearing from behind the double doors, offering Cindy a glass and grinning conspiratorially, she held a finger over her lips and said, 'But don't tell Dicky that I drink so much. I don't want him thinking I'm a dropeless hunk.'

They both giggled.

'You're a dropeless hunk?' Cindy laughed.

'I meant hopeless drunk,' Melissa told her. She made a concentrated effort to say the phrase accurately this time. 'I think I'm getting my words muddled. I might have had one too many this evening.'

'Your secret's safe with me,' Cindy promised. 'I won't tell Richard you're a dropeless hunk.'

Melissa placed a hand on Cindy's shoulder.

'You're not the cow I thought you were going to be,' she sniffed.

Cindy laughed. The sound was deadened by the kitchen's flat acoustics. Her mirth sounded forced and strained and not wholly appropriate. Cindy wasn't sure she found Melissa's comment funny but nervousness and the alcohol combined to make laughter the only response she was able to manage. 'Why the hell would you think I'd be a cow?'

'Dicky jus' goes on about you so mush,' Melissa told her. She retrieved the hand from Cindy's shoulder and made a pathetic attempt to straddle the stool at the breakfast bar. The task might have been accomplished if she had dared to let go of her highball. Instead, after one ungainly lurch that almost had her falling to the floor, she shook her head and belched.

Blushing, placing a hand over her mouth as though that would retract the sound, she flashed an apologetic glance in Cindy's direction and said, 'I think I need to go to the loo and freshen up.'

Cindy nodded. She sipped at her drink and was thankful there were no ice cubes in this one to give away her nervousness. Even through the veil of alcohol-induced fug, Cindy knew that Melissa's trip to the loo could be the last journey the woman ever made. She tried to sit still in her chair, not wanting to make any movement or gesture that could alert Melissa to her impending doom.

Melissa staggered towards the door with far less style and composure than she had exuded at the beginning of the evening. Every step was an exercise in reluctant and overcompensating balance. She used the worktops for support on her journey and then clung to the door as though she would fall if she didn't grip its handle with vicious ferocity.

Cindy pushed her stool back and tried to stand up. The feet of the stool dragged noisily against the tiled floor. The sound was like a giant's dry fart. Cindy giggled as the simile crossed her thoughts. She looked up to find Melissa glaring at her with unconcealed suspicion.

'You're not following me, are you?'

Cindy stifled a moment's panic as she shook her head. She was still intending to go ahead with Richard's murderous plan. In a moment of drunken paranoia she silently hoped that nothing she had said or done had given away her intentions. Seeing the penetrating glare that Melissa shot her, she thought it was likely she had said or done something to reveal the secret.

'No,' she said quickly. 'I wasn't following you. I was just needing to—'

'You're not tryin' to follow me upstairs, are you?' Melissa demanded.

She lurched back towards Cindy. She had one hand gripped in a tight fist around her glass of JD. Her other hand reached out in a talon of polished, glossy fingernails. Hastily, she clutched at Cindy's shoulder.

'You're not tryin' to follow me to my bedroom, are you?'

The question was accompanied by a wet spray of spittle that spattered against Cindy's jaw and décolletage. Her breath was a wet rush of ripe bourbon fumes. 'Did you intend gettin' me alone and makin' a pash at me? Is that what you were plannin'?'

'Of course not.'

'Shame.'

Melissa pushed herself away from Cindy. Without needing to rely on the worktops for support this time, she managed to make it to the kitchen door. Cindy watched her disappear from the room, and then shook her head in disbelief.

Melissa had been coming onto her.

Making lewd suggestions.

And the idea had not been wholly repellent.

If she was being honest with herself, Cindy could feel a tingle of fresh warmth nestling in her loins as she thought of herself and Melissa kissing, embracing and slowly undressing. She'd never had sexual thoughts for a woman before, but she figured if she was going to have them about any woman, it was as well to be having them about a woman as perfect and beautiful as Melissa.

She swigged the remnants of the bourbon from her glass and then put the highball down by the side of the sink. Shaking her head to clear her thoughts she remembered that nothing was going to happen between herself and Melissa. If his last text message had been correct, Richard would now be waiting at the top of the stairs, ready to push Melissa to her death. Cindy was no longer sure if that was something she thought Melissa deserved but she also knew the decision did not belong to her.

This was Richard's home.

It was Richard's wife.

And it was Richard's murder plan.

All she had to do was sober up whilst they waited for the authorities, explain that it had been a horrible, tragic accident, and do her best to look upset, confused and surprised. If Richard really did pluck up the courage to push Melissa down the stairs, Cindy did not think it would be difficult for her to look upset, confused or surprised.

Slowly and quietly, Cindy crept out of the kitchen.

'DICKY! Dicky! Are you up there?'

Cindy rushed stealthily down the unlit corridor that led to the hall of Melissa Mansion, following the sound of Melissa's plaintive voice. Melissa hadn't bothered to turn on any of the house's lights. She climbed the stairs in darkness. When Cindy reached the hall she saw the whole scene being played out with Melissa as a moonlit silhouette walking through midnight darkness.

Her eyes slowly adjusted to the lack of light.

She could see Melissa's frail figure laboriously mounting the stairs. The woman still held tight to her glass of JD with her left hand. With her right, she kept grabbing at the banister and then hauling herself up to the next step on the staircase.

Squinting into the shadows, trying to make sense of the charcoal, black and navy shapes she was seeing, Cindy noticed that Melissa's oversized wellies were making the ascent precarious.

Cindy held her breath.

She wondered if Melissa was going to make it to the top of the stairs. Considering the way her boots kept slipping from each step, Cindy thought there was a good chance Richard would have no need to push her down the stairs. It seemed more likely that the stupid bitch would fall backwards and save him the trouble of having to become a murderer by breaking her own stick-thin neck on the staircase.

'DICKY!' Melissa screamed. 'Where the fuck are you, Dicky?'

Although it was dark, Cindy could see that Melissa was a mere couple of steps from the top of the staircase. She glanced at the long and curving route that the stairs followed and felt suddenly ill at the idea of Melissa's body bouncing down such an unforgiving descent.

The idea of shouting out to Richard crossed her mind. Cindy had no idea what she could shout, but she wanted to tell him that she was having second thoughts about the murder plan. She thought it would be best if they found a way for him to escape from his marriage without resorting to such extreme measures. But it was impossible to think how she could call that message up the stairs without alerting Melissa to the truth of what they had intended.

'DICKY!' Melissa bellowed.

'I'M HERE!' He screamed.

Cindy saw his shadow loom at the top of the stairs. She watched Melissa stagger back in surprise. Unwilling to watch the inevitable, Cindy closed her eyes. She waited in claustrophobic darkness to hear the sound of Melissa's agonised scream, or the gut-churning clatter of broken bones bouncing against marble steps. In the black silence she was almost deafened by the pulse beating just behind her ears.

'You arsehole,' Melissa shrieked. 'You absolute fuckin' arsehole!'

Cindy opened her eyes and saw that somehow – she had no idea how – Melissa had managed to keep her place on the top step. The woman teetered there like an unnerving exhibition of tightrope walking.

But she hadn't fallen.

Cindy released a sigh of grateful relief. The lights came on. They were as spectacular and wonderful as the mood lighting that illuminated the kitchen. Cindy could see the whole scene with disturbing clarity. Richard's face was flushed. The tendons on his neck stood out like cords. He leered over Melissa from his position at the top of the stairs, looking like he still intended to push her.

'You scared the shit outta me,' Melissa bellowed. 'I coulda fallen and broken my fuckin' neck"

'That was the intention,' Richard snapped, bitterly.

She stared at him with pained eyes. There was an instant where Cindy felt a rush of genuine sympathy for the woman. Melissa-who-had-everything was suddenly faced with the reality of discovering that her husband wanted her dead. It was a single pinprick that burst the balloon of her whole shallow existence. Her shoulders fell and her face crumpled.

'You don't mean that,' Melissa whispered.

'I fucking do,' Richard roared.

She retaliated with a speed that was surprising. Going from defeated to defiant in the space of a heartbeat, Melissa raised a hand and aimed it for the side of Richard's face. Taking a step back to place extra weight behind the blow, she lost her balance and began to topple down the stairs.

Cindy drew a shocked breath.

Melissa went back in an arc that was almost graceful. With one leg extended, and the other folded behind her, she looked vaguely like a ballerina as she swooned back and down. It wasn't until her skull met a marble step midway down the flight that her movement looked anything less than choreographed and composed.

Cindy heard a brittle sound that reminded her of autumn twigs breaking underfoot. It was a crisp and brittle clip, accompanied by Melissa's soft grunt of protest. The woman's legs continued to fly through the air, even though her head remained lodged against one single step. The angle of her head in relation to her shoulders went from looking pained to impossible. Then, when her feet had finished their idle curve, her head flipped up and she began to re-enact the first fall. This time she clattered down the remaining stairs without the polished finesse of her first attempt.

She's like a human slinky. The idea threatened to inspire a manic wave of giggles. Cindy suppressed the sounds before they could make her appear insane. But still, the thought would not go from her mind: *Melissa the human slinky.*

As if to prove Cindy wrong, Melissa collapsed into a semi-foetal ball on her second full impact with the stairs. She rolled to the bottom of the staircase, bashing from the banister rails to the wall. The sickening sound of snapping bones seemed to accompany every jarring thud that the woman made against the stairs. She lay there for an instant, covered in a pall of deathly silence.

'Fucking hell,' Cindy gasped.

'Fuckin' hell,' Richard echoed.

In the same instant they both ran towards her fallen figure.

'She went down like a sack of shit,' Richard muttered as he hurried down the stairs. 'She just went arse over tit, and down and—'

'Melissa?' Cindy called. 'Melissa? Are you OK? Are you all right?'

'She's dead,' Richard said. He managed the last few steps with a lack of effort that made a mockery of Melissa's ungainly descent. 'She has to be dead after a fall like that,' he insisted. 'No one could survive a fall like that. She went down like a sack of—'

'Dicky?'

They both stopped dead when they heard Melissa's voice. Exchanging a swift glance, neither of them sure if they had heard the word or imagined it, Cindy glared at Richard. She silently urged him to do something manly.

'Dicky,' Melissa sighed. 'I think I've spilt my drink. Can you get me another one?'

As one, Cindy and Richard rushed to Melissa's side.

Melissa's expensive dentistry now looked like it had been a waste of time and money. Her brilliant, whiter-than-white smile had become a bloodied and shattered grimace. Her perfectly sculpted nose was flattened and gushing blood over the right side of her cheek. One leg was twisted under her body at an angle that a contortionist would never have managed. The other looked like it had miraculously developed a second knee, allowing it to bend in conflicting directions.

'Only a drunk could have survived a fall like that,' Richard marvelled.

'My drink, Dicky,' Melissa wailed plaintively. 'I need another drink.'

'I didn't even have to push her.' He sounded incredulous. 'I just—'

'I saw what happened,' Cindy told him.

'Why won't one of you get me a fuckin' drink?' Melissa complained. 'I need a drink after doin' that. Get me a drink.'

'Should I phone an ambulance?' Richard asked.

Cindy glared at him again. She was surprised he couldn't see what so obviously needed to be done. She was more surprised that he seemed unable to finish the plan he had set in motion. 'No,

Richard,' she said patiently. 'You can't phone an ambulance yet. Melissa's not dead.'

A puzzled frown crept over his stunned features. 'What do you mean?'

Cindy nodded towards the fallen woman at their feet. It looked as though Melissa was finally beginning to register some of the pain that had to be racking her body. Her eyes looked wide and frightened. Instead of demanding a drink she was now starting to whimper. The sound came out of her bloodied lips on half-chugged breaths.

'Dicky?'

Richard ignored her. Glaring at Cindy he asked, 'What do you mean?'

Cindy could see he was no longer going to be any use in the situation. Realising the onus of getting the job done properly now rested on her shoulders, she stepped behind Melissa and urged Richard out of the way.

'What are you doing?' Richard demanded.

Cindy placed a hand under each of Melissa's armpits and began to lift.

Melissa groaned.

'What are you doing?' Richard insisted. 'Cindy? Will you please tell me what you think you're doing?'

Cindy managed to drag Melissa up one step before pausing and turning to glare at him. 'I'm getting this job done properly,' she explained. 'And, since that first fall down the stairs didn't kill her, I'm going to drag her back to the top and throw her down again until it does kill her.'

Richard stared at Cindy with wide-eyed disbelief.

Melissa moaned. 'Dicky,' she murmured softly. Her words were muffled with blood and the threat of tears. She struggled to escape the hold Cindy had on her but it was a futile and uninspired attempt. 'Dicky,' she sobbed. 'I think I've broke a fingernail.'

20

For Cindy, the nightmare began on Wednesday morning.

Her mobile emitted the familiar shrill beep that said she had received a text message. Cindy had elected not to go into the office on Monday or Tuesday, accepting Raven and Skull's unexpected offer of a brief period of compassionate leave. Obviously, she hadn't been related to Melissa but she had been in the woman's home when she died and, contrary to popular opinions, Raven and Skull was not operated by unfeeling monsters.

Cindy drove to the office alone. She parked in the spot reserved for carpool sharers, like herself and Richard, and then went through the process of getting to her desk and trying to remember how to do her job.

It was not easy.

The events of Friday night continued to wend their way through her thoughts in an unwanted slow-motion replay. She saw herself peeing in front of Richard. She revisited the moment where he blessed her with a passionate and penetrative wet kiss. Then she was sitting in the kitchen with Melissa and the huge fridge and the hidden bottle of Jack Daniel's. She was thinking of using the meat cleaver on the woman. And then she was watching Melissa tumble down the stairs again and again.

Cindy massaged her forehead with her fingertips, trying to ease away the threat of a headache that nestled there. Her upper body ached as though she'd overdone it at the gym. Her shoulders were stiff. The muscles of her chest felt sore, tender and bruised. Her first thought was that she'd caught some sort of cold or the flu. Then, when she remembered the exertion of dragging Melissa's damaged body up the stairs, Cindy realised her aches were attributable to nothing more than simple muscle strain. The thought made her clutch a hand over her mouth.

She called Tony Wade and told him that, due to his bereavement, Richard would be off for the rest of the week. Tony said that Roger Black had already informed him about the incident

.

'Of course,' Cindy said. Not wanting to ask the question, but feeling sure she should show some degree of compassion, she asked, 'How's Mr Black taken the news?'

There was silence from Tony's end of the telephone. 'You know Roger Black,' he said quietly. 'The guy looks permanently angry. He gives the impression he would kill an admin assistant for bringing him coffee with milk or sugar.'

'Yeah,' Cindy agreed.

Her mouth was dry.

It was suddenly difficult to form words.

'Mr Black was pretty fond of Melissa,' Tony went on. 'She was his only niece and I think he's ready to make someone suffer. I know I've been staying out of his way since I found out about her death.'

Cindy's stomach tightened.

'How are you bearing up?' Tony asked.

Cindy and Richard had decided, in order to best conceal their secret, they needed to be as open and honest about all that had happened as circumstances would allow. They would tell anyone who asked that Cindy had been at the house on the Friday evening. They would not try to hide the fact that she'd been drinking with Melissa and they'd tactfully allow that Melissa had drunk one too many before she made her final fatal descent on the stairs. Richard had pointed out that they wouldn't be lying if they said Melissa had lost her footing at the top and tumbled back down. The only parts of the story they were going to keep secret were the details about Richard trying to startle Melissa into falling and the pair of them twice dragging Melissa to the top of the stairs to throw her back down.

'Cindy?' Tony sounded concerned. 'Are you still there? How are you bearing up?'

After Melissa's third tumble down the stairs – a tumble that made her neck snap, and finally stopped her from complaining about her broken bloody fingernail – Richard had immediately called an ambulance. He and Cindy had patiently awaited its arrival.

Paramedics came.

Then a police car.

And, then a harried-looking legal executive from Raven and Skull assuring Richard that Roger Black was on his way over. When he arrived Cindy was bundled back to the sanctuary of her own apartment with the promise that her car would be returned to her the following morning. A police officer took her statement, repeatedly assuring her it was just a formality in these circumstances. And then she spent Saturday and Sunday alone in her apartment and waiting for a call from Richard. When he finally did make contact on Sunday evening, the message she received was disquieting and distant.

DONT CALL BK. IM USIN A DSPOSBLE MOB TO SND THIS MSG. DONT FONE OR CALL. ILL B N TOUCH AS SOON AS THE HEATS DIED DOWN. RICH XX

'Cindy?' Tony pressed. 'How are you bearing up?'

'It wasn't pleasant,' Cindy said, honestly. 'I'm just trying to shut it from my thoughts and get on with things.'

'You know where I am if you need anything,' Tony told her.

Cindy thanked him and then placed the phone back in its cradle. The mobile on her hip emitted its shrill series of beeps. She considered reading the text message, and then decided her body needed another fix of caffeine first.

It was unlikely to be a call from Richard.

He was clearly trying to avoid contacting her to any degree that could be regarded as suspicious. His last message had made that much painfully clear. And, although she desperately wanted to hear from him, Cindy knew that Richard was right. They had to go out of their way to make sure there was no suspicion of foul play.

Stepping out of her office, walking past her secretary, Margaret, and heading towards the canteen, she was surprised to see so many vaguely familiar faces study her with sympathetic frowns. Cindy had always known that gossip and bad news travelled faster and more effectively than any other means of communication she controlled under the auspices of Raven and Skull's CNS department. But she still found it difficult to accept that everyone in the whole office building already knew the superficial details of what had happened to Richard's wife.

'Cindy?'

'Are you OK, hon?'

'We heard what happened. How are you, babes?'

Becky, Heather and another girl stood in front of her. Cindy thought there was something horribly familiar about the third woman, although she couldn't quite recall where she had seen her deathly pale face before. All three of the friends looked tearfully concerned and Cindy couldn't decide whether to be thankful for their companionship or annoyed by the nuisance of their questions.

'I'm OK,' she said, thickly.

The third woman reached out to place a hand on Cindy's shoulder. Recognition came to Cindy with a rush of horrified revulsion. The woman reaching out to her looked exactly like Melissa. Cindy had never seen the woman in the offices of Raven and Skull before but she didn't think it was possible that one human being could look so exactly like another. She shrank from the threat of the woman's touch. Stepping hurriedly back, deciding she could manage the morning without her needed fix of coffee, Cindy turned away and rushed back to her office.

The fax machine in the corner of the room hummed to life as she stepped into the room. Cindy could hear the beep and whirr of electronic communications interacting. At the same time, her mobile spat another trill series of beeps that told her she had received another message.

Sighing wearily, and resigning herself to the fact that she needed to start dealing with the morning's workload, Cindy turned on her PC and typed in her password. Whilst she was waiting for the machine to go through the slow process of booting, she walked over to the fax machine. Unfastening the mobile from her hip she glanced at the first message and saw it was from an unknown number.

She wondered if it might be from Richard. The tone of his last message had made her think that he would keep communication to a bare minimum. But if something had changed in the situation, she suspected he would try to tell her as soon as possible.

Silently, she berated herself for not checking the text message as soon as it landed. Urgent haste made her fingers fumble over the mobile's keypad. She hit the wrong button twice and quietly cursed her own shaking hands. Forcing herself to work slowly, trying to operate the keys the way they were supposed to be pressed, Cindy realised her entire body was drenched with nervous perspiration.

The intercom on her desk buzzed loudly.

Cindy shrieked and dropped the phone. It bounced against the floor. For an instant, Cindy thought she would get off lightly from the incident. As the phone flew through the air it seemed undamaged by the rough treatment of its first fall. It was only when it hit the floor for a second time that she heard something break. A hairline crack appeared across the screen. That single sign of damage told her the phone would likely be rendered unusable.

'Shit!'

She could immediately see a morning filled with the problems of completing all the necessary paperwork for getting her company-issued SIM transferred to another mobile phone, having all the apps she used reinstalled in a new unit, and waiting until some overpaid undergrad from resources finally turned up at the end of the day with her newly working mobile and a backlog of overdue messages.

The intercom on her desk buzzed for a second time.

Cindy pressed the button on the machine and snapped, 'What is it, Margaret?'

'Mr Black is on his way to see you,' Margaret sniffed. 'He told me to cancel all your appointments for this morning. He said you two have a lot to discuss.'

'Lucky me,' Cindy said, bitterly. She released the button on the intercom, glanced at the fax machine and then remembered she needed to deal with her mobile. Picking up the phone from the floor, shaking it, as though such brutal treatment might bring it back to life, Cindy accepted that the phone was dead. She dropped it into one of the padded envelopes for internal mail. Sealing the envelope, then addressing it with a sticker that said IT HARDWARE, she placed the broken mobile in her out tray and walked over to the fax.

A handwritten message was being spat into the paper tray. It looked as though it had been scrawled in wet ink before being sent. Cindy had no idea what colour the ink was when it went into the fax machine but it was coming out a greasy, oily black. Not that the wetness of the ink troubled her. The most disquieting thing about the message was not even the trembling handwriting in which it had been written. From what she could see, the most distressing aspect of the message was the meaning implied by the single word that ran diagonally down the page.

K
   I
      L
         L
            E
               R

21

Roger Black didn't bother knocking when he entered the office. Closing the door behind himself he took a seat facing Cindy, sat down and released a breath that sounded positively feral.

'This is a grim fucking business,' he growled.

Cindy nodded. She gripped the arms of her chair with determined ferocity, adamant Black would not see any symptoms of her nervousness.

'Grim,' she repeated.

'I knew Melissa liked the odd drink,' Black went on. 'But I didn't think she was the sort who could get so pissed she'd start doing pratfalls down the fucking staircase.'

Pratfalls.

Black's word echoed inside her mind. Cindy wondered why everyone thought he cared so much about Melissa when he was able to use such a callous phrase to describe what had happened.

'A grim, grim business,' Black said, wearily. He shuffled forward in his seat and studied Cindy's face, solemnly.

Cindy had seen Roger Black around the offices of Raven and Skull and had always considered him a man to avoid. It wasn't just that he was physically unattractive. Squat, dark and constantly frowning, he looked like the embodiment of a thug. The fact that he always wore a suit only made him look like a thug on his way to make another court appearance. Yet Cindy knew Roger Black didn't just have the physical power of a thug: he also had the power that came from being a controlling partner in Raven and Skull. Roger Black had chaired the panel when she was interviewed for her position with the company. Roger Black was currently listed as acting CEO of the company due to Charles Raven having a medical condition that left him heavily incapacitated. Cindy didn't know much about the company's structure from before she had arrived but, nowadays, she knew that whenever anyone spoke of senior management they were only ever talking about Roger Black.

'What happened, Cindy?' he asked. 'Tell me what happened on Friday night.'

She sighed and tried to think of a plausible reason why she shouldn't tell him. In the stillness of the office she heard the fax machine begin its ritual whirr of beeps and shrill whistles as it accepted another message. Her gaze immediately flashed in that direction.

'Deal with your workload later,' Black instructed.

She guessed he was trying to be soothing and sympathetic but it was clear that those were not traits that came easily to him. His words were barked like instructions. His manner was harsh and he made no attempt to disguise his impatience.

'Just tell me what happened last Friday night so I've got a full picture of why my niece is getting buried at the end of this week.'

'The funeral is on Friday?'

'It's a private service,' Black said, quietly. 'Although you're welcome to attend if you wish. I can organise a car for you and—'

'Thank you,' Cindy said, quietly. 'I'd like... I mean... I appreciate that.'

Black grunted. He pulled a diary from his breast pocket and made a note inside. Cindy saw the flash of something fat and metallic that was also inside his jacket pocket. She quickly closed her eyes and told herself she had not seen anything there. It was enough to try and cope with what she and Richard had done on Friday. Trying to get her mind to deal with the discovery that Roger Black carried a concealed weapon would be one more detail than her rational mind could handle.

The fax machine made the familiar scraping sound that always came when it was collecting a new sheet of paper. With her eyes closed Cindy could easily imagine the sheet of paper being pulled up by the traction of the machine's black rubber wheels and fed through the internal mechanism that allowed the fax's ink to be sprayed onto the page. The prospect of receiving another message like the one she had received earlier made her bowels clench tight. Roger Black was in the room and she did not want him to latch onto the idea that she might be a killer.

'Friday night,' Black prompted.

When Cindy opened her eyes she could see that Black had put the diary back into his pocket. He stared at her with eyes as dark as polished beetles.

'You were going to tell me what happened,' he reminded her.

'You know what happened,' Cindy told him. 'Melissa had too much to drink. She was going to the loo. She made it to the top of the stairs and then she... she fell.'

The fax spat out its sheet of paper. The machine sighed as though the process had been arduous. Cindy stopped herself from glancing in that direction.

'Why was Melissa drinking?' Black asked.

'She was just being sociable, I guess,' Cindy tried. 'She'd asked me into the house to have a girls' talk and we just ended up drinking more than was sensible.'

Black nodded. 'You were friends? Melissa never mentioned that to me.'

'No. Yes. Well, not really.' Confusion and embarrassment caused a blush to rise up from beneath Cindy's collar. 'It's complicated.'

'I've got all morning. All day, if that's what it takes.'

'I give Richard a lift to work each morning,' Cindy began. 'That way I get one of the carpool spaces and Richard doesn't have to worry about getting to and from work.'

'Why can't he drive himself?'

'Banned.'

Black nodded. His features were inscrutable but Cindy got the vague impression that Black approved of Richard's driving ban. He studied her expectantly and she realised he was waiting for her to continue.

'I give him a lift home at the end of the day too,' she went on. 'And I was just dropping him off when Melissa asked me to join her for a drink.'

'Even though you weren't friends?'

'She wanted–'

'Didn't it strike you as odd?'

'Yes. No. Well, not odd. But out of the ordinary.'

'And you just said yes.'

'What else was I supposed to say? I'd got a lonely weekend stretching ahead of me. The opportunity for some human company didn't seem that unappealing. And the few times I'd spoken to Melissa before, I thought she was kinda nice. So, I said yeah.'

Silence stretched between them. Cindy had no idea what else Black wanted to hear from her and she didn't want to start babbling for fear that she might something incriminating.

'What did she want to talk about?'

'Why are you asking all these questions, Mr Black?'

'What did she want to talk about?'

'Is there something suspicious about Melissa's death?'

'What did she want to talk about?'

'She wanted to talk about Richard.'

Cindy dared to glance towards the fax machine. She could see that there was a page resting in the tray but, from her position, she was unable to see what was printed on the page.

'Melissa wanted to ask you questions about her husband. Why? Were you fucking him?'

Cindy knew there was a guilty blush rising from her décolletage to her throat. She could feel it burning her cheeks and bringing a rush of tears to her eyes. She madly wondered if Black was gullible enough to interpret her colouring as a blush of outrage rather than a symptom of embarrassed guilt. Even as that thought was tumbling through her mind, Cindy knew it was pathetically optimistic.

'It's Richard's birthday next week,' Cindy said, stiffly. 'Melissa was undecided about the gift she should get for him. She wanted my advice.'

Black's dark eyes regarded her with stubborn, animal wariness. 'Why would she ask you?' his voice was soft. 'She's been married to him for seven years. She doesn't know you. Why would she ask you, a stranger, what her husband might want for his birthday?'

Cindy stood up and started towards the fax machine.

Black grabbed her wrist. The force of his grip was strong enough to stop her from taking another step.

'Why?' he repeated.

'I spend two hours each morning driving Richard into the office,' she spat. 'We don't sit in silence on that drive. We talk about stuff. The same happens every night when we're driving home. Two hours of talking about stuff. That's four hours a day or twenty hours a week. If me and Richard happen to have lunch during a day, or if we attend the same meeting, that means I can sometimes spend more time with Richard in a week than he spends with his wife. Considering we spend so much time together, I think it made sense for her to ask for my opinion on which present he would prefer.'

Black released his hold on Cindy's wrist whilst nodding towards her chair. She understood the spoken message and, with only a bitter glance in the direction of the fax machine, Cindy silently returned to her seat.

'What did you tell her to buy him?'

'Excuse me?'

'Melissa wanted advice on what present to get her husband. What present did you tell her to buy him?'

'Melissa was torn between treating Richard to a holiday in Africa or a Caribbean cruise. She was asking which I thought he would prefer.'

'Which did you say?'

'I think she was deciding on Africa,' Cindy admitted. 'Although I don't think either of those choices would have been ideal for Richard. He's not really got the sort of complexion that suits too much sun.'

'Did you tell her that?'

'I was trying to,' Cindy lied. 'But it wasn't something I could say at first without sounding really rude. If I'd blurted something like that as soon as she invited me into her kitchen it would have sounded like I was trying to tell the woman I knew her husband better than she did.'

Black sat back in his chair. He considered Cindy in silence.

Cindy couldn't recall the last time she had been studied with such close and daunting scrutiny. She resisted the urge to scratch her itching flesh, fold her arms across her chest or make some attempt to hide herself from Black's unwelcome interest. Instead she sat as still as she was able and struggled to meet his gaze.

'I'm sorry for all the questions,' Black said, eventually. He rubbed a stubby-fingered hand against his face and added, 'It's been a long weekend.'

'Tell me about it,' Cindy agreed.

'It's probably best if I don't,' Black countered.

There was an eerie expression on his face. On any other human being Cindy would have identified the curl to his lips and the twinkle in his eyes as a smile of some description. Because this was Roger Black she knew it couldn't be one of those. Wrenching her gaze from the disconcerting depths of his eyes she saw that her PC screen had finally sprung to life.

As head of CNS, Cindy had her PC set so the machine activated her email programme when the computer was switched on. She watched the familiar screen load and saw that her machine was receiving a barrage of emails. With each one the computer whispered conspiratorially, '*You've got mail. You've got mail. You've got mail...*'

Her complexion grew pale as she saw what she was receiving.

Cindy reached over and punched the mute button on her keyboard. The electronic announcements stopped, although she could see the emails continued flooding into her inbox.

'I'll leave you to your work,' Black said. 'You've clearly got a lot to do.' He stood up and offered his hand across the desk.

For one horrifying moment Cindy was struck by the idea that Black could see her monitor screen. The incoming emails all seemed to have the same subject header: TO THE KILLER.

Cindy took Black's hand. His grip was hard and uncompromising.

'I'm sorry for your loss,' she said earnestly. She glanced over to the fax machine, wondering if she could read its message from where she now stood. The contents of the page remained at a maddening angle that was impossible for her to see. 'I'm really sorry.'

Black nodded. 'A car will pick you up from here on Friday morning.' He started towards the door and then stopped abruptly. Turning around, fixing her with a grim glower, he said, 'It's a shame Melissa didn't get to know you better. I'll bet the two of you would have been famous friends.'

'Famous,' Cindy agreed.

Black slammed the door closed behind himself.

Cindy counted to ten after he had gone. She counted the numbers slowly and with lengthy pauses between them. As soon as she reached ten, Cindy decided that Black would not be returning. But she still locked her office door to be on the safe side. Turning to her PC she saw the machine had received 4,036 messages. Each one bore the same subject header: TO THE KILLER.

22

Deleting the messages was no good. As fast as Cindy could delete them a fresh batch of messages would arrive. Each bore the same subject header: TO THE KILLER. She examined one, trying to see who had sent it, but there was no helpful clue there. The sender's email address was a blank and she knew that could mean it was part of a virus or that the email had been sent from an account where the user was deliberately keeping their identity a secret, or that some other unexplained forces were operating. That latter option wasn't one she normally liked to consider but, since taking a position with Raven and Skull, she had come to accept that there were occasions when the only justification that could be offered was the glib phrase: *unexplained forces*.

Admittedly, as head of CNS she had subordinates who could possibly have found out where the email had come from. But if any of her staff saw the subject header of those emails, Cindy knew the rumours would begin circulating faster than any email in history and she was not going to lay herself and Richard open to that sort of scandal.

The message of each email was identical: a single six letter word repeated over and over and over again. *killer, kill…* When the fax machine whirred into life, Cindy snatched her gaze away from the mesmerising lines of text.

She went over to the tray and saw she had received two faxes, both daubed with the identical slanted message: *KILLER*. She plucked the sheets of paper from the tray and took them to her personal shredder. Feeding through the pages slowly, then shaking the box beneath the shredder's jaws so that the segments of freshly made confetti were forced to mingle together, she watched the next page being spat out of the fax machine bearing exactly the same message.

Cindy stooped to the side of the fax machine and wrenched the machine's telephone connection from its socket. The fax machine whistled discordantly. It sounded as though it was in pain. The noise made her shift from one foot to the other, waiting for it to end. Cindy tore the half-printed sheet of paper from the fax's feed and then stuffed that page into the shredder's whirling, ever-hungry jaws.

The tip of her middle finger touched against the steel blades. Too late, she snatched her bitten hand away from the teeth. A pinprick of blood stood red against the pale flesh. She watched it swell to the size of a full stop, then a pea, then the droplet was falling to the floor and being replaced by another.

'Shit! Shit! Shit!'

The shredder continued to munch its way through the page.

Cindy glanced back at the computer monitor and saw that her email inbox now contained 13,306 messages. She didn't bother to check if they all bore the same subject header. Instead, she dropped to her knees and wrenched the computer's CPU free from its space beneath her desk. Unplugging the kettle lead from the back, tearing at all the other tendrils of cables that slithered from the unit, she lifted the metal box high in the air, and then smashed it to the floor. Satisfied by the hefty metallic thud, Cindy lifted the box and dropped it again.

Then again.

And again.

There was the sound of something loose scratching on the inside of the unit. Cindy smiled with grim satisfaction and pulled herself from the floor. The stillness of the office was broken by the shrill buzz of her intercom.

Cindy pressed the intercom's button.

'What do you want, Margaret?'

'I heard some noises coming from your office. I wanted to make sure you were OK.'

Cindy glanced at her hand. The tip of her finger continued dripping blood. 'I've cut my finger on the shredder,' she admitted. 'But it's nothing serious. Can you get in here?'

'On my way.'

As Cindy walked over to the door, unlocking it in readiness for Margaret, she heard the muffled ring of her mobile phone. The five shrill beeps it emitted suggested it was receiving a text message. Glancing at the sealed, padded package, Cindy acted without hesitation. She picked up the envelope, dropped it to the floor and then stamped on it with all the force she could manage. The heel of her shoe went through the bag and she heard it smash through the body of the mobile phone.

The phone continued to beep.

Cindy raised her foot and stamped again.

And again.

'Is everything OK?' Margaret asked as she stepped into the room.

Panting, exhausted from the effort, Cindy stepped away from the envelope. The telephone had stopped ringing and she could see part of its shattered mechanism now peeped through a tear that penetrated both sides of the envelope.

'I think everything's OK,' Cindy lied. The words came out in a strained rush. She knew if she tried to say them again, she was going to burst into a flood of hysterical giggles. 'But I need my mobile taking down to hardware.' She picked up the envelope from the floor and placed it in Margaret's hands. 'I'll also need a replacement PC fitting,' Cindy said, nodding towards the misshapen box in the centre of the room. 'That one seems to have a problem. I think it might be hardware related, although I expect the lab rats will blame it on the software.'

Margaret glanced at the broken box and then turned to study Cindy. Her face was as inscrutable as Roger Black's had been, although her features lacked the hard edge of brutality and potential violence. 'Have you tried pressing Control, Alt and Delete?'

Cindy wanted to laugh. She bit back that response for fear it would come out as a spiralling manic cackle. 'I'm just going for a coffee,' she said. The words sounded strangled. 'I'll be back in a minute or two. See if they can get the replacement stuff hurried along.'

Margaret nodded. She held a notepad and scribbled on it as Cindy rushed out of the office. 'Do you want me to get in touch with Human Resources too?' she asked. 'See if they have a psychiatrist on standby?'

Cindy didn't bother responding. She figured she was probably beyond the help of a psychiatrist.

23

The canteen was deserted. The rows of empty tables and forgotten coffee cups reminded Cindy of documentaries she had watched concerning the fate of the *Mary Celeste*. Cindy walked to the main serving area and, seeing no one there, sighed heavily and then looked around for a coffee machine. She didn't particularly care for the dusty taste of powdery, processed machine coffee. But she was desperate for a drink. She fumbled through her purse and found change for the machine.

An LED display sat above the coin slot. She watched the words on the unit spread their constant message of coffee-related advertising. 'ENJOY A REFRESHING ESPRESSO. THIS MACHINE ACCEPTS 10P, 20P, 50P AND £1 COINS. WHAT DO YOU WANT TO DRINK, KILLER?'

Cindy stepped back from the machine in shock.

The words disappeared from the LED screen.

'Did you just want a coffee?'

The polite enquiry was called from the canteen's main serving area. Cindy didn't shriek when she heard the voice but she came close to releasing the sound. Trying to steady her nerves, needing to get a drink so she could sit down and work out what was happening, she staggered back to the counter and said, 'Yes. Coffee. Strong and black, please.'

'Do you need a breakfast?'

'No.'

'We've got full English.'

'No, thank you.'

'I can do you a sausage sandwich–'

'No, thank you.'

'Or a bacon sandwich–'

'Just the coffee, please.'

'Or you could throw me down the stairs a couple more times.'

Cindy finally glanced at the woman's face. She didn't normally bother to look at the serving staff who worked in the canteen. They were usually the grinning dregs of society, making minimum wage and seeming offensively cheerful despite their lowly employment status. Dressed in a rumpled white uniform that was meant to imply cleanliness, the kitchen staff invariably wore paper hats to keep their cheap haircuts from contaminating the food.

The woman serving Cindy wore a hat. Her head had been lowered when she'd first caught Cindy's attention and that was why Cindy hadn't seen her face. She had only seen the top of her paper hat. But now, now that the woman had raised her head and tilted it at an awkward angle that suggested her neck was no longer doing its job properly, Cindy recognised the woman.

'Melissa?'

'Do you just want coffee? Or would you like to throw me down the steps at this place? We're on the fourteenth floor so, if we get to the fire escape stairs, I'd bounce down and down and down and...'

Cindy took a step back, away from the counter.

The woman stared at her with eyes that were flat and devoid of expression. Her flesh had an unhealthy pallor that was too pale to consider. It was as though the blood had stopped flowing through the veins beneath the skin. She held up one hand with fingers that were bent to obscene and frightening angles.

'Of course, you'd get knackered from the strain of having to drag me back up here. But, if it meant you could get your filthy little hands on my possessions, I don't think that would trouble you too much, would it?'

'Melissa?' Cindy murmured.

She took another step back.

'What do you want, Cindy? Coffee? My house? My money? My husband?'

Something touched Cindy from behind. She whirled to see who was standing there, dropping her purse to the floor in the same movement. The clatter of coins was deafening in the stillness of the canteen. Cindy saw that Roger Black had been standing behind her. Unable to suppress the sound, she wailed in dismay.

'Cindy?'

She pushed past him and hurried out of the canteen. Running blindly, she didn't stop until she'd reached the lift doors. A swarthy dark-haired figure stood outside the lift. He placed his foot against the side of the open door. Cindy recognised Shaun from Customer Services but she couldn't bring herself to say anything to him to acknowledge that recognition.

'You want to go down on me?' he asked. His leering grin made it obvious that he was attempting lewd innuendo.

Cindy stared past him and saw that there was a woman waiting inside the lift already. She took a step back when she recognised her. No longer wearing the uniform of a canteen worker, now dressed like one of Raven and Skull's maintenance staff in a plaid shirt, jeans and a hard hat, Melissa stood inside the lift doors and extended a beckoning finger. There was no nail on the finger. There was only a bloody bed of raw flesh where the nail should have been.

'Come on in, Cindy,' Melissa urged. 'Go down with us.' She laughed, a sound that came out horribly strained through mangled vocal cords.

'Are you getting in?' Shaun asked.

Cindy stared at him in amazement, shocked that anyone could contemplate riding in the lift with Melissa's ghost. Shaking her head, using the movement to propel herself into action, she hurried away from the lifts to a door marked EMERGENCY STAIRS.

'Crazy bitch,' Shaun muttered. His voice was loud enough for Cindy to hear the words. A part of her figured he might be right in that assessment of her faculties, although she thought he was equally crazy for taking the lift with Melissa. Pushing through the doorway to the EMERGENCY STAIRS, Cindy took a moment to savour the silence before considering the enormous task that now lay ahead of her.

The stairs were utilitarian concrete with fixtures of stainless steel rails.

The crisp echo that followed every sound told Cindy that, if she stumbled, the stairs would be hard and unforgiving. She stared down at the angular route they took, winding round and down and round and down until they continued beyond the range of her vision. If a person fell down those steps, she thought, their body would continue until the corpse landed in hell.

From somewhere in the main building there was a muffled explosion.

Cindy flinched.

The movement made her lurch towards the first step of the staircase and she gripped the banister with desperate ferocity. Her cut finger blazed in protest. A stiffer shard of pain came from the snap of her fingernail. The sudden sting was so shrill she yelped.

A siren began to wail. The noise was migraine loud and accompanied by the hiss of sprinkler water cascading around her ears.

'What the hell happened?' she wondered.

Behind her, from the main building, Cindy could hear similar questions and exclamations being called. Someone burst into the emergency stairwell and rushed past her. A second figure followed the first. Both sets of footsteps clattered against the concrete steps as they hurried down the winding descent. Neither of them paid any heed to Cindy as she clutched the banister and tried to summon the courage to continue her journey downward.

'It sounded like a bomb,' one of them called.

'I think it was the lift,' the other shouted back. 'I was standing by the doors and a shit load of debris just blew through them.'

'Fuck! Was anyone inside?'

Cindy could have answered that question. Instead, gripping tightly onto the banister, she started to descend the stairs one slow and terrifying step at a time.

24

Two hours later Cindy had reached the bottom of the stairs. It was an agonising journey that left her shaking from exertion. Her fingers ached from gripping the banister, her legs trembled from the effort of taking her down each step in a slow, desperately safe descent. Her thoughts were a constant tug-of-war between the urge to rush down the stairs and get out of the building and the insistence that, unless she was ultra-careful, she would lose her footing, stumble and fall to her death.

Most of Raven and Skull's staff had rushed past her at some point during her journey. They were chattering excitedly about the tragedy of the lift breaking. Cindy heard various theories being proposed, and heard the aftermath experts telling anyone who would listen that lifts could never just plummet to a catastrophic end. But for everything that she heard, the reality remained as uncertain as the faltering rise and fall of the distant ambulance sirens.

'Shaun from Customer Services,' someone shouted.

In the hollow acoustics of the stairwell it sounded like the voice was coming up from hell.

'Shaun from Customer Services was in the lift. He's dead.'

'Was anyone else in there with him?'

Cindy listened intently for the response. Her fingers gripped more tightly onto the banister.

'Someone says they saw a woman in there with him.'

'A woman? Who?'

'*Yes*,' Cindy thought. She didn't dare ask the question herself but she listened desperately for the response. '*Who?*'

'Dunno. I guess it'll be difficult for them to make a positive ID. That was a really bad fall.'

Cindy closed her eyes and dared to hope. She wasn't sure if a ghost could die, but she clung to the idea that Melissa's ghost might have come to its end at the bottom of the lift shaft. Melissa's ghost had been in the lift, beckoning for Cindy to join her. Now the lift was destroyed at the bottom of its shaft. Cindy knew nothing about ghosts but she clung to the hope that Melissa's ghost would be discovered dead in the remains of the lift alongside Shaun.

By the time she reached the ground floor her body ached as though she had been beaten. The remnants of a crowd remained in the bustling foyer and a string of red and white warning tape cordoned off the lift doors.

An ambulance stood outside the office's main doors. It was parked on the pavement at a jaunty angle, whilst a pair of paramedics leant against its side, chatting idly. A fire engine, its livery a virulent orange that made the rest of the day seem more grey, was parked by the side of the ambulance.

'You look like shit,' one of the paramedics told Cindy. 'Are you OK?'

She swallowed and nodded. The movement hurt. 'I just had difficulty getting down the stairs.'

'I found it easy getting down the stairs,' the paramedic's assistant told her.

Cindy glanced at the woman.

Melissa.

Now wearing a paramedic's uniform, tilting her head to one side so that it lolled at a grotesque angle, Melissa said, 'I found it easy to get down the stairs the first time and then, the second and third times, it got even easier those last two times because you were so kind as to carry me up.'

Cindy fled to the car park. She jumped into the Ford Focus and, for one horrible moment, she feared she didn't have her keys with her. She remembered dropping her purse in the canteen and panic made her think that she had also dropped her keys. The idea of having to make the miserable journey back up the stairwell, to see if someone had found her keys and handed them to lost property, was enough to make tears well on her lower lids.

It was not something she would do.

It was not something she could do.

Now that she was out of the offices of Raven and Skull she was determined never to return. She would walk home if that was what was needed. She would leave the car behind and walk the whole forty-five miles away from Raven and Skull back to her own apartment.

As she patted the pockets of her jacket she felt the familiar shape of her car keys. Cindy released a sigh of absolute, heartfelt gratitude.

The Focus started first time.

She paused for a moment, shivering in the car seat and savouring the relief of sitting in a comfortable and safe environment. Then, having to use extra effort to stop her arms from shaking, she guided the car out of the car park.

The satnav sprang to life. The electronic voice, antiseptic and vaguely feminine, said, 'At the roundabout, in one hundred yards, take the third exit, *killer*.'

Cindy shrieked. She tore at the small unit and wrenched it from its dashboard housing. The coloured screen turned black.

Outside the windscreen she saw that her car had veered onto the other side of the road. The blare of an approaching horn forced her to steer hard to the left. There was a squeal of brakes, a momentary lurch and the sound of metal scraping rustily against metal.

'You fuckin' loony bitch!'

Cindy heard the cry come to her as she continued to drive onward. Ordinarily, she would have raised a finger and flipped the other driver off. With her hands gripping tight around the steering wheel, she didn't have the energy to make the gesture. Instead she carried grimly on, following the route home that was as much a part of her daily routine as sitting behind a desk at Raven and Skull.

It took fifteen minutes to get to the motorway.

An overhead sign warned of impending delays. Cindy read the message from its electronic display and was not surprised to see the words change. At first it read: DELAYS AT JCT 6. After a slow blink, the message changed to: CINDY IS A KILLER.

She turned off the motorway immediately.

Daring to turn on the radio was a mistake. She recognised the soothing voice of the female DJ. It was a woman whose show preceded the drive-time slot that she normally listened to with Richard on their journey home. The show was made up of unusual news stories and phoned-in dedications.

'This next song is being played for Cindy,' the DJ announced.

Cindy glared at the radio. The LED display on the radio player usually said the name of the station she was listening to. This time it simply flashed the word KILLER.

'This one comes to Cindy from Melissa,' the DJ announced. 'And she's asked us to play *Tragedy* by Steps.' The DJ laughed and added, 'Melissa says the title and the group are really appropriate for Cindy because Melissa says she had a tragedy this weekend and it happened on some steps. I don't know what that means but Cindy, if you're listening, Melissa says that you really killed her this weekend and she's looking forward to getting her own back on you.'

Cindy turned off the radio and drove on in silence.

She was away from her familiar route but she felt confident that she was headed in roughly the right direction. Even though every road sign was now useless, only displaying the word KILLER followed by a set of useless numbers, she felt sure she could remember her way back along the roads.

An articulated lorry drove past her. The side was a long advertising board. Its yellow colour made her think it should have been advertising Weetabix or Cornflakes. Instead of the familiar brand, Cindy saw that it announced to the world: CINDY IS A KILLER.

She pulled the Focus to the side of the road and turned off the engine.

Stepping out of the car, chilled by the day's cool breeze against her sweat-lathered flesh, Cindy took a deep breath and stood helpless in the centre of the road. Every muscle in her body was fatigued from exertion. Her fingertip continued to bleed with sullen, determined ferocity. She was thirsty, tired and confused and wanted only to weep and collapse and remain motionless until all her problems had gone away.

She looked up to see a car bearing down on her.

The temptation to remain in its path and allow the inevitable impact to end her suffering was almost irresistible.

Instead, she fell against the side of her Focus.

'You crazy cow!' the driver called.

In her ear, a voice whispered, 'Next time you won't be so lucky.'

She sat down by the side of the road and tried to gather her thoughts. The grass was wet against the seat of her skirt but she figured, the way things had been going today, a damp arse was probably going to be the least of her worries. More important, for the sake of her own sanity, she needed to work out what was happening and how she could best deal with the situation.

Reminding herself that she worked in CNS, Cindy decided to tackle the problem as though it was something that had landed on her desk. She was renowned for getting things done in the office and she told herself it was time to stop panicking and rely on those skills that had earned her the nickname, FED-EX.

It was impossible to say whether or not all that had happened to her this morning was because she was being haunted by Melissa's ghost, or because she was being haunted by her own guilt over Melissa's murder. Regardless of which was causing her suffering, Cindy knew she only had to deal with the effects and find the answer to one question.

Will you get away with it?

The messages that had come in on her mobile, through the fax machine and on her PC might have been figments of her imagination, or they could have been real and from a supernatural source. She knew that there might be other explanations but, reflecting on all that had happened since she first reached the offices of Raven and Skull that morning, Cindy reasoned that those two options were the only ones that needed to be considered. More importantly, when she asked herself the important question (*will you get away with it?*) the problem did not seem so daunting.

Her email account was password protected so no one was going to read any of the thousands of accusations that would be now filling her inbox. Her mobile was out of commission and none of the lab rats in the IT Department would have any cause or reason to read her messages once the unit was repaired. Her fax machine was unplugged and there was no one at Raven and Skull who had any need to plug it in. Every message she had received was private and personal and, even those that had run the risk of being seen by others had mysteriously been overlooked.

Roger Black had clearly not seen any of the accusatory messages and he was a man who missed nothing. She didn't think he'd even been aware of the ghostly-cafeteria-worker-Melissa who had been standing behind the canteen counter.

Shaun from Customer Services had seemed oblivious to the presence of the ghostly-maintenance-Melissa who had been in the lift with him whilst making her hateful accusations. Cindy thought this suggested that she was the only one who could see the woman. She mentally revisited all that had happened: the satnav, the DJ and the traffic signs. They had been messages that only she had seen or heard. No one else seemed to be responding adversely to the motorway's warning messages or the unhelpful and repetitive road signs.

Will you get away with it?

Cindy could feel her confidence soaring. It didn't matter whether the messages from Melissa were coming from her own subconscious or from some supernatural source. The important thing was that the messages were only being seen by her.

Will you get away with it?

She smiled when she realised she had an answer to her question. She was getting away with it. Her secret was safe and she was getting away with murder. The notion allowed her to take a deep sigh of relief.

'You won't get away with it,' Melissa told her.

Cindy nodded.

She was not surprised to see Melissa sitting in the passenger seat of the Ford Focus and staring out at her. Cindy was no longer even scared by the woman's grisly presence, or the finality of her depressing message.

'I probably won't get away with it,' Cindy agreed.

'You *certainly* won't get away with it,' Melissa corrected.

Cindy nodded again. 'But that's not going to bring you back to life, is it?' She stood up, patted remnants of cut grass from her backside, and tried not to think that her buttocks were clammy from sitting by the roadside. After all she had endured since arriving at work that morning, Cindy figured the nuisance of a damp backside was a minor inconvenience. She climbed into the driver's seat and turned the key in the ignition.

'Do you know where you're going?' Melissa asked.

'I'm going home.'

'Do you know how to get there?' She ran her broken fingers over the empty dashboard housing where the satnav had been. 'This isn't your usual route, is it?'

Cindy pointed at a sign by the side of an approaching junction. 'I'm only thirty miles from KILLER,' she observed, wryly. 'I think, if I take a left at KILLER, then I'll be just half an hour from going through KILLER and then I should be home.'

Melissa played with the radio's buttons.

Cindy drove her fist into the front of the radio. Her hand was turned into a ball of agony from the action but it stopped the machine from playing anything further.

'I'm not in the mood for listening to music,' Cindy told Melissa.

'What are you in the mood for?'

Cindy did not respond.

25

She drove her car onto the driveway of Melissa Mansion and parked outside the front door. Cindy remembered that the last time she had placed her vehicle in this particular position had been on that fateful Friday evening that had ended with Melissa's death.

'What the hell are you doing here?' Melissa demanded. 'I thought you said you were going home?'

Cindy considered telling the ghost that, very soon, Melissa Mansion would be her home. She decided that revelation was likely to cause some anger and stopped herself. In a quiet voice, Cindy said, 'I want to see Richard.'

'Dicky won't be happy to see you,' Melissa warned her.

'I'm not here to make him happy.' She climbed out of the car and walked towards the door.

'I don't think he's in,' Melissa said, following. There was a note of desperation in her voice as she added, 'I'm sure he's gone out somewhere.'

Cindy continued. She could see the door was ajar and, without worrying that it might be construed as trespassing, she pushed her way into the house.

'Come on in,' Melissa sneered, sarcastically.

Cindy didn't bother glancing at her. She didn't want to give Melissa the satisfaction of knowing she was unnerved. The last time she had visited this house was the night when she had become a murderer. Now she was returning to the scene of the crime. Shivering a little, Cindy glanced around the spacious hallway and tried to think if there were any changes she would make to the decor once it belonged to her and Richard.

'Make yourself at home,' Melissa sneered. 'Oh! Wait. You've already done that by murdering me and claiming this place for yourself, haven't you?'

'RICHARD!' Cindy called. 'Where are you?'

'He's not in,' Melissa snapped. 'Perhaps you should just get back in your nasty little car and piss off home?'

'RICHARD!' Cindy tried again. 'It's Cindy! Whereabouts are you?'

'He's probably in the bedroom, violating my marital bed with another of the staff,' Melissa suggested, airily. 'Did he ever tell you that was his hobby?'

'RICHARD!'

'He gets a particular thrill from fucking commoners and the working-class,' Melissa explained. 'I expect he got a real kick out of riding your fat arse.'

Cindy started towards the kitchen. The room was eerily silent. She was reminded of the evening she had spent in the room with a living and less embittered Melissa. That evening seemed to have happened a long, long time ago.

'He's not here,' Melissa exclaimed. 'How many times do I need to tell you that?'

'Would you like me to pour you a bourbon?' Cindy asked. She was blackly amused to see Melissa scowl at the suggestion.

'And why would I want you to do that?'

'You've been talking to me for the last couple of hours or more,' Cindy reminded her. 'I figured this must be a new record for you. Is this the longest you've been without getting a drink inside you.'

'You really are a nasty cow, aren't you?' Melissa marvelled.

'I'm a nasty cow with a pulse,' Cindy returned. 'What have you got, Melissa? You can send me poisonous email messages. You can send accusatory faxes to my office and those horrid texts to my mobile. But now I'm standing in your kitchen, and we're face to face with each other, you can't even raise a hand to strike me.'

Melissa's scowl was black with impotent fury.

Laughing bitterly Cindy said, 'You've got no corporeal presence, Melissa. You can't do anything to me, so stop pretending that you have any control over my destiny.'

Cindy didn't bother waiting for Melissa's response.

Instead she started out of the kitchen calling, 'RICHARD!'

He wasn't to be found in any of the downstairs rooms. Cindy went from one to another. She was still marvelling at the size and splendour of Melissa Mansions and repeatedly telling herself that all the ostentatious glamour she was walking through would soon be the property she shared with Richard. The idea was a balm to her thoughts after the panicked anxiety of the morning she had suffered.

Will you get away with it?

I have got away with it, she thought, triumphantly.

'RICHARD!'

It was annoying that he wasn't responding, but Cindy used the nuisance as an opportunity to properly explore her new property. The two reception rooms on the ground floor were large and luxurious. She ventured down a set of stairs and found the house's basement was divided into two delightfully spacious rooms. One of them contained a large pool table. The other was a darker affair, housing a boiler and gardening equipment and dusty old packing cases.

'RICHARD!'

She returned uneasily to the hall. Although she was struggling to remain defiant, Cindy couldn't help but feel uncomfortable to be standing where she had been whilst watching Melissa take her first ungainly tumble down the stairs. Even though it was now daylight, and that dramatic fall had taken place in oily darkness, it was impossible not to remember how dreadful the moment had been. She was struck by the idea that if she listened to the silence for long enough she would be able to hear the wet slap of bruised flesh hitting the marble stairs and the crunch of snapping bones still echoing through the hallway.

'RICHARD! ARE YOU UPSTAIRS?'

'You're going to have to go up there and see, aren't you?' Melissa whispered. Her voice was filled with hateful glee. 'You're going to have to climb those stairs and see if you can find him up there.'

Cindy didn't bother turning to face the woman.

'I think I can manage a flight of stairs.'

'You didn't seem so confident back at Raven and Skull.'

Cindy said nothing. The arduous descent of the emergency stairway was an episode she didn't want to brood on. The blind terror and rising panic were now behind her but, she knew, if she tried to remember those emotions, it would be too easy to recall the dark and desperate fear that had come when she'd tried to manage those brutal, unforgiving stairs.

'You don't want to fall,' Melissa chided. 'It hurts like a bitch. It will look awfully suspicious for Richard if a second woman is found dead at the bottom of his staircase. It will almost look like he has a habit for making these things happen.'

'I'm not going to fall,' Cindy repeated.

'You don't want to,' Melissa agreed. 'When you die, you're going to spend eternity in hell. That's what happens to all those who've sinned as egregiously as you.'

'Egregiously?' Cindy repeated. 'Is that one of the words they taught you at Cambridge?' She flashed an insincere smile and said, 'I wouldn't know such complicated words. I'm just a working class girl with a fat arse.'

Melissa sniffed.

'You're going to hell when you die so you'll want to delay that happening for as long as possible. I may not have a corporeal presence on this plane. But, when you're in hell, I'm going to be one of those demonic bitches that makes your suffering legendary.'

Cindy mounted the first step on the staircase. It was secure beneath her foot and, even though her legs felt tired, she was sure she could manage the full flight without incident. 'Is hell likely to be worse than having you talk to me all the time?'

Melissa did not respond.

Cindy half turned and was surprised to discover that the woman was no longer in the hallway. She took another step up the flight of stairs, still staring down into the hall, and wondering if Melissa had now decided to leave her alone. When she turned to face up the flight of stairs Melissa stood before her. The woman's shattered face was so close that Cindy almost screamed from the fright. Her aching fingers instinctively gripped tighter onto the banister. The fact that her body tried to pull backwards was enough to make her realise she had come close to falling down the stairs.

'Did I make you jump?' Melissa asked, sweetly.

Cindy drew a ragged breath. She paused, gripping the stair rail tight, and waiting for her staccato heartbeat to finally slow.

'Go on,' Melissa encouraged. She stepped out of Cindy's path and said, 'Climb a little higher. Let's see if you can make it all the way to the top.'

'Are you jealous?' Cindy asked. She tried not to let her breathlessness come through from her speech. 'Are you jealous that I've got a fully functioning body? Even when you were alive the best your body could ever manage was to open the fridge and pour another Jack Daniel's.'

'You bitch,' Melissa breathed.

'Living bitch,' Cindy said, absently. She didn't bother waiting to see if the remark caused any upset. Instead, struggling to make the task seem effortless, she put one foot in front of the other and made her way to the top of the stairs. It was not as arduous a climb as she had feared. When she realised she had managed the chore without incident, Cindy breathed a heavy sigh of satisfaction.

'RICHARD!' she called. 'Are you up here, Richard? It's Cindy!'

A figure loomed onto the landing in front of her. It was male, tall and rushing with wild urgency. After it had sped past her, Cindy recognised Richard. But he was clearly preoccupied with his own problems and didn't see her standing at the top of the steps. It was instinctive to want to step backwards to avoid the inevitable collision but, because the dreaded stairs were behind her, Cindy fought the urge. Instead, she stepped to one side and allowed Richard to go rushing down the staircase.

Melissa came rushing at Cindy. She too was running and her path was on a collision course with where Cindy stood. Reminding herself that Melissa was a harmless, insubstantial ghost, Cindy held her ground and stared levelly at Melissa to show she was not intimidated.

When the woman pushed into her, knocking her backwards and into the empty air above the stairs, Cindy's first thought was a panicked refusal that this was happening. She flailed to reach out for something. She needed to clutch anything that might slow her descent. Her feet kicked aimlessly in the air. She began to plummet down towards the marble stairs. A shriek of protest built up in her throat. Before she could release the sound, Melissa's voice whispered in her ear, 'Lucky me! I do have a corporeal presence.'

Will I get away with it?

Cindy was trying to think how she could now answer that question as she fell backwards on the same route that Melissa had taken on Friday night. The world turned upside down and her head connected with a hard, angular step. In that moment she understood that she wasn't going to be as fortunate as Richard's former wife when it came to surviving that first agonising descent. But it was only when her body had reached the floor at the bottom of the stairs that she understood her plight.

'Cindy,' Melissa said quietly.

Cindy could see that the woman was kneeling over her.

Melissa reached out and took the fractured remains of Cindy's right hand. She lifted it in the air. Cindy tried to exercise some control over the arm, tried to retrieve her hand from Melissa's grip, but the ability was beyond her.

'Cindy,' Melissa whispered conspiratorially. 'Cindy. I think you might have broken a fingernail.'

'I don't get it,' Becky complained. 'How can you tell us a story about how you died, when you're here talking? That doesn't make sense.' She glared angrily round at the others and said, 'I'm right, aren't I? That doesn't make sense. It doesn't make any sense.'

'It made as much sense as your story,' Richard observed.

Cindy was indignant. 'Are you calling me a liar?'

Richard tightened a comforting hand against her shoulder. 'No one's calling anyone a liar,' he said firmly.

'The thing that doesn't make sense,' Heather broke in, 'is that Cindy said she didn't want to hear another story about Raven and Skull, and then goes on to tell us about her affair with someone at Raven and Skull, and what a shitty Wednesday she had going crazy in Raven and Skull's offices. What was that about, Cindy? How come your story took us straight back there?'

Cindy looked set to snap back with a vitriolic response. Before she could say anything, Geoff spoke quietly from his seat in the corner.

'The reason for that is because everything leads back to Raven and Skull. No one can escape the place. And, once you're in their clutches, they take over your existence.'

'Have you got a story?' Tony asked.

Geoff pursed his lips.

'Half now. Half when you hand it over to me.'

Geoff didn't stare at the stranger. He could only look at the contents of the tote bag that had been dropped onto the table in front of him. Sitting in a corner booth at Shades, enjoying some discretion from the rest of the room, his stomach muscles tightened. It was automatic to glance over his shoulder and assure himself that no one else in the pub had seen this element of their transaction.

There were a handful of locals in the pub. Most of them were burly men dressed in snug T-shirts pulled taut over bulging beer-bellies. A few of them stood at the bar, chatting and drinking. A couple of them lazed in front of pints glued to nearby tables. The open door revealed a glimpse of the triptych of smokers who stood outside Shades beneath the sickly green glow of the pub's illuminated sign.

No one was looking in the direction of Geoff and his corner booth.

No one had noticed that he was involved in an illicit transaction.

Still, it was impossible to loosen the coil of anxiety that tightened in his stomach. He knew that people had been killed for a lot less than the bundle of notes concealed inside the flimsy tote bag. The idea that he could become another statistic because of the money made his bowels twist as though he had received a knife blade to the guts.

'Is it a deal, Mr Arnold?'

The stranger was an imposing figure. His casual jeans, worn with a hooded fleece beneath a leather jacket, were uniform standard for rough urban pubs like Shades. Geoff had seen a dozen men dressed identically this evening and he didn't consider himself particularly observant. The stranger wore a skull-hugging grey beanie. It was pulled down far enough to hide the tops of his ears. His face looked battle-hardened with the memories of scars criss-crossing one cheekbone and acne pockmarks making an alien landscape around his mouth. There was a day's worth of razor stubble dirtying his lantern jaw, adding to the impression of strong physical ability. The only thing about him that struck Geoff as peculiar was the fact that the man carried a vague scent of incense. It was a fragrance that was musky, sweet and vaguely religious.

'Is it a deal, Mr Arnold?'

Geoff continued to study the contents of the tote bag without moving. The situation wouldn't become real until he placed his hand inside the bag and touched the crisp, dry notes. Until his fingers made contact with the money his commitment to the deal remained no more than a half-joked suggestion, a quip that intimated he might be able to do as the stranger had asked. Until he did that much, until he placed his fingers on the notes and accepted that the money was his, Geoff could consider himself good, honest and innocent.

'Mr Arnold?'

'Geoff?'

Geoff glanced up at the sound of Nicola's voice. He passed her a thin smile. Reaching across the table, ignoring the money for a moment, he squeezed her hand and then returned to his contemplative silence. It was an enormous decision and he refused to be rushed.

'What am I getting myself into here?' he asked, eventually.

The stranger rolled his eyes.

'Geoff!' Nicola protested.

'I'm just asking what I'm getting into.'

The stranger reached for the tote bag. He grabbed both handles and started to slide the money out of Geoff's reach forever. Geoff was ready to let him. If the money was gone, the temptation to accept it was taken away and he would no longer have to make the decision to become a thief.

Nicola glared at him. Although she remained silent she shook her head. Her lips shaped the word, 'NO.'

The stranger regarded Geoff with a cold, murderous gaze. His contempt and the loss of his respect should have meant nothing. Geoff didn't know the man's name. He had only met him once previously. But a part of him felt politely apologetic for the inconvenience he had caused.

'I'll see if I can find someone capable of this job,' the stranger grunted. He flashed his glower in Nicola's direction and said, 'Your boyfriend should not organise introductions with amateurs.' The last word was invested with the contempt normally reserved for the vilest epithets.

Geoff placed his hand on the back of the stranger's wrist. The skin felt cold, clammy and dead beneath his touch. It was like touching a fat slug. 'Leave the money there.'

The stranger hesitated.

'The more I know, the better chance I have of doing this job properly,' Geoff explained. 'Do you really have issues with me doing this right?'

'You're acquiring something for us from Charlie Raven's desk,' the stranger said stiffly. 'I thought we'd already established this fact.' He glanced from Geoff to Nicola, then back to Geoff. 'Wasn't that clear? Didn't we sort out all these details at your boyfriend's restaurant, the House of Asher?'

'Usher,' Nicola corrected.

Geoff sipped his drink so the stranger couldn't see his smirk. He liked the man's evasive use of language. The stranger wasn't asking Geoff to steal something: he was paying him to *acquire* an item. Geoff wasn't even being asked to *acquire* the item for the stranger: the man's careful vocabulary suggested he represented a group of people who would likely share the burden of avoiding responsibility if the shit hit the fan.

The item itself remained nameless.

Geoff noted the way the stranger reminded them that it sat on the desk of Charlie Raven, a wheelchair-bound invalid. The stranger made no mention of the fact that the daunting spectre of Roger Black was now the man who usually worked from behind Raven's desk. The stranger was shaping his words so carefully, and openly concealing so much, Geoff had to wonder how much the man was keeping to himself.

Geoff wondered how much he had already missed.

He placed down his drink and regarded the tote bag. Making a momentous decision, he pushed his hand inside and grabbed a bundle of notes. Pulling them out, feeling the paper touch his fingers and knowing that he could no longer convincingly describe himself as innocent, he thumbed at the corners of the notes for a moment and savoured the sensation.

'This is fifty thousand?'

'That's correct.'

'And there'll be another fifty thousand when I give you the item?'

'That's correct.'

The division of the money had been settled a month earlier at The House of Usher. From the hundred thousand Geoff had been promised, Don, Nicola's boyfriend, would receive ten per cent for organising introductions between Geoff and the stranger. Nicola was due to get twenty grand because Geoff had insisted on having her help him. With those expenses out of the way, Geoff would be left with an even seventy thousand once the job was successfully completed.

Thumbing the bundle of notes, relishing the sensation of having illicit money in his hands, he supposed that seventy grand seemed like a reasonable amount for the gamble he was planning. He knew that there could be three possible outcomes from this endeavour. The chance of coming away from the situation better off by seventy thousand pounds made them all seem worth the risk.

The best result would be if he acquired the item, got the remainder of his money, and could continue working for Raven and Skull until he decided to do something different and more exciting with his life. With seventy thousand pounds in the bank he would be able to afford the few luxuries that made existence bearable. He would not have to worry about annual appraisals, savings accounts, pensions schemes and all those other drains on his financial and spiritual resources that preyed on his thoughts through the long and miserable hours of sobriety.

If things didn't go as he hoped, and he found he was no longer able to continue working for Raven and Skull, Geoff figured that seventy grand would be enough to finance a satisfying new start in life. He could go anywhere in the world if he wanted. He could enjoy any adventure that appealed to him.

He was savvy enough to understand that going anywhere in the world might be a necessity if he had earned the displeasure of Roger Black. But he refused to brood on the possibly negative elements of his plan. If he had to leave his comfortable position at Raven and Skull, Geoff was determined that a new start would incorporate the thrills and excitement that were currently absent from his life. It did not seem unreasonable to think that avoiding the wrath of Roger Black could be considered as a level of excitement.

Ultimately, if things went badly wrong and the shit really did hit the fan, Geoff figured that prison would provide him with three nutritionally balanced meals a day and the chance to study with the Open University. Even that option, with the unwelcome opportunity of making intimate friends in a prison shower block, had to be better than the grey and worthless existence of an office drone that he was currently calling life.

'What makes the gold-plated skull on Charlie Raven's desk worth one hundred thousand pounds?'

The stranger glowered.

Nicola rolled her eyes and looked away.

The stranger reached again for the pile of money.

This time, when Geoff stopped him, he was more forceful. Ignoring the natural distaste that came from touching the man's cold, dead flesh, he said, 'I'm doing the job regardless of how you answer. I just want to go in there with as much knowledge as you can possibly provide. The more prepared I am, the more likely it is that I will acquire the item for you without incident. Doesn't that make sense?'

The stranger considered him, warily. 'Do you know anything about the Church of the Black Angel?'

28

'I suppose it falls on me to make introductions,' John Skull began.

Skull sat at the head of the board. To his right sat his partner and the newest recruit to the Skull and Raven management team. The visitors to his office sat on his left. Skull's secretary, Fiona, slowly circled the room anointing, and then lighting, the ritual candles. At the foot of the table a translator repeated Skull's words in Haitian Creole. He pointed at Skull when the man spoke, in case any of those listening to the translation were unsure whose words he was translating.

Fiona conducted her work with methodical and unostentatious efficiency. Even though it was late at night, with no one else in the office building and dark outside, she had still taken the precaution of drawing the blinds at the office windows. Approaching each knobbly black candle she immersed the wick with a citric sweet balm of van van oil. Whilst the blend of lemon grass, citronella and ginger grass trickled down the uneven sides, she rubbed a special composite of High Jon powder into the length of the candle. Her small, slender hands worked sensuously against the wax, as though she was intimately massaging a lover. Her fingers shone with the oily lubrication as they worked their way up and down the hard length, blending the powder and oil into the wax. Fiona mumbled quietly to herself as she went about her work. Those close enough to hear her caught snatches of a mumbled dialect not too dissimilar from the one being used by the translator.

'Going round the table,' Skull began, 'we have Charlie Raven, who I'm sure you all know.'

Each of the visitors turned to study a grinning Charlie Raven whilst the translator repeated Skull's words. There was a lit Woodbine smouldering in the corner of Raven's mouth and he waved a cheerful greeting.

'It's a pleasure,' Raven muttered.

'Charlie is my junior partner in this company,' Skull explained. 'And it's through his hard work and the resources of his contacts that we've been so swiftly able to establish our prominent position within the city.'

Skull paused, allowing the translator a moment to reiterate his message and giving everyone else the chance to politely acknowledge the wunderkind that was Charlie Raven.

Raven seemed to bask in the adulation. His grin grew wider.

'Beside Mr Raven we have the newest recruit to our management team,' Skull went on. 'This is Mr Roger Black.'

Roger Black nodded gruffly.

'Mr Black has shown a level of competence for our style of business trading that far exceeds the expectations of his youthful appearance,' Skull explained. 'Aside from graduating *summa cum laude* from Cambridge last year, he's also shown a penchant for planning and execution that match well with our company's ethos.'

There was a moment's confusion. The translator was questioned by one of the visitors and he shook his head. Staring at Skull he said, 'You must excuse me. The houngan says, in his language, the word 'execution' can mean 'to kill.''

Skull considered this before nodding. 'It can mean the same thing in our language,' he agreed. Saying no more on the subject, gesturing towards Fiona, he said, 'The young lady working her way around the room will be familiar to you all. Fiona has been my secretary for the past five years and she's spent the last month researching the nuances of voodoo and educating the rest of us on its technicalities so that we're all properly prepared for this ritual.'

Involved in her work, Fiona didn't bother to acknowledge Skull's flattering introduction. The visitors glanced in her direction but no one spoke.

'To complete the formalities,' Skull continued. He gestured towards the figure sitting closest to the translator. 'This is Houngan Despre, a very powerful *bokor* who most of you have already met.'

The visitor nodded solemnly. He was tall, dark skinned, with a timeless quality to his features that made it impossible to estimate his age. He mumbled through an over-white smile and the translator said, 'It is an honour.'

'Next to Houngan Despre is Mambo Rillieux.'

Skull waved his hand in the woman's direction.

Everyone turned to stare at the elegant Creole woman.

'Mambo Rillieux, also known as Queen Juliet, is a special visitor to our country due to our government's lack of cultural sympathy for her religious beliefs. I trust, since it will be to our advantage, we can all show her a more hospitable welcome than that provided by the authorities.'

Rillieux nodded gracefully as the translator repeated Skull's words.

'And finally,' Skull said, 'We are honoured to be in the presence of Supreme Houngan Manumishon. Manumishon is the gentleman who, if our plans are successful, will be—'

Manumishon raised a hand. 'Mr Skull?'

The translator echoed his words.

'May I interrupt and say that we are not able to do as you ask. This meeting is a waste of all our times and many of your resources. You ask from us that which is impossible.'

Skull's smile remained on his lips. His eyes continued to sparkle with a glimmer of barely suppressed amusement but they also contained the hint of a threat. 'I'm aware that I'm asking a lot, Supreme Houngan…'

'You are asking the impossible,' Manumishon countered.

'… but I think you should hear what it is we want. If you all think it's impossible, we can discuss the matter and see if there's a solution to our requirements. A solution that the three of you can propose as an alternative.'

Behind Skull, Fiona had finished anointing and lighting the final candle. Without a sound, she took the ceremonial chalice she had been carrying and placed it beneath the final candle. Carefully, she took a blade from her pocket and passed it once through the candle's flame. The blade was long, sharp and its length was asymmetrical. Fiona pressed it to her lips, then placed it carefully into the chalice. There was a sudden thrill of electricity in the room and the air turned heavy. Fiona took a glance around the room, assured herself that all the flames were burning appropriately, and then slipped through the open door. She caught the light switch as she left, leaving the occupants in the muted glow of the fluttering candlelight. She returned a moment later holding the handle of a large box. Placing it discreetly on the floor by Skull's feet, she stood behind him and began to unfasten the buttons on her blouse.

Despre leant forward. Turning his attention between Skull and Manumishon, he spoke quickly and with impassioned urgency. The translator stumbled over some of the words as he tried to keep up with the man's impassioned outburst.

'Of course this is impossible. These people are outsiders and know nothing of voodoo. They think that their money can build us a church here in their United Kingdom. In return, they expect to be touched by *Bondyè*. I can't believe that one of the lesser *mistè* would piss on these ignorant *farang*.'

Rillieux laughed.

Manumishon glowered.

Skull passed a glance to Raven who shook his head, as his smile grew broader. Raven scribbled something on a notepad and left it on the desk where Black could read the words.

Behind Skull, Fiona had removed her blouse and was stepping out of her skirt. Seemingly unnoticed by everyone in the room, she began to remove her bra and then her panties. Her modest breasts swayed lightly as she tried to maintain her balance and step out of the undergarments. When she stood up, revealing herself naked, no one looked in her direction until she spoke.

'No one here expects to be touched by *Bondyè*,' Fiona said, sharply. She glared at Despre and said, 'You will not insult us by condemning us as *farang*.'

The visitors glared at her. The translator glanced in Fiona's direction, noticed her nudity, and then blushed. He repeated her statement in Haitian Creole.

'Messers Skull, Raven and Black are aware that *Bondyè* does not trouble himself with the matters of this world,' Fiona went on. 'They know that spiritual matters in voodoo are dealt with through the *loa*–' She paused and glared at Houngan Despre. '*Mistè,* if that's how you prefer to describe spirit liaisons for *Bondyè*.'

Despre shrank back into his seat.

Fiona gestured to Skull, Raven and Black. 'These gentlemen are trying to bestow generous gifts on you. They wish to help you promote the name of your church to a wider parish. They have invested a lot of time and effort in arranging this meeting. And you repay them with insults?'

'*Ayizan*,' Rillieux whispered.

Manumishon and Despre drew sharp breaths.

Raven shook his head. He held up a hand and looked set to argue with Rillieux and assuage the doubts of her companions.

Skull leant close to him and placed a hand on his arm. In a lowered voice he said, 'Rillieux thinks our Fiona is possessed by the spirit of *loa Ayizan*. Let's not spoil Rillieux's delusion.' Speaking directly to the translator, Skull said, 'You can see that the *loa* favour us with their presence. If the *loa* have faith in Skull and Raven, surely their church's representatives can extend us the courtesy of hearing our proposition?'

The translator held up his hand. Studying Skull carefully he said, 'I do not know these terms *loa*, *Bondyè* and *Ayizan*.'

'You don't need to understand them,' Skull growled. 'Just translate.'

The translator shook his head. 'I'm working with a Creole language here.' He sounded agitated and out of his depth. 'I understand that every word I say here is very important. I don't want to make a mistake.'

'*Bondyè*,' Fiona said slowly, 'is the one supreme vodun god. The name is a Creole formation from *Bon Dieu* – Good God.'

The translator nodded. His gaze was locked on Fiona's face, purposefully ignoring her bare body.

'*Loa*,' she continued, 'are the spirits who respond to vodun prayers. *Bondyè* does not concern himself with mortal matters. But the *loa* listen to prayers and they answer them if they receive appropriate compensation.'

'Loa,' the translator repeated. 'Spirits.'

'That's a very simplistic definition, isn't it?' Manumishon enquired.

'It's as much as the translator needs to know,' Fiona returned. 'Unless you think he needs to know more?'

Manumishon shook his head and settled back in his seat.

The translator still stared at Fiona's eyes. 'Ayizan?'

'Ayizan is the *loa* responsible for commerce and trading.' Fiona's smile was tinged with a bitter edge of smugness. She looked as though she was settling herself into a role as she added, 'Ayizan is one of the more powerful *loa* and easily able to possess any mortal she chooses. Because of her interest in commerce it's appropriate that she's here tonight.'

The translator muttered a thank you.

'Tell us what you want, *loa*,' Despre said, softly.

As the translator reiterated Despre's words, Skull touched Fiona's wrist and said, 'They think you're possessed by Ayizan.'

Fiona smiled down at Skull. In a soft voice she said, 'And you don't think I'm possessed by Ayizan. I wonder who might be correct.' She didn't wait for his response. Instead, she walked to the seat that had been set aside for her and climbed onto the table. Kneeling, with her back to the translator, she pointed at Black, Raven and then Skull.

'You three will give your gifts to the houngan now. They will accept your generosity. They will build the Church of the Black Angel here in this United Kingdom and they will perform the ritual that will guarantee your company's further success.' Glaring at Skull she said, 'The initial sacrifice is in the box by your feet. The kris sits in the chalice behind you.'

From behind Fiona, the nervous babble of the translator's words was a constant undercurrent to her commands. Raven and Black turned to glance at the kris, the ceremonial dagger, which Fiona had left in the chalice behind Skull. Its handle was gold and encrusted with jewels. The blade of the kris was long twisted and looked wickedly sharp. Skull continued to stare at Fiona with an expression of amused satisfaction. When she stepped close to him he caught her elbow and pulled her ear close to his lips.

'This isn't a one-way journey for me, is it?'

She laughed at the suggestion. 'Haven't I answered that question before?'

'Several times,' he admitted. 'But I want to hear your reassurance again.'

She pulled away from him and turned to the visitors as Raven and Black climbed from their chairs. Raven headed out of the office and Fiona knew he was going to retrieve the money from the safe. Black went for the box at Skull's feet. The content's clucked in despair, as though the chicken inside knew that its fate was now in the hands of Roger Black.

'What do you want from us?' Manumishon demanded. 'Haven't we already said that what you're asking is impossible?'

'Their demands have changed,' Fiona said, quietly. 'These gentlemen simply want to give you one hundred thousand pounds so you can start the Church of the Black Angel here in this beneficent country. They will arrange new identities for each of you, so that you no longer have to worry about any outstanding issues you may have with the authorities.'

Manumishon and Despre exchanged glances. Rillieux's nostrils flared when the translator reiterated those words. Grudgingly, she nodded agreement.

'In return for their generosity,' Fiona went on, 'you'll arrange for the prayers to be made to the spirits so they bless this company's fortunes and protect their investments. In return for their generosity you will also convince the spirits to accept Mr Skull here as a *loa*. Do you understand what you're being asked to do?'

Whilst Fiona waited for the translator to finish speaking, she began to casually rub van van oil into her bare flesh. Starting with her shoulders, unmindful of being naked in the centre of the room, she eased the lubricant against her skin and relished its sweet fragrance. As she continued to massage herself with the van van her skin shone gold in the candlelight.

'Do you understand what you're being asked to do?' she asked again.

Manumishon shook his head and glared at her. 'We can't make this man into a *loa*,' he exclaimed. 'He is alive. Do you propose that we should kill him?'

Fiona glanced at Skull.

Skull's grin was broad and voracious. He turned to Manumishon and said, 'At last, supreme houngan. I think you finally understand what we want from you.'

29

Geoff sat in the passenger seat of Nicola's convertible Mercedes. Technically, he supposed, the vehicle wasn't Nicola's. It belonged to Nicola's boyfriend, Don. But, since Nicola was driving, and seemed to have constant access to the car whenever it was needed, he thought of it as being hers. The tote bag in the back of the car technically belonged to the stranger. And, of the money inside the bag, he supposed that even the thirty-five thousand that was his share wouldn't technically belong to him until he had completed the job. Technically, he decided, even though he was sat in an expensive car, alongside a beautiful woman, and carrying fifty thousand pounds, he was still the same office drone he had been at the beginning of the day. The world may have shifted on its axis, and he might have agreed to become a thief. But there was no reason for him to believe he was now any different to the man he had been at the start of the evening.

'Did you believe any of that stuff he was telling us?' Nicola asked.

'Vodun? *Bokor?* Ayizan? Severed heads? Naked women? Voodoo sorcerers?' He drew a deep breath and tried to push the images from his thoughts. 'I've never heard such a load of horseshit in my entire life.'

'That bloke looked like he believed in it all.'

Geoff nodded. 'Believing is everything,' he said, tiredly. Ignoring the question, ignoring everything except for Nicola's large, expressive eyes, he said, 'Is Don cool with this?'

They sat in the car park outside Shades. They could see the doorway from their seat inside Nicola's car beneath the shadow of the car park's trees. A handful of smokers congregated in the orange glow of light from the pub's windows. Above them, the glowing green sign that said SHADES spluttered softly in the night. The initial letter winked on and off.

'Don doesn't mind the occasional deal that skirts south of being legal,' Nicola said lightly. 'He employs a couple of migrants in the kitchens at The House of Usher and I know he's paying them peanuts cos they're not supposed to be in this country. I've also seen him sell a couple of bits and pieces to his regular customers that would land him in jail if the police ever found out that he's dealing in–'

'Is Don cool with you working with me?' Geoff asked, flatly.

Nicola wrenched her gaze from Geoff. She stared out of the Mercedes' overlarge windscreen. 'He's not said he objects to that.'

'Does he know that you and I have a history?'

Nicola shrugged. 'He knows that we went out together for a while.'

Geoff closed his eyes and thought for a moment. Nicola said the words so easily it was almost possible to believe that their torrid relationship could genuinely be described as them going out *together for a while*. The bland phrase slipped over the fact that they had developed an immediate sexual connection. It didn't even hint at the idea that Nicola had a voracious appetite for sexual deviance that matched Geoff's prurient tastes. With his eyes closed he was treated to a montage of images where Nicola's slender body was oiled, bound and savagely disciplined. Her mouth was half-open in a sigh of ecstasy and, when she did speak, she was urging him to go further, do more, break taboos and take her to new and undiscovered extremes of satisfaction. The intensity of the memories was so vivid that it did not surprise Geoff to discover, when he opened his eyes, he was sporting a semi.

'Don was the one who suggested your name for this job,' Nicola said quickly. 'Don knows that we did more than kiss…'

'We did a lot more than kiss,' Geoff grunted.

'… and he trusts me not to fool around behind his back any more than he's fooling around behind mine.'

Geoff digested those words as he studied the darkness outside the vehicle. It was a cloudless night with a sprinkling of stars making shapes in the sky overhead. He wanted to dwell on the vastness of the universe and remind himself that his own actions were small and most likely irrelevant and meaningless in the great scheme of things. But he couldn't shake the idea that he was on the verge of being involved with something onerous.

'I'll take all the money,' he decided.

Nicola squealed. 'I thought part of it was for me and for Don!'

'There's fifty grand there,' Geoff said thoughtfully. 'If I manage to do this job right, if I manage to get that skull out of Charlie Raven's office, and into that weirdo's hands, I need to have some sort of leverage that gets me the remainder of the money.'

Nicola chewed on her lower lip. 'Don won't be happy.'

'I'm relying on Don being unhappy to ensure that he puts the pressure on our religious friend and forces him to pay up.'

'Don't I get any of the money?' she asked with sudden brightness.

She leant over from her position behind the driver's wheel and placed a hand between his legs. The gesture was absurdly intimate, although Nicola managed to make it look almost chaste. The inside of her wrist rubbed against the crotch of his pants. In contrast, her face was a mask of innocence as she blandly studied him and asked, 'Don't I get anything up front?'

'I'm so tempted to give you something up front,' Geoff admitted.

They both giggled.

Geoff could taste in an electric tang in the air between them. He felt sure, if he took a deep breath, he would be able to drink the sweet and succulent flavour of Nicola's arousal. Her lips were so close he could see the smoothness of the tempting gloss that coated their surface. He could almost taste the flavour of the Bacardi Breezer she had sipped inside Shades. If their lips touched and his tongue slipped inside her mouth, he knew he would be able to devour every sweet taste that her nearness promised.

'I'm so tempted to give you something up front,' he sighed. 'But if I did that, it would raise Don's suspicions, so it's not something I can do.'

Nicola snatched away her hand and slumped back in her seat. All her facade of playful teasing evaporated as though it had never been there. The atmosphere of charged arousal vanished leaving Geoff with a rising blush and a waning erection.

'So how are we going to do this?' Nicola asked eventually. She glanced at the money on the back seat and added, 'What's your plan?'

'Drive me home and I'll see you for lunch tomorrow,' Geoff promised. 'I'll have sorted out all the details of how we're going to do this by then. We'll be taking the skull within the next week or two but, for now, I'm only certain that it will be happening on a night time and it won't be happening until I'm good and ready.'

30

Geoff took the money out of the tote bag and counted it on the kitchen table. There was fifty thousand pounds. No more and no less. The sum gave him a vague sense of reassurance that the Church of the Black Angel would not try to cheat him. He reasoned that anyone who went to the trouble of counting out exactly fifty thousand pounds was clearly representing an organisation that understood every penny mattered. It was clearly an organisation that knew a deal was a deal and what was right was right. But, whilst those thoughts were comforting, Geoff knew he would need to rely on something more substantial than a vague sense of reassurance if he wanted to be sure of receiving the full amount that was due to him once he had completed his part of the arrangement.

He placed the counted money in a metal biscuit tin. The tin was decorated with images of Edinburgh Castle, a West Highland Terrier, some thistles and a kilt-wearing bagpipe player. The edges of the box were embellished with a tartan print and, inside the box there was a lingering fragrance of all-butter shortbread. Sealing the lid shut with a strip of duct tape, Geoff went into his bedroom, pulled open the door of the fitted wardrobe, and then fell to his knees. Tearing at a loose corner of carpet at the back of the wardrobe, ignoring the money spider that ran over the back of his hand, he pulled the carpet back and exposed a pair of loose-fitting floorboards. Once the loose fitting floorboards were removed he had exposed a space between the joists below that was just wide enough to accept the biscuit tin.

Carefully, almost reverently, Geoff slid the tin into its hiding place. He covered the tin with the boards and then concealed the boards with the carpet. He then pushed a pair of battered trainers and an old T-shirt over the corner of carpet and closed the wardrobe doors. Absently, he kicked some spare laundry against the wardrobe doors then sat down on his bed and tried to decide if the hiding place was adequate. An hour later he was still sitting there. Pragmatically, he told himself it was time to go to bed and get some sleep in readiness for Monday at the office.

Maddeningly, sleep evaded him.

Lying in the darkness, trying to shut his thoughts away for the night, Geoff's mind kept returning to the problem of how he would be able to take the skull from Charlie Raven's office and whether or not he would be able to manage the theft without being detected.

It was not something he wanted to think about.

He didn't want to be brooding on the issue because he was tired and knew there would be time enough for some serious planning in the morning when he was rested and refreshed. But his mind refused to see the situation in such simple terms. His mind kept returning to the problem and revisiting the intricacies of how to get into Charlie Raven's office and how to walk out with John Skull's skull.

Geoff supposed it wouldn't have been so bad if his thoughts reached a satisfactory conclusion. Instead, his mind seemed content to have him envision every internal detail of the Raven and Skull offices and reconsider them afresh. It was almost as though he was starting work early and being forced to endure the ritual of his nine-to-five day through the last of the weekend hours when he was supposed to be asleep.

He could see the cubicle where he worked in the accounts office, sharing workspace with Shaun from Customer Services. He could even see the monitor of his own computer, the screen hidden behind a corporate screensaver that had the Raven and Skull logo bouncing lazily from one side of a black background to the other. He saw his own reflection in the monitor's black screen and was surprised that he did not appear in his work's suit with neatly tied tie and stylishly fashioned coiffure. Instead, the reflection showed a Geoff who was wrapped in a tatty blue bathrobe, wearing Homer Simpson slippers, with his hair looking like an untidy thatch.

As sleep continued to elude him, Geoff was able to walk into Charlie Raven's office and walk idly around the room. John Skull's skull grinned at him from its place on the desk. The gold plate gleamed dully. The hollow eye sockets gleamed with a dark and malignant glee. Not usually prone to flights of fancy, Geoff could have easily given into the belief that the skull's eyeless gaze was following him as he patrolled the office. The thought made his stomach fold.

He lay restless in bed, wishing he'd used some of the stranger's money to buy himself a bottle of scotch. It crossed his mind that he ought to get out of bed and make himself a soothing drink of instant cocoa. But, even though that idea might have helped him achieve a restful night, he still thought it sounded like too great an effort.

His imagination took him into the company's boardroom.

The blinds were drawn. Candles illuminated the room. There was the scent of sickly sweet plants, sweat and smouldering smoky flames. Instead of being empty, the boardroom was playing host to the scene the stranger at Shades had described.

Geoff considered closing the door and backing out of the room. Curiosity made him linger. Skull, Raven and Black sat on one side of the boardroom's impressive table. A nervous translator sat at the foot of the table. The bespectacled man's lips were moving in a constant but soundless babble. The three formidable Vodou *bokor* stared blindly at Geoff as he entered the room. Their expressions bore an intensity that suggested they could see him, but they had no interest in really looking at him.

Geoff resisted the urge to wave.

In the centre of the boardroom table, Skull's naked secretary held a curly-bladed knife. Geoff wanted to admire her naked figure. She was attractive with curvy hips and hard, long nipples. Her freshly oiled flesh looked gloriously inviting. Her bush had the overgrown appearance of the untamed thatches he had seen in vintage seventies porn. But that was only a small detail that did not deter his interest. His gaze was drawn away from the allure of her bare breasts and exposed sex. Instead, he found himself watching with reluctant admiration as she commanded the attention of everyone in the room.

Fiona's fingers were wrapped tight around the ceremonial handle of the kris. She pressed the tip between her breasts and gasped softly as it penetrated flesh. A dark bead of blood, turned black and oily in the guttering candlelight, blossomed beneath the blade. It drew, a slim dark line as it spilt down her torso.

At her feet, Geoff could see the headless corpse of a chicken. When he raised his gaze to study Fiona's face he saw that her lips were a rouged and messy smudge.

He couldn't remember how much the stranger at Shades had said about the ritual in Raven and Skull's office, or *Skull and Raven* as it had been then, but Geoff felt sure he hadn't heard this level of detail. Had Fiona gone all Ozzy Osbourne and bitten the head from the chicken? Or had she simply drunk the fresh, warm blood straight from the chicken's brutally severed neck? He could almost taste the hot gush of thick coppery fluid rushing over his tongue and down his throat. It was impossible to dwell on either idea without needing to quell a rising wave of nausea.

When he glanced again at Fiona's face he saw the woman had changed. The blade remained pressed between her breasts. Her eyes were open wide and, Geoff realised, Skull's secretary had been replaced by Nicola. Her pretty, kissable mouth was open in a shock of surprise. She pushed the kris deeper and then began to drag it downwards.

Raven and Skull exchanged a nervous glance.

Rillieux nodded approval.

Geoff took a moment to admire Nicola's body. It was as perfect as he remembered from their short and torrid relationship. Little had changed about her except, in this dream, she now had a tattoo on her hip. The mark was a red and black design: a dagger penetrating a heart with the words beneath it saying *Don 'n' Nicola*. Geoff wrenched his gaze further downwards to Nicola's feet. He saw that one bare foot was almost touching the severed stump where the chicken's head had been. He wanted to mutter a warning, tell her not to let her skin touch the unpleasantness of that wet, bloody flesh.

But the words refused to come.

And he could see that the chicken had changed into something that looked vaguely human. A headless corpse at her feet. Sprawled across the boardroom table. Blood pooling from the raw stump of its severed neck.

Geoff opened his eyes and sat upright.

His bedroom was held in darkness. For an instant, as the shadows pressed in on him, he could still smell the scents of van van oil, High Jon powder, naked flesh and fresh spilt blood. There was a tinge of smoke in the room that brushed his nostrils. From somewhere in the depths of the shadows he could have sworn he heard a sultry, feminine chuckle.

Scrabbling to turn on the light, he was treated to the sight of his own, drab bedroom. A tumult of laundry festered in one corner. A seldom-worn tatty blue dressing gown hung on the back of the door. The curtains lay flat and unmoving against the window. The whole room was so still and silent he had no doubt that everything he had seen had come from the eerie depths of his hyperactive imagination.

Checking the alarm clock by his bed, Geoff was dismayed to see that it was close to five in the morning. He couldn't recall sleeping properly through a moment of the night. His body ached with weariness and his flesh was tacky with greasy perspiration. Repulsed, Geoff dragged himself out of bed and stumbled into the shower hoping the hot water would prove invigorating.

Over a breakfast of coffee and toast, Geoff decided that he would set off to work early. Battling against the shroud of weariness that hung over his thoughts, he dressed for the office and told himself that getting there early might present an opportunity for him to simply take the skull. If he could simply walk in and snatch the skull before the day had properly started, he knew it would stop the theft from weighing on his thoughts.

Two hours later, with his eyes feeling grainy and his head throbbing from the lack of sleep, Geoff started his regular walk down the street that led to Raven and Skull's offices.

The road was already gridlocked with traffic. A bustle of early morning zombies trudged the pavements. They were the physical embodiment of his own absence of enthusiasm to get to work. Because this was an hour earlier than his usual routine, Geoff took time to pity the wage slaves as they crowded the streets, gliding easily between each other like well-choreographed dancers.

The thunderstorm rattle of a shutter startled him from his musings. He turned to see what had caused the noise and watched a slender brunette opening the security blinds from one of the High Street shops. As she pushed the grey metal covers into their housing at the top of the shop's facade, Geoff saw the place was named: L 4 LEATHER. It wasn't a place he had seen before and he stepped past the slender brunette and into the darkened interior.

'I'll be two minutes getting my float sorted,' the brunette told him.

'Just browsing,' Geoff assured her.

He walked once round the shop when the idea hit him. A second circuit of the place was long enough for the plan to be firmly in his thoughts. He selected a pair of leather gloves, took them to the counter, and waited patiently for the brunette to serve him. Whilst she was taking his money and counting out his change, Geoff tore the price tag and the labels from the gloves and pulled them onto his hands. He accepted the change and then walked back around the store and selected a pilot's case from L 4 LEATHER's extensive range of bags and cases.

'Did you want to see how the gloves would look with the case?' the brunette asked.

'No.' Geoff flashed a disarming smile. 'I'm just making sure my fingerprints aren't on there.' He paid in cash, and was pleased with the way the shop assistant seemed uncertain as to whether or not to treat his remark as a joke. He opened the case on the shop counter, tossed out the small pack of silica granules, and adjusted the combination lock to a setting of 444 and 444.

'Why that number?' asked the assistant.

Geoff raised an eyebrow. 'If someone really wanted to get inside this case, they could cut their way in with a good knife. If someone wants to take a sly peek without raising my suspicions, they're going to have to guess the combination. If they try to do it in a logical sequence, most likely they'll start from the 000 setting. To my reckoning, it should take as long to get to 444 if a person starts at 000 and works upwards or if they start at 999 and work their way down.'

'You're clever,' the assistant smiled.

Geoff nodded. 'Let's hope so.' He removed the last of the packing materials from the case, as well as the labels and price tag from its handle, then stepped back onto the street.

He could see Raven and Skull's offices in the distance. The building stood like a dark and ominous tower on the horizon. The sight made him feel as though eyes from the office had just watched his transaction inside L 4 LEATHER. That thought sent a shiver tickling down his spine. He tore his gaze from the Raven and Skull offices and walked two doors along the High Street before stepping inside a grocery shop.

Calmly, unhurriedly, he searched the aisles for sugar. A plan was formulating inside his mind and he felt comfortable going with the intuitive hunches that were guiding him rather than over-thinking the situation. Buying two bags of sugar, placing them securely inside the pilot's case, Geoff tested the combined weight and decided that would be as heavy as he was likely to need.

'You don't want a carrier bag?' the shopkeeper asked.

'They're OK in here,' Geoff told him.

'If those bags of sugar split they'll make a mess inside your briefcase.'

Geoff could have pointed out that it was a pilot's case, not a briefcase. He could have explained that he had specifically purchased the pilot's case for its extra width. But he didn't bother to say as much.

A conversation like that would likely have him explaining that one bag of sugar was approximately the same weight as a human skull. Two bags of sugar would compare to the weight of a gold-plated human skull that might be made heavier by any other unexpected surprises in its composition. Confident that the shopkeeper did not need to know such nuggets of information, Geoff simply fumbled to get a note from his wallet whilst wearing his new gloves.

He made his way out of the grocery shop and walked into a beating.

31

Geoff didn't see either of the men approaching him until it was too late.

Obviously he had noticed them. They were both so large and broad it would have been impossible to miss them. Dressed in the fashionable borderline debonair stylings of nightclub doormen, with sunglasses, black overcoats and heavily-blinged knuckles, they both had shaved heads and the sort of lumbering gait that suggested a formidable amount of physical power. But, because they seemed preoccupied with the conversation they were having, Geoff dismissed them from his vision as peripheral parts of the scenery.

The Raven and Skull offices loomed larger on the horizon. Geoff braced himself to go in there and put in a full day's worth of unremarkable work. It was something he'd been doing without effort or enthusiasm for the past five years and he reasoned that today should be no different.

A large hand slipped beneath his left armpit.

As he turned to find out what was happening, another hand slipped under his right armpit. Before Geoff could splutter a word of protest he was dragged backwards through a shop doorway. The ring of the door's overhead bell sounded at the same time as he asked, 'What the fuh?'

A large hand grabbed his face, cutting off the expletive before it could be fully formed. Geoff was pushed backwards and, as the floor fell from beneath his feet, he found himself sitting heavily on a chair. He had a moment to realise he had been pushed into a dingy and relatively unoccupied cafeteria.

A fat waitress stood behind the counter. She chewed gum and looked bored. A cheery pop song played in the background from a tinny portable radio. The sound of the singer's happiness was eerily faraway.

Aside from the two burly bouncer-types who had dragged him there, Geoff saw that Don was also in the cafeteria. He was as tall as the bouncers but not quite as broad. Dressed in a loose shirt with the throat unfastened, he sat, composed, at a table near the counter. His frown was a leer of forced menace.

'Good morning, Geoffrey,' Don said. His voice was crisp. He was clearly trying to sound business-like for the benefit of his thugs. 'I'm glad you could join me for this meeting. Would you care for a cup of tea?'

Geoff shook his head. Panic and confusion pounded inside his head to make his headache worse. He wanted to protest being dragged into the cafeteria but he had an idea that the less he said, the more likely he would be able to get out of the dingy cafeteria without suffering too traumatic an ordeal.

'Four cups of tea,' Don told the waitress. 'And take your time making them in the back room. Away from here. Out of earshot.'

'Mr Chin insists that I stay here whilst the shop is open,' the waitress told Don. 'He says, as long as there's a chance customers might come in, I have to stay in here and keep an eye on the door.'

One of the burly, bald-headed men went to the door and dropped the door's latch. As an afterthought he turned the OPEN/CLOSED sign.

Don flashed a shark-like smile for the waitress. Reaching inside his coat for his wallet, he produced a fifty pound note and tossed it on the cafeteria's dirty counter. 'Keep the change,' he said, sweetly. 'And stay in the back room until you hear the shop bell ring again.'

The waitress hesitated for an instant.

Geoff whispered a silent prayer that she would refuse to do as Don asked. He hoped she would threaten to call the police. A wave of disappointment rushed over him when she snatched the money and then disappeared out of sight.

Geoff was sorry to see her go. He took a deep breath and tried to ready himself for whatever trouble he now faced. He suspected, no matter how long he tried to prepare, he wouldn't be ready for whatever it was that Don wanted to throw at him.

'Good morning, Geoffrey,' Don said pleasantly.

He stepped towards the chair Geoff had been thrown into and placed his foot on the seat. The sole of his shoe appeared between Geoff's spread thighs. The toe of the shoe hovered dangerously over Geoff's crotch. When Geoff made an attempt to move, the two doormen stiffened. It was enough of an unspoken threat for

Geoff to realise he had to sit where he was and endure whatever torment Don thought necessary.

'I believe you've got some money of mine,' Don began.

'No,' Geoff assured him. 'I've not got any of your money yet.'

The fist came from nowhere.

If he had thought he was likely to be punched, Geoff knew he would have braced himself for the impact. Because it struck like a flash of summer lightning, he was simply slammed back further into his seat. His head snapped backwards. The back of his skull smacked hollowly against the brick wall behind him.

'I think that was the wrong answer, Geoffrey.'

Don's voice sounded hatefully pleasant. Geoff could hear the man's words through the dull ringing that now clanged inside his aching head.

'I think you might have ten grand of mine and I'd like it now please, before I lose my patience.'

'That's not the arrangement,' Geoff started. 'You get your cut when I've received the full payment.'

Don nodded.

Geoff was lifted out of his chair and then punched back into it. The blow to his stomach left him breathless, winded and gasping for air. The forehead that smashed into his nose left his face an exposed sore of agony. Fresh panic rippled through his thoughts as he realised he was at the mercy of the three violent men who had him trapped in the cafeteria.

'Now,' Don said quietly, 'it seems we've had a little confusion here because you've misunderstood when I should get my money. I think, now that the misunderstanding has been resolved, you're going to hand it over, aren't you?'

Geoff looked at him incredulously. His vision was a little out of focus. Geoff suspected that he needed a few painkillers before his sight would sort itself out. But it was still impossible to believe that Nicola's boyfriend could be dumb enough to believe he was carrying ten thousand pounds on his Monday morning trip to the office.

'I don't have that much with me,' Geoff explained.

'Then what's in the briefcase?'

'It's a pilot's case,' Geoff corrected.

Don slapped Geoff across the face. The blow bit like a wasp sting. It was more humiliating than any of the punches or the head-butt because it reminded Geoff he was at the mercy of a man who could simply slap his face whenever he chose.

One of the doormen snatched Geoff's pilot's case from the floor. He placed it heavily on the dinette table next to Geoff and began to toy with the dials on the combination lock.

'444,' Geoff prompted. 'It's the same for both dials.'

The doorman glanced at Don, who nodded for him to continue. Geoff waited patiently as the doorman went through the tedious process of lining up all the numbers to the same location.

'Is the money in there?' Don asked.

'No,' Geoff said. 'I just told you I don't have that much with me.'

Don raised his hand with the threat of another slap.

Geoff fell silent.

Glancing at the doorman, waiting for him to align the numbers on the combination dial and then open the case he asked again, 'Is the money in there?'

'No.' The doorman sounded puzzled. 'There's just two bags of sugar.' He lifted them out and showed them to Don.

'Maybe it's not sugar?' the other doorman suggested. 'Maybe its drugs he's carrying?'

'Inside bags of sugar?'

'Concealed.'

The doorman holding the bags of sugar pushed his finger through one of the paper packets. As a hiss of sugar sprayed to the floor he put his finger into the contents and then licked it.

'Sugar,' he declared.

Without being told, he performed the same inspection on the second bag and proclaimed the same result. Seeming at a loss for what to do with the bags he tossed them both into the pilot's case.

Don stared at Geoff. Now, instead of looking angry and menacing he looked genuinely puzzled. 'What sort of 'tard carries two bags of sugar in a Samsonite briefcase? Are you a diabetic? Or have you got special needs or something?'

'It's not a briefcase,' Geoff said, sullenly. 'It's a pilot's case.'

Don's fingers curled into a fist. 'Why?' he demanded.

Geoff massaged his jaw before responding. He could have told Don that the sugar was in the case so that his arm got used to its weight. When he did manage to swap the sugar for the skull from Charlie Raven's desk, Geoff didn't want to raise anyone's suspicions because they had noticed he was previously holding his case as though it was lighter or heavier. Rather than supply that explanation to Don, Geoff simply said, 'I'm taking care of the job I've been asked to do. If you insist on having your money up front, I guess I've got no choice except to do as you ask—'

'Damned right,' Don agreed.

'So I'll make sure you get the money this evening.'

'I want it now,' Don insisted.

'I haven't got it on me now,' Geoff sighed.

'One of my friends here will drive you home so you can get it.'

Geoff struggled to get out of the chair. Staring solemnly at Don he said, 'No.'

Both of the doormen squared their shoulders. Geoff saw they both made fists with their fat, pink hands. Considering the amount of heavy gold jewellery each wore on their knuckles he knew that a punch from either would be enough to land him in hospital. The prospect of impending pain was heightened by a shiver of protest from every bruised muscle in his body.

'No?' Don repeated. He was smirking. 'Is that your final word on the matter?'

'I'm not going back home now,' Geoff said firmly. 'Part of what I'm trying to do involves me being seen as the ideal employee for the next week. That means I should be appearing at work on time and putting in a full day's work. I'll have your money delivered to your restaurant this evening, as soon as I've finished being an ideal employee.' He stepped towards the door and found the way blocked by both of Don's subordinates.

'What if I insist?' Don asked.

'You were the one who put my name forward for this job,' Geoff reminded Don. 'If you insist on fucking up my plans, then I'll have to pull out of the job and your contacts will get pissed at you for recommending the wrong man.'

He didn't bother looking at Don whilst he spoke. Instead, he stared at the glimpse of cafeteria doorway that was visible between the burly shoulders of the two doormen.

'I'll look forward to seeing you at the restaurant this evening,' Don said easily. 'If you haven't turned up there by nine o'clock, I'll have you tracked down like a dog and then one of my friends here will remove your testicles.'

'The money will be with you by nine o'clock,' Geoff said, stiffly. He started towards the door but neither of the doormen made an effort to move out of his way.

'And,' Don continued, lightly. 'Since we're being frank and honest with each other here, I'll warn you now: if you ever put your dick anywhere near my girlfriend again, I'll have my friends here remove that as well your testicles. Do you understand?'

32

Geoff tried to regain his composure on the brief walk that remained to take him to the offices of Raven and Skull. His head ached. Humiliation burnt inside his chest like acid indigestion. The irrational need to go back to Don and force a violent confrontation was overwhelming. Cautioning himself with the unwelcome knowledge that such an argument would only lead to his own brutal battering, Geoff made his way into the office and settled himself behind his desk. His computer was already switched on. The corporate screensaver was active, bouncing the Raven and Skull logo back and forth across his monitor. Geoff found the sight eerily disconcerting.

'Have you got a black eye?' Shaun asked.

Geoff ignored him. Taking a bottle of painkillers from the drawer of his desk he dry swallowed three. 'I'm going for a coffee,' he growled.

'Are you going for a smoke?' Shaun asked. 'I'll come with if you are.'

'I'm just going for a coffee,' Geoff said, coldly. 'If anyone comes in looking for me you tell them I was in half an hour early this morning and I've only just gone for a coffee. Do you understand?'

'Yeah,' Shaun agreed. 'I'll also tell them you wanted to spread smiles and sunshine around the canteen.'

'Fuck off, Shaun.' He didn't like saying the words. He knew he was taking out his anger at the unassailable Don on the more pathetic figure of Shaun. The weakness of his own impotent character left his mood black with self-loathing. Entering the canteen he wanted to turn around and return to his cubicle when he saw Nicola.

'Jesus, Geoff,' she gasped. 'You look like shit. What happened?'

'Your fucking boyfriend and two of his Neanderthal buddies,' Geoff snapped. 'That's what happened to me.'

'Shit!' She blushed and put a hand on his arm. 'I think that might be my fault,' she whispered.

Geoff shrugged his arm free and ordered a coffee. Taking the drink to an empty table in the corner of the cafeteria he was annoyed to discover that Nicola was following him. She took a seat facing him and leant conspiratorially across the table.

'Don asked me if we'd ever *done anything.*' She stressed the last two words in an ultra-soft whisper. 'That's probably why he was pissed at you.'

Geoff sipped at his coffee.

'What did you tell him we'd done?'

'Nothing.' She wasn't looking at him. Eventually she said, 'Nothing much. I just said we'd gone out together for a while.'

Geoff stayed silent. He knew that Nicola had already said this much to Don. He waited for her to explain what else she had said. He took another sip from his coffee and hoped the painkillers would soon start to take some effect.

'Last night he asked if we'd ever fucked,' Nicola went on.

Geoff rubbed his aching forehead. He couldn't imagine why it would trouble any man that his girlfriend had been in a previous relationship with someone. However, it was easy to believe that someone with Don's possessive personality would consider it an affront that his girlfriend was not a vestal virgin.

'You told him we'd only ever held hands?' Geoff said, hopefully.

'I said I gave you a pity fuck once.'

Geoff groaned.

'I said I only gave you the pity fuck because you seemed desperate, I felt sorry for you, and you have such a tiny cock.'

'Gee,' Geoff said thinly. 'It's nice to know people have been saying such good things about me behind my back. Do you happen to know the telephone number for the Samaritans?'

'He saw you as a threat.' Nicola spoke with quick anger. 'I had to say something that would make it sound like I had no sexual interest in you whatsoever. I wasn't going to tell him that you're hung, able and extremely competent in the sack.'

Geoff accepted this compliment grudgingly.

'That's why I told him you're hung like a hamster and you smell of chlamydia.'

'I smell of…?' Geoff didn't bother finishing the question. He wasn't sure chlamydia had a distinctive aroma and, if it did, he certainly didn't want people thinking it was a smell that could be associated with him. But he could see no point in saying that to Nicola. He took another sip at his coffee and then decided it was time to get to his desk.

'OK,' he told Nicola. 'I understand what you're telling me. Don's insecure. I'll make sure I don't do anything to upset his precious self-image. Is there anything else you wanted to share with me before I take my small cock and my chlamydia smell back to my desk?'

She nodded. Glancing around the cafeteria before speaking she whispered, 'It can't happen at night.'

He didn't need to ask what she was talking about. 'Why not?'

'All the doors are locked. You'd never get in.'

'There's a guy in janitorial who owes me a favour,' Geoff started. 'I plan on borrowing the key from him today, getting a copy made this lunchtime and–'

'I've been talking to my friend Chloe,' Nicola said, stiffly. 'She's been working overtime for the past month. She knows what goes on at night in this building and she says that every door is locked. You'd need to copy all of the janitor's keys and then spend a month learning which was which. Trust me. You can't go in at night.'

'Great,' Geoff growled. He swigged the remnants of his coffee. 'This is proving to be one of those days, isn't it?'

'It's about to get worse,' Nicola warned him. 'I hear that Roger Black wants to see you in his office this morning.'

33

Geoff sat opposite Roger Black and wondered how the man could be so intimidating.

This morning he had been beaten by Nicola's boyfriend and accosted by two physically capable thugs. The memory of that incident was still fresh enough to leave him nauseous if he brooded on the episode for too long. Yet Geoff knew he would rather go back to the small cafeteria and face those three than be sitting on the opposite side of a desk from Roger Black.

A small part of him believed, if Don and his henchmen had been charged with tackling Roger Black, they would have immediately backed down and left the man to his own devices. But he supposed that particular stand-off was one he was never likely to witness.

'What the fuck is wrong with you, Arnold?' Black's gruff manner was daunting at the best of times. This morning, Geoff struggled not to leap from his chair and run screaming from Black's office.

'There's nothing wrong with me,' he stammered.

'Your face looks like shit,' Black growled. 'Someone's been punching you. Who? Why? What's been going on?'

'I got mugged on the way here this morning,' Geoff said, quickly. It wasn't the truth but it wasn't an outright lie. Because of this morning's event he knew he was going to be ten grand worse off by the end of the day.

'Fuck,' Black grunted. 'Have you reported it to the police?'

'Would that do any good?'

Black sighed and shook his head. 'You've got a point, Arnold. What did they get away with?'

'About four pounds,' Geoff admitted. He didn't bother explaining that they were four pounds of sugar. 'I seldom bring large sums of money with me on my way to the office.'

'I guess that's quite wise,' Black conceded. 'Do you need me to get a first-aider to take a look at you?'

'No.'

'I can have someone get painkillers or–'

'Really,' Geoff broke in. 'I'm all right, Mr Black. I've taken some painkillers. I'm just trying to get on with my work and not let the whole shitty incident trouble me anymore than it needs to.'

Black raised an eyebrow. 'It's a shame we've not got more with your spirit of dedication in these offices.'

Geoff waved the praise away.

They were sitting in Charlie Raven's office. Now that Black was acting CEO of Raven and Skull it was common knowledge that he used Raven's office as his own territory. The gold-plated skull on the desk stared morosely at Geoff. The black, empty sockets looked impossibly deep. The row of even teeth was set in a voracious grin. Geoff tried determinedly not to stare at the skull but the only other alternative was to raise his eyes and meet Black's intimidating gaze.

'I'm serious,' Black assured him. 'You've obviously taken a pretty bad beating. I can see that your head is swelling up like a barrage balloon. But, instead of whining about it, or spouting some bullshit story about how there were two of them or something–'

'There were three of them,' Geoff interjected.

Black ignored him. 'Instead of whining about it, you're in the office, you're getting on with your work, and you're making the rest of the staff here look like a bunch of pikey losers. Well done, Arnold.' He thrust a hand across the desk and said, 'If we had an employee of the month award going on, you'd be a shoo-in for this month.'

Geoff tried to grin as he shook Black's hand. 'Raven and Skull don't have an employee of the month award though, do they?'

Black shook his head.

Geoff laughed. 'This day just keeps getting shittier, don't you think?'

Black's eyes clouded over for an instant. Then he opened his mouth and began to bray laughter. Geoff had never heard Roger Black laugh before. He supposed, in the whole of Raven and Skull, there were probably fewer than a handful of people who had ever heard Roger Black guffawing with laughter. The sound was so terribly malevolent that Geoff began to wish he wasn't one of those who had heard the sound.

The skull continued to regard Geoff with its fixed, ever-hungry grin.

Geoff wondered if now would be the ideal opportunity for him to acquire the skull. Black was momentarily distracted. Geoff could snatch the skull from the desk and run. He would be out of the building before Black realised what had happened. Admittedly, it wouldn't be a clean theft. There would undoubtedly be consequences. But if he stood up now, grabbed the skull from the desk and tucked it hard against his torso like a fly half going for a try, he could bolt from the office and the skull would be his.

The skull will protect you.

He didn't know where that thought came from but it seemed less like an insane idea and more like a promise. The suggestion seemed to say, if he took the skull now, it would work like an amulet and protect him from any harm or danger as long as it was in his possession.

The empty sockets beckoned Geoff to make his move.

Geoff wiped one sweat-soaked hand against the thigh of his trousers. He licked his over-dry lips and glanced guardedly at Black. The man was still laughing and sufficiently distracted to allow Geoff his opportunity.

The skull will protect you

Geoff remained in his seat. If he took the skull now there would likely be police waiting for him at home when he returned. If he took the skull now there was no way he could return to the offices of Raven and Skull to resume his grey little job, and his grey little life with its grey little wage packet.

Black wiped his eyes and slapped a hand on his desk. He finally seemed to have his laughter under control. 'I like you, Arnold. I'll be watching out for you.'

Geoff stopped himself from making a comment. He hadn't thought the day could get much worse but he figured the news that Roger Black was now 'watching out' for him had to rank as the base note of the morning. How the hell was he supposed to steal the skull if he had now appeared on Roger Black's radar? The idea was enough to make him want to sob with despair.

'You haven't yet said what you wanted me here for.'

Black nodded. He was clearly impressed with Geoff's efficiency and this question just seemed to improve his high regard. 'End of year is approaching,' he grunted. 'Is your department ready for their accounts' audit?'

Geoff had no idea. Nevertheless, because he knew that Black would not tolerate any vacillation, he nodded as though the end of year accounts' audit had been at the forefront of his thoughts. 'I'll make sure they're ready for this weekend,' he promised.

Black nodded. 'Good man, Arnold.'

The words struck Geoff as ironic. He did not feel like a good man. He was planning to steal from the only person he had spoken with this morning who had shown him any genuine sympathy. Roger Black wasn't trying to beat Geoff up. Roger Black wasn't wandering around the offices of Raven and Skull telling anyone who listened that he had a small cock and a lingering smell of chlamydia. Roger Black was only offering him praise and validation.

The idea that he could so easily abuse someone's trust struck Geoff harder than any of the punches he had received at the hands of Don and his two doormen friends.

Geoff wondered how long he had been so shallow. Despondently, he realised he had only become so self-serving since he first touched the stranger's money. Since then, it had been a constant downhill slide. The one reassuring thought that crossed his mind was the idea that he probably couldn't sink much lower.

34

'You could do it during the day,' Nicola told him.

It was lunchtime. They sat on opposite sides of a canteen table amid the teeming bustle of their fellow, faceless colleagues. Nicola had a plate of salad in front of her. Geoff didn't feel up to attempting much more than a bowl of soup, and that was only to line his stomach as he chewed on more painkillers.

'Good idea,' he agreed. 'I steal the damned thing during the day. That way the guards reviewing the CCTV cameras won't have any trouble recognising me when the police are going through the records. That should make everybody's job a lot easier. I might even save everyone a whole lot of time just by walking straight down to the police station and turning myself in. What do you think I should wear? A stripy sweatshirt, an eye-mask, and maybe carry a big bag that has SWAG written across the side?'

'You're really in a mood today, aren't you?'

Geoff slurped a spoonful of soup. It tasted as though it had come from a rusty tin. 'Having your boyfriend kick the shit out of me, and then threaten to cut my bollocks off if I go near you, is not something that is likely to put anyone in a good mood.'

He took another spoonful of soup. The taste had not improved.

'Don's the jealous type,' Nicola said, lightly. She said the words as though this explained and excused his behaviour. Lowering her voice she added, 'And if you can put Don out of your thoughts for a minute, have a think about what I'm saying. Why not do it in broad daylight? All the office doors are unlocked during the day. It would be the ideal time.'

'And the CCTV cameras?' He pointed towards the unit that covered the canteen. It was an antiquated piece of machinery that sat large in the corner above the canteen doorway. A single red light beneath the camera showed that it was working and recording events in the room. 'What would I do about the CCTV cameras?' he asked.

She shrugged. 'Take them out.'

'Yes,' Geoff agreed. 'Why didn't I think of that before? I should just take out the CCTV cameras. Oh! Wait a minute! I know why I didn't think of that before. It's because I don't live in one of those *Ocean's Eleven* movies.'

He dropped his spoon into his soup bowl. It landed with a heavy clatter that had other diners in the canteen startled and staring at him. Geoff glared ferociously at the faces fixed in his direction until they each turned back to their own business.

'Did you know the CCTVs were fitted in here ten years ago?'

'How interesting.'

'Did you know that the cabling was installed without compromising the incumbent structure of the architecture?'

Annoyed with himself, Geoff studied Nicola. He could sense she was building to a point and he wanted to hear it. It occurred to him that she'd clearly spent a productive morning researching ways for the theft to go ahead whilst he had been wallowing in self-pity and doing nothing more productive than chewing painkillers and typing names into Google.

Not that he considered his morning to have been unproductive. He had typed the names Despre, Rillieux and Manumishon into the search engine, and discovered several interesting facts about the founders of the Church of the Black Angel.

Despre was the most innocuous of the trio. Affiliated with a handful of radical groups, Despre was only suspected of murder, human trafficking, drug running and kiddie-fiddling. His whereabouts were currently listed as unknown, although the two websites that Geoff had consulted both suggested he was somewhere near the Amazon.

There were pictures.

They were old, sepia-tinted images, clearly scanned and uploaded from a private collection of black and white photographs. Some of them showed Despre scowling at the camera. One disturbing image showed Despre smiling with a gaggle of sad and frightened urchins kneeling at his feet. Another showed Despre holding a naked woman. The woman's posture was so relaxed Geoff couldn't work out if she was drugged or dead. But the most disturbing things about the images of Despre had nothing to do with what the man was doing. The most disturbing thing was that Geoff thought he recognised the man's face. Geoff wasn't sure if the stranger in Shades had described Despre to such a level of detail but he felt certain, staring into the images of the houngan's cold eyes, that he knew the man and had seen him recently.

Juliet Rillieux was a more controversial figure. She had turned up dead in London fifteen years earlier. Geoff discovered that she had been on the run from Haitian authorities, who had not taken kindly to the extortion rackets she organised in Port-au-Prince. She left behind a following of devout believers, who were possibly spurred on in their worship by her threats of curses and hexes. Rillieux, according to one website, left behind an army of effigies. Each effigy was adorned with human hair. Each was penetrated by at least three pins and each was responsible for a brand of suffering that could only be attributed to the black arts. Rillieux, according to another website, had often been seen in the company of an entourage of her own private slaves. The associates were made up of those she had raised from graveyards. Rillieux, it was said, could make the rich and famous succeed or bleed, depending how much they paid her. Geoff read one article where the author said Rillieux was the only *bokor* they had ever witnessed who could genuinely call on Baron Samedi – *loa* of the dead – and have him do her bidding.

Geoff read the words from his monitor. He wished he didn't believe what he was reading. He also wished he wasn't reading about people who were clearly more successful than himself. Even though Juliet Rillieux had died fifteen years earlier, the fact that she had once had the ability to control spirits, life and zombies suggested it might still be wise to regard her as a potentially formidable opponent.

There had been no available photographs of Rillieux. The few places where he had expected to see images had been websites where the picture refused to download and, instead of showing her face, displayed an empty oblong. One link promised it had a photograph of the elusive woman but, when Geoff tried to open that page, his PC crashed. Not wanting to run the risk of making his enquiries known to the IT department, Geoff decided he had discovered enough about Queen Juliet Rillieux. He concentrated the remainder of his search on the remaining founder of the Church of the Black Angel.

Manumishon, the supreme houngan, turned out to be more of a mystery figure than his associates. Whereas Despre and Rillieux apparently had control over life, death and the afterworld, Manumishon's skills extended to the internet. Even though Geoff invested an hour in trying to search for the man's name in an article, blog or linked to a photograph, he found nothing at all relating to any vodun, voodoo or vodou practitioner with a name remotely resembling Manumishon's.

Manumishon, it transpired, was a common surname amongst those descended from former slaves. The name was derived from the noun *manumission: formal release from slavery or servitude*. Geoff had read the definition and told himself it would be one of those words that he would never be able to use in a sentence. That thought had been immediately proved wrong when he realised that, stealing the skull from Roger Black's desk would be the first step on his manumission from Raven and Skull.

'Are you listening to me here?' Nicola asked. She snapped her fingers in front of Geoff's face, bringing him back to the noisy reality of the canteen. 'Do you understand what I've just told you about the CCTV cables in this building?'

'Explain it again,' Geoff advised. 'Pretend that I wasn't listening.'

Nicola did not bother hiding her frustration. 'The CCTV cables were laid inside existing conduit so as not to compromise the architecture. Also, because the equipment is more than a decade old, there's no wireless stuff. There's none of this special fibre-optic stuff inside inaccessible plastic housings. Are you with me so far?'

Geoff nodded. He had understood the words but he couldn't yet see her relevance or the point she was trying to make.

'All the cables from each floor are linked together in one big snaky bundle,' Nicola explained. She lowered her voice so there was less risk of anyone overhearing and said, 'They're linked together in a big snaky bundle that feeds to the main security network downstairs.'

'So?'

'So,' Nicola now sounded impatient. 'If you take out the bundle of cables for this floor, the CCTV cameras won't see a thing of what you're doing. And taking them out should be as easy as cutting through a bunch of cables.'

Geoff shook his head. 'Pointless,' he snapped. 'As soon as the cameras went off, there'd be a team from security patrolling the offices until they found out what the problem was.'

'They wouldn't get up here straight away,' Nicola argued.

'They'd get here soon enough,' Geoff snapped. 'It certainly wouldn't leave much spare time in case there were delays or setbacks.'

'Delays or setbacks?' she scoffed. 'Like what?'

'Like, maybe Black being in his office,' Geoff suggested. 'Or someone who knows me maybe being around Raven's office, stopping me from getting in there, or asking me what I'm doing there?'

'Shit,' Nicola muttered. 'I hadn't thought about stuff like that.'

Geoff said nothing.

'What you need,' Nicola decided, 'is for the cables to be cut at exactly the same time as there's a massive distraction that has everyone rushing out of the building.'

'Yes. That's exactly what I need.' Geoff sighed heavily and said, 'Or, in other words, I might as well give up now.'

Nicola considered him guardedly. 'Are you seriously thinking of backing out?'

Geoff shrugged. 'What have I got to lose?'

'You owe Don ten grand. And he's going to want that money regardless of whether you do the job or not–'

Geoff opened his mouth to protest that Nicola was being unfair. If he simply gave the money back to the Church of the Black Angel, surely Don could accept that he wasn't going to get his money and everyone could forget about Geoff's limited involvement in the planned robbery. He closed his mouth when he realised that Don would never accept such a situation. Geoff had touched the stranger's money and accepted the responsibility of stealing the skull. He was now committed to a course of action regardless of whether or not he wanted to continue.

'I also want my twenty grand,' Nicola continued. 'And I'll use every resource at Don's disposal to make sure I get it.' She stared solemnly at Geoff and said, 'Are you really thinking of backing out?'

'Not anymore,' he sighed, bitterly. 'Not anymore.'

35

Geoff's journey home was exhausting.

He supposed he was tired from not having slept properly the night before. And he reasoned that the tiredness was making him paranoid. But, whilst that argument made sense to the rational part of his mind, it didn't lessen the anxiety that accompanied him on his walk to the station, or his bus ride home.

The cool caress of an unseen gaze grazed the back of his neck. The disquieting sensation that he was being watched made Geoff study every stranger with wary hostility. Judging by the puzzled expressions being flashed in his direction, Geoff supposed he looked like one of the evening's typical bus-travelling lunatics but it wasn't until he caught a glimpse of his own reflection in the bus's window that the thought was confirmed. One eye was almost swollen shut from the blow Don had landed at his head. His cheek was a raised and black landscape that, on anyone else, he would have attributed to dirt or disease or both. Grudgingly, he conceded that the reason he thought everyone was staring at him was because he looked strange enough to merit their curiosity. And, whilst that thought offered some reassurance, it didn't shake the idea that there was one set of eyes fixed on him that belonged to someone with sinister intentions.

He climbed off the bus, walked half a mile home, and then slipped into his flat. With the kettle on, and a change of clothes thrown into the bathroom for when he'd finished showering, he tried to shake some of the day's worries from his shoulders. His entire body was stiff. Those parts that didn't ache with cuts and bruises shook from the tension of being held in a position of tight and nervous readiness throughout the day.

He went into the bedroom without touching the light switch. The room was held in shadows but he reasoned if he was being watched, he didn't want to alert anyone outside the building that he was going into his bedroom. He knew the thought was irrational and paranoid. But he also knew that, sometimes, irrational and paranoid people were being watched. Common sense told him that acting irrational and paranoid was the most sensible option for someone who was dealing with criminals and planning to steal a hundred-thousand-pound artefact from his employer. Pulling clothes away from the front of the wardrobe door, he moved the shoes and jumble he had placed in the corner, lifted the edge of the carpet and then removed the two loose floorboards.

The biscuit tin was missing.

The moment's panic was almost enough to stop his heart from beating. Geoff came close to screaming. His mind raced through the ways that his tin of money could have been stolen. His fingers scrabbled against joists, dust and spider webs as he tried to blindly find the tin. The sting of an old and rusty nail scraped across his knuckles. The pain was sudden and intense but barely registered on his thoughts as his search continued.

And then his fingers found the side of the tin.

The smooth metal was reassuringly cold.

The relief was so strong it left him light-headed.

The tin hadn't gone. It hadn't been stolen. He simply hadn't been able to see it in the darkness. Dragging it from its hiding place, wrenching the duct tape from its lid, he carried the tin into the kitchen and left it on the table whilst he made himself a coffee.

The gashes across three fingers of his right hand surprised him with the amount of blood they produced. In his panic to find the tin he hadn't realised he had cut himself so badly. Running the cuts beneath a cold tap, trembling with the pain of cleaning the wound, his gaze constantly returned to the tin of money on the kitchen table.

He dried his hand on a kitchen towel, made a quick coffee, and then opened the tin. There was one disquieting moment, just before he removed the lid, where Geoff thought he would find the tin empty. In his mind's eye he could picture the shiny interior staring up at him and containing nothing more than the scent of long-forgotten biscuits and a reflection of the kitchen light. When he saw that the money was still there, he released a breath that he hadn't realised he had been holding.

Quickly, as quickly as his trembling and aching hands could manage, Geoff counted out ten thousand pounds. His coffee turned cold whilst he was counting the sum for the third time.

Once he had assured himself that he had accurately counted out five hundred twenty pound notes, Geoff placed the money to one side and then took five of the twenties for himself. He found an empty envelope for Don's money and then put his own meagre hundred into his wallet. The amount he had taken for himself almost covered what he had spent on gloves, sugar and the pilot's case.

It took another ten minutes to reseal the biscuit tin, return it to its hiding place, and then conceal the fact that the hiding place existed. By the time he returned to the kitchen he realised the evening was slipping away from him. The need for a shower and a warm coffee were like desperate cravings. But the memory of Don's casual threat was a more powerful motivator. Methodically, Geoff stuffed the envelope containing Don's money into the bag he usually used for taking his sports gear to the gym. The bag had a vague fragrance of sweat and old laundry but it looked tired enough to be considered innocuous. Trying not to let himself worry that the time was fast approaching nine o'clock, and that Don's deadline was looming ever closer, Geoff left his apartment, twice checked that the door was secure, and then headed for The House of Usher.

He walked half a mile towards the nearest bus stop. When he passed a group of loud, arguing teenagers, their faces hidden by hoodies and their bodies concealed inside designer tracksuits, he suddenly grew uncomfortable with the idea of carrying ten thousand pounds through the darkening city streets. As soon as he was able, Geoff hailed a passing taxi.

The driver asked where he was headed, and then fell into silence.

Geoff supposed, given the way he looked, the driver couldn't think of much to say. He caught a glimpse of his reflection in the cab's glass partition and realised he looked grotesque. With his face still battered and a wild expression in his one visible eye, he could sympathise with the driver's preternatural silence because he wouldn't have known what to say to someone who looked so desperate. He wanted to use the journey to think his way through the complexities of trying to steal the skull. However, with the fear of missing Don's deadline growing larger with each passing second, Geoff couldn't concentrate on the problem.

The driver pulled up outside The House of Usher and slid the partition back. 'Thirteen quid.'

Geoff paid for the ride with a single twenty and told the driver to keep the change. Then, standing alone outside the restaurant, he wondered what mad impulse had made him agree to steal the skull.

The House of Usher was a large, detached building. Fronted by plate windows the warm interior lights presented a middle-class utopia filled with couples, families and friends who were laughing and eating in cosy splendour. The soft lighting suggested a warm, ambient welcome. Touches of gold trim on the rich red furnishings hinted at the comfort and reassurance of wealth. He could see the restaurant's courtyard from where he stood. A huge fountain stood in the middle of the courtyard, burbling pretty patterns of water for the solitary couple sat by its edge.

Shivering as he stared into the restaurant from the cold outside, Geoff could not recall one moment in his life when he had felt so lonely and miserable. He was watching affluent diners enjoying their spoils at the end of the working day. His own world involved scrabbling in the darkness of his pokey flat, counting out money for thugs, and constantly fretting that someone knew his thoughts or was readying themselves to steal his belongings.

'*Why are you doing this?*' he wondered.

It was a question he could no longer answer. If there had been a way to withdraw from the theft without causing himself financial hardship or more suffering, he would have clutched it with both trembling and aching hands. Tearing himself away from the bitterly enviable scene of the restaurant's front window, Geoff walked to the side of the building and stepped through the open door that led to the kitchens.

Bright lights were reflected from the shiny white wall tiles and stainless steel kitchenware. A torrent of rich and overlapping scents filled his nostrils. He caught wafts of acidic spices, tempting garlic and pan-fried heat. The clatter of pans, the chatter of voices and the sizzle of cooking were all deafeningly loud. But there was one raised bellow that was louder than all the other sounds.

It rattled from the walls and Geoff recognised Don's voice instantly.

'What the fuck do you call this?' Don demanded. 'You are a worthless piece of dog shit and I ought to kick you in the bollocks from now until judgement day.'

Geoff could see Don towering over a quivering underling. Don was wearing his kitchen whites. Geoff reluctantly conceded that the man looked impressive in the uniform but he quickly followed that thought with the personal reassurance that he still loathed and detested Don.

'I'm sorry, chef,' the underling muttered.

'You will be fucking sorry,' Don thundered. He pushed the plate close to the underling's face. 'Tell me what this is. Tell me what this piece of shit is supposed to be.'

From his position near the door Geoff could see the interaction clearly. He thought the item on the plate looked like a nice piece of steak. He quickly conceded that he wasn't an expert. Any steak that was warm and looked sufficiently brown on the outside was one that he would consider a nice piece of steak. But it was obvious that Don was not happy with the quality of this steak and he seemed to believe the kitchen hand incurring his wrath was solely responsible for his disappointment.

'Why don't you just take a shit on a plate and send that out to my customers?' Don demanded. 'Is this the sort of filth you've been trained to cook? What sort of worthless fucking cretin are you?'

The kitchen hand tried stammering responses but Don was clearly in no mood to hear answers. He tossed the steak and the plate into a corner of the kitchen. The plate clattered noisily: broken on impact. The steak adhered to one of the white-tiled walls and sat there like the world's largest slug. Don pushed his face threateningly close to the kitchen hand's. He grabbed the throat of the underling's shirt and pulled the poor man closer.

'The cost of that broken plate is coming out of your wages.'

'Yes, chef.'

'You're going to clean up that piece of shit–'

'Yes chef.'

'And you're going to do the job you've been told to do.'

The kitchen hand nodded and trembled as he tried to make his contrition sincere. Geoff watched the whole scene; quietly wishing the kitchen hand would rebel.

'Do it properly this time,' Don continued. 'And never let me catch your worthless arse working to such a low standard ever again. Have you got that through your thick fucking skull?' He rapped his knuckles on the kitchen hand's forehead with three sharp taps.

Geoff flinched in sympathy, as though he had received the light assault. He fervently wished the kitchen hand would simply snap, grab a convenient knife, and then start to butcher Don with the frenzy of a human chopping machine.

It was impossible for Geoff to be unmoved by the injustice of the situation. Geoff told himself that, if he had worked for any employer who treated him with such contempt and disdain, he would have told the man to stick his job up his arse. Being honest with himself, he supposed he might not have said something so confrontational to someone with Don's ferocious temper. But he would certainly have left the kitchen and never returned to face a future humiliation of such severity.

And yet, as those indignant thoughts rushed through his mind, Geoff remembered he had been in many menial jobs where an overbearing employer had humiliated him with the same ferocity that Don had just inflicted on the kitchen hand. Geoff also remembered that, when he had been suffering the brunt of an employer's wrath, he had simply accepted the belittling experience. True, he had muttered threats and grandiose claims of retribution to fellow colleagues after the event. But he knew that he had always accepted the unjust humiliation with little more than a meek and pathetic protest and the wheedling excuse that it hadn't been his fault.

The kitchen hand mumbled another apology.

Geoff felt a wave of contempt swell up in his stomach. He tried not to be disgusted. He knew the fear of failure and unemployment were enough to leave anyone at the mercy of brutal, egotistical employers. But it was impossible not to share Don's low opinion of a man who could be so easily cowed into acquiescence.

As the kitchen hand bent to pick up the shards of discarded plate from the corner of the kitchen, Geoff realised this was why he wanted the money that would come from selling the skull that currently sat on Charlie Raven's desk. He wasn't planning the robbery because he was greedy or driven by the aimless goal of simply acquiring wealth. He only wanted to have the necessary resources that would allow him independence.

He had floated through enough menial jobs like the kitchen hand's to suffer the unjust wrath of dozens of belligerent bullies. At the moment there was no one in the Raven and Skull hierarchy who abused their authority in such a way. But Geoff knew that it would only take one ill-advised promotion for the drudgery of his life to be transformed into a living hell.

If he managed to acquire the skull, and trade it for the outstanding fifty thousand, Geoff knew he would have the financial security that would mean he never had to worry again about the mood swings of an overbearing employer. Grinning for the first time in days, Geoff realised that was why he needed to steal the skull.

'What the fuck do you want?' Don snarled.

'I've brought you your money.' Geoff raised the sports' bag in the air, as though this proved the truth of what he was saying.

'And you think I want it in the kitchen?'

'You threatened to cut off my bollocks if I didn't get it to you by nine o'clock this evening,' Geoff reminded him. 'I figured I would bring the money to you regardless of where you were, even if you were on the plop, just so long as it kept my balls where they're supposed to be.'

'You think you're quite the funny man, don't you?'

Geoff opened his mouth to answer. He was thinking of making a remark about Don's Gordon Ramsay impression. Common sense, and the glint of murderous encouragement that sparkled in Don's eyes, told Geoff to close his mouth without saying a word.

'Bring it with you,' Don grunted. He gestured for Geoff to follow him through a door that led out of the kitchen and away from the main body of the restaurant. 'Hurry it up,' Don snapped. 'I haven't got all fucking night.'

Despising himself for doing as he was told, Geoff obediently hurried to follow Don. The room they walked into was decorated in a more homely fashion than the sterile, anodyne kitchen. The walls were covered in flock wallpaper that Geoff guessed was a leftover from the restaurant's last overhaul. The predominant colour was an austere black, glamorised by suggestions of silver.

Aside from a desk, an old PC and a comfy chair, Geoff noticed a huge cast-iron safe squatting in one corner of the room.

Nicola lounged in one of the comfy chairs. She was naked save for a tiny thong that barely covered her sex. The smouldering joint in her fingers told Geoff she was stoned before he even caught a glimpse of the vacant expression in her eyes. He wrenched his gaze away from her before Don thought he was staring at the perfect, tempting mounds of Nicola's bare breasts.

'Hi Geoff,' Nicola giggled.

'Nicola.'

'Cover yourself up, you fucking slut,' Don snarled. He threw a piece of cloth in Nicola's direction.

Nicola dropped her joint into an ashtray and fumbled to cover her breasts with the cloth Don had thrown at her. Geoff was dismayed to see that everyone in The House of Usher responded to Don's demands.

'Don't just cover your titties,' Don barked. 'Cover up your minge too. I don't want you flashing your twat to this tosspot.'

'I'm wearing knickers,' Nicola argued.

'Those aren't fucking knickers,' Don sneered. 'I've fucked you once tonight without needing to take those off.'

Geoff's stomach rolled with a fresh wave of disgust.

'Just get yourself dressed,' Don sounded as though the matter was no longer of any interest to him. 'Get yourself dressed and stop taunting this worthless sack of shit with the sight of your titties and your pussy.'

He turned his back on Nicola, and only Geoff got to see the woman flip him off. Don fell to one knee and began to fumble with the combination lock on the safe. He started to turn the dial, then glanced over his shoulder and glared angrily at Geoff.

'Stop fucking watching me,' he grunted. 'I don't want you knowing the combination to my safe.'

Rather than argue the point, Geoff simply turned away. He could see Nicola was smirking, as though she enjoyed watching Don's childish displays of authority. Her eyes shone with wicked malice as she teased the tip of one finger against her exposed nipple and then shivered as though thrilled by the sensation. Licking her lips in an overly suggestive fashion, she snaked one hand down her bare stomach, towards the top of her thong. Geoff watched her fingers slide over a red and black tattoo on her hip. It showed a dagger penetrating a heart with the words beneath it saying *Don 'n' Nicola*.

Geoff was unable to tear away his gaze from her.

Nicola shifted in her seat, spreading her thighs wide apart. She ran her middle finger over the centre of her thinly sheathed sex. She arched her neck back silently, then teased the edge of the thong to one side. The perfect pout of her pussy lips was revealed to Geoff.

'Give me the money,' Don demanded. He was staring into the safe. He had a hand stretched out behind him and he snapped his fingers with theatrical impatience. 'Now. Hurry it up.'

Nicola allowed her thong to slide back over her sex. She pulled on the top that Don had thrown to her. All the time she kept smiling slyly in Geoff's direction.

Geoff passed Don the bag he had been carrying.

'This bag smells like arse,' Don muttered.

Geoff wanted to ask if Don was a connoisseur of that particular fragrance. Staring at Nicola, mesmerised by the bold invitation in her eyes, he stayed silent.

'Are you sure there's ten grand here?' Don demanded.

'Count it if you like,' Geoff said. It was a struggle to stop himself from stuttering. He had a raging erection and it was nearly impossible to pull his concentration away from Nicola.

'I'll take your word for it,' Don said, graciously. 'Although, if this safe is down by a single penny, I'll be coming after you for that amount.'

Geoff found his hand had curled into a fist. He could imagine driving the fist into Don's handsome face. From this position, it would be easier to kick the man from behind, force his head to smash violently against the cast-iron safe, and then keep kicking at him until the man was no longer able to retaliate. But the image of driving his fist into Don's face was the most tempting one that filled his thoughts.

Of course, the repercussions of such stupidity were obvious. He knew that any violent action towards Don would be akin to suicide. Yet still, the idea was sorely tempting.

Nicola winked at him. Her painted lips formed the shape of a kiss and she silently blew it in his direction.

'CHEF!'

The cry came as the door burst open.

Geoff flinched as though he had been caught doing something wrong.

He recognised the kitchen hand who had been the victim of Don's wrath as the man hurried into the room.

'There's trouble front of house, chef,' the kitchen hand gasped. 'You'd best come quick.'

'Fuck,' Don grunted. 'What is it?' He was moving as he spoke. Pushing past Geoff. Bursting through the doors and following in the wake of the kitchen hand.

'There's a customer choking,' the kitchen hand explained.

And then the sounds of their conversation were gone as the door closed behind them.

Geoff found himself alone in the restaurant's office with a near-naked Nicola and an open safe. It was, he thought, a dictionary definition of the word *temptation*. He stared at the open safe for a moment, sure that he was seeing something important but not quite sure how his brain ought to process the information.

'Isn't that bizarre,' Nicola murmured.

When Geoff glanced up he saw that Nicola was following the line of his gaze and studying the open safe.

'He's forever leaving the safe open and unguarded when he gets distracted. You wouldn't think anyone could be so stupid, would you?'

Geoff said nothing. He didn't think *anyone* could be so stupid. He realised that, with the right distraction, *everyone* would be so stupid.

A smile split his lips.

He walked over to the safe, kicked it closed, and secured the lock.

'Why did you do that?' It sounded as though Nicola's high was wearing off. She looked petulant and scornful. 'It's not like I would have taken anything from Don's safe,' she said, indignantly. 'Did you lock it because you suddenly don't trust me?'

Geoff shook his head. 'There's nothing sudden about it,' he admitted. 'If I'm being honest, Nicola, I've never trusted you.'

36

They fell on him as he was walking out of The House of Usher. There were two of them and they were large and swift. They stepped out of shadows and bore down on him with obvious determination.

Geoff's first thought was a rush of gratitude.

The enormous amount of money he had been carrying earlier was now locked securely inside Don's safe. Those notes that had weighed him down so heavily on his journey to The House of Usher could not be taken from him.

Then, as large hands grabbed at his armpits, and his feet lost contact with the floor, he thought, '*not again.*'

Darkness shrouded him.

He got the impression that someone had thrown a cape over his face or tugged a bag over his head. There was a scuffle of footsteps. A familiar fragrance of incense. And then the sound of a rusty vehicle door being opened.

He was taken out of the night's cool air and bundled into somewhere warm and unfamiliar. His back was pushed hard against something he guessed was the interior side panel of a van. The wall was solid against his spine but he could feel that it wasn't wholly robust. When he started trying to stand up his legs were pulled from underneath him so his backside hit the floor with a solid thump.

Geoff groaned.

He was about to say something, raise his voice in complaint or make his distress known in some way, when the bag was pulled from his face and a super-bright torch was shone into his eyes.

He tried to raise a hand to cover his eyes. His arms were pulled down and held firmly at his sides. The hands holding his wrists were strong and unrelenting.

'Is this the one?'

Geoff squinted against the light. The torch beam was so powerful and strong that it hurt. Behind the light he could make out only silhouettes and faltering shadows. His mouth was dry and his pulse had accelerated. The comical notion of relief was no longer in his thoughts.

'You've been charged with retrieving the sacred relic for our church.'

He'd been grabbed by the client, Geoff guessed. Was there no one in this whole sorry mess who didn't feel a need to hold him against his will or threaten him with physical violence?

'Where is it?' The voice was thickened by a foreign accent. The words sounded as though they were being deliberately articulated. 'Where is it? You must tell us right now.'

'I haven't got it yet.'

'Our mystics tell us that you touched it today.'

Mystics? Now there were mystics involved? How much bullshit did these people believe?

'I was close to it today, but I couldn't get hold of it. I couldn't take it.'

'He's wasting our time.' This was another voice. From the way the torchlight faltered with the words, Geoff guessed the person speaking was holding the torch. These words were spoken in an uncaring rush, as though the speaker didn't care if his articulation was accurate or otherwise. 'He's wasting our time. I say we should sacrifice him.'

Sacrifice? Geoff pressed his back hard against the unrelenting wall of the van. He pressed his heels firmly against the cold metal floor and, although his wrists were still being held, he prepared to pull himself free. He stopped because he thought he heard something in the voice that sounded like a bluff. Would they really pay him fifty grand one day and then threaten to sacrifice him the following day? That didn't seem likely.

'I've said I'll get it, and I will,' Geoff snapped, irritably. 'You'll have it within the next couple of weeks. You'll have it sooner if I get lucky.'

'Lucky? You think that this matter relies on a little bit of luck?'

'No,' Geoff lied. He pulled his hands free and shaded his eyes. 'I think this matter relies on skilful planning *and* a good deal of luck.'

'The fates have said that you will be able to do this.'

'If the fates have said I'll do this, then why are you snatching me off the street and threatening to sacrifice me?'

'The fates want you to keep the unnecessary deaths to a minimum-'

Minimum? Geoff thought uneasily. 'There aren't any unnecessary deaths in my plan.' No one seemed to be listening. The voice from the darkness simply spoke over him.

'We're puzzled as to why you haven't done it already.'

'I'm planning it and I'm doing it my way,' Geoff said, firmly.

He struggled to get to his feet. His head touched the roof of the van but he was moving slowly and stopped himself from banging into it. Standing stoop-shouldered, with the torch beam still landing bright on his eyes, he tried to decide what to do next. Someone tried to push him down but this time Geoff thrust their hands aside. He glowered menacingly into the shadows.

'I've had enough of this shit,' he growled.

The words sounded ludicrous coming in his own voice. It was a melodramatic and macho exclamation and unlike his usual meek way of addressing people. Yet, for some reason, the words carried enough weight to make the shadow hands disappear back into the darkness.

'You've already said that I'm expected to keep the unnecessary deaths to a minimum,' he reminded them. 'You'll open this van door now if you don't want to become statistics in those unnecessary deaths.'

There was a muffled discussion and then the van door was pushed noisily open. The breeze from the cool night was a refreshing balm on Geoff's cheeks. He wanted to sigh with gratitude. There had been a brief moment when he wondered if he would escape the van. Now he could see that his first hunch had been correct: they were simply trying to intimidate him.

'Why didn't you snatch it today, when you had the chance?'

Geoff thought about the moment when he had been sat at Black's desk. The idea of grabbing the skull at that point had seemed almost irresistibly tempting. He even recalled thinking, at the time, the skull had been promising to protect him if he should grab it and run.

'I'll get the skull when I think the time is right.'

'We need it urgently.'

Geoff jumped from the van and started walking into the night. 'Keep kidnapping me and threatening my life,' he grumbled. 'That's going to make it happen with much more urgency.'

37

He used brandy to help himself sleep. The bottle had been a present from someone who didn't know his drinking habits. Geoff suspected that the brandy was one of those gifts that had been passed from one giver to another and to another. For six months it had sat in the same cupboard where he kept tins of beans and packets of crisps, gathering dust on its slender shoulders. Geoff would have probably passed it onto some other hapless recipient if he hadn't decided to open the bottle one night when he had been tired, a little drunk, and in need of something alcoholic to slake his thirst.

Geoff had managed a single measure of the brandy and then decided the fiery taste on his throat, and the scent that stung like vinegar in his nostrils, was more than his delicate palette could tolerate. But, to give proper credit to the drink, the brandy had helped him sleep on that occasion.

He pulled the bottle from its place beside the crisp packets and poured a generous measure. Hopefully it would help him sleep this evening. He thought of diluting the bitter flavour with Coke or lemonade before deciding he was sufficiently manly to tolerate the drink neat. He downed it in one and imagined his breath was suddenly dragon-like with the flames that burnt his throat. Once he'd stopped coughing, Geoff poured himself a second shot and began to sip at the liquid with tentative urgency.

He did worry that it was dangerous to be drinking.

He had taken an excessive amount of painkillers throughout the day. He had taken so many that he worried that his body could react badly to the combination of drugs and liquor. He was also worried in case one of the many people who were currently trying to beat him up decided to break into the house whilst he was inebriated. When he was sober and in a position to protect himself, Geoff knew he remained a fairly easy mark for any thug who wanted to lay into a human punchbag. This evening, exhausted, aching and a little bit pissed, he figured kittens and children could easily beat him insensible.

And yet, as much as that thought worried him, Geoff knew it was also true that he needed to get a proper night's sleep. His rest had been broken and wearisome the previous night. He'd endured a difficult day where the world was made foggy from his unrelenting weariness. He didn't think he could tolerate a second day that was made so unbearable. If his need for sleep meant he had to finish the entire bottle of brandy, even though the liquid tasted like rusty robot piss, he was determined to do whatever was necessary.

He passed out in his chair with a late night poker game on the TV.

'You're a murdering bastard, Geoff Arnold. A murdering bastard.'

Geoff shook his head. He wasn't a murderer. Couldn't the stupid bitch understand that?

There was the citric sweet scent of van van oil. He caught notes of lemon grass and citronella along with the pungent taste of ginger. The room seemed to be lit by the flickering light of a candle.

But he was no longer in his room.

He was in the Raven and Skull offices.

'You're a murdering bastard, Geoff Arnold. A murdering bastard.'

Nicola was shouting the words at him. She did not look happy.

'I'm not a murderer,' he told her.

He looked around and guessed that the time was close to midday. That thought was confirmed when he saw a desk clock with the second hand creeping slowly towards noon. As the second hand of the clock touched twelve there was a tremendous explosion. He turned and glanced in the direction of the sound. Something horrific had tortured the wall that housed the lift shaft.

Alarm bells were ringing in a siren wail. Sprinklers, seeming sympathetic to the distress, began to shower a shock of ice cold water over everyone and everything.

Murdering bastard.

He ignored Nicola's words and pulled himself from his chair. Earlier, he had thought the room was lit by guttering candlelight. Now he could see he had been mistaken. The offices were lit by fluttering fluorescents, struggling to illuminate the room after whatever power surge had caused the catastrophic explosion.

Murdering bastard.

He climbed slowly out of his chair and waited for a moment. Others from the shared office of the accounts department and customer services were already leaping out of their chairs and hurrying to the site of the disaster.

Roger Black stepped coolly from his office.

'What the hell's going on?' Black called. 'What's happening?'

'The lift's exploded.' The person who replied was raising their voice to be heard above the alarm. 'The lift's exploded and I think Shaun was in there. I think there was a woman in there with him as well.'

Black shook his head.

'Abandon the building,' he declared. He stepped into the accounts department and told Geoff to abandon the building. Then he headed off in the direction of the CNS department to give them the same command.

Geoff watched a flood of staff, soaked from the sprinklers and ducking from the noise of the alarms. They were all heading towards the staircase doors.

You murdering bastard.

Geoff walked over the Roger Black's office and stepped calmly inside. He found himself grinning at the gold-plated skull on the desk. There was a smear of something red on the jawbone but he ignored that. Instead he lifted the skull and was surprised to discover that it barely weighed anything.

Is this all I have to do?

You're a murderer. You're a murdering bastard.

He shrugged off the accusations. Nicola always tried to be melodramatic whenever she thought she could get away with it. Even in his dreams it seemed she felt a need to act like some lunatic portent of doom. He hurried out of the office and headed through the doorway marked EMERGENCY EXIT: STAIRS.

He woke up muttering the words, 'I'm not a murderer. I'm not a murderer.' And, whilst he wasn't sure why he should be saying such a thing, he felt as though he now had an idea for how to acquire the skull.

38

Geoff was zombied through his Tuesday.

He woke up and made a breakfast of burnt toast and tepid coffee whilst continuously yawning. Even though he remembered a series of striking and vivid dreams from his night in bed, a series of dreams that were somehow disturbing and mysterious yet enlightening, it felt as though sleep had evaded him.

His eyes were grainy.

The world around him seemed grey and bleak.

His body was plagued by all the aches and pains that came from his previous day's beatings. He interrupted his morning shower to take painkillers and grimly chew them. The pressure of the water's jet was too intense on his bruised face. It hurt to soap his chest because he suspected he was now the owner of a freshly broken rib or two. His knuckles, which he had scraped bloody when he feared his money had been stolen, were still a raw mess of slowly-healing flesh. Studying the blackened edges of his torn skin, flinching from the sight of the exposed pink underskin that looked so painful when he flexed his knuckles, Geoff wondered if he had picked up an infection.

What if I just take the money and run?

The idea sauntered temptingly across his tired thoughts but he knew it wasn't worth considering. Don would track him down and beat him to a pulp for the affront of embarrassing him. More likely, if Don caught up with him, the sadistic thug would do a damned sight worse than merely beating him to a pulp. Don had already threatened Geoff's genitals. Geoff didn't know if that was symptomatic of the man's repressed homosexuality, or simply indicative of the most terrifying threat the man could make. Regardless of Don's reason for making the threat, Geoff didn't want to find out the man's motives: he simply wanted to avoid the risk of having his favourite parts damaged by a malevolent psychopath.

Not that Don was the only thing that Geoff had to fear. If Geoff did decide to flee with the remaining forty thousand in his possession, he guessed the Church of the Black Angel would want to do something about recovering their losses. He didn't think the members of the church were particularly well-organised but they had managed to track him down quite easily the previous evening. Geoff wasn't sure if supernatural forces genuinely guided them, but considering the way they had snatched him from the street and used the word 'sacrifice', he felt sure they would have no qualms about exacting a bloody and sadistic revenge if he crossed them. Without needing to dwell on the thought, he knew that vengeance from the Church of the Black Angel would involve candles, fragrances and wicked, curly knives.

'Take the money and run?' He shook his head. 'Not a good idea.'

He dressed in the cleanest clothes he could find and hurried out the door. The skies were heavy with the prospect of thunderclouds. The day promised to be long and bleak. The journey was made tedious because he shared it with irritating busloads of school-bound teenagers and the miserable thumping ache over his bruised and blackening eye. Painkillers had eased the stiffness in his ribs to a mild nuisance but they hadn't touched the raw discomfort of his face. He arrived half an hour early and settled himself behind his desk to try and deal with the Raven and Skull accounts in readiness for Roger Black's audit.

The accounts were a chore made demanding because they were so monumentally tedious. Six members of staff were working on completing the input of the year's purchase ledger and sales ledger invoices. Once the ledgers were finalised and signed off they would then be passed on to the company's external accountants. The company's external accountants would then be able to export the information into pretty little graphs that Roger Black could likely understand. Geoff was behind on the portion of data input he was expected to complete but that knowledge didn't worry him. Rather than fretting about the data input, he was spending his time slyly snooping around the offices so he could draw his own schematics of the building and get a better understanding of how to steal the skull.

Nicola saw him making the drawing during his lunch break. He was nursing a mug of extra strong coffee and half a pack of painkillers.

'What are you drawing?'

He glanced up at her and shook his head in disbelief.

He was sitting in the Raven and Skull staff canteen and he wasn't going to say aloud that he was drawing a diagram of the building's CCTV cables so he could work out how best to commit an undetected robbery. As Nicola sat down facing him he folded a clean sheet of paper over his drawing and took a slow swig from his mug of coffee.

'You look like shit,' Nicola told him.

'Yeah,' he agreed. 'Although, on the bright side, I've not been beaten up so far today.'

'Donny shouldn't have done that yesterday. He can be a prick.'

She placed a concerned hand on his.

Surprised by the contact, he allowed it linger there.

'Donny wasn't the only one that tried beating up on me yesterday.'

He told her about his encounter with the Church of the Black Angel. He mentioned the van, the suggestion of a sacrifice, and the way he had felt lucky to escape with his life.

Nicola stared at him with slack-jawed amazement.

'They had you in a van? And there were four or five of them? And you just got up and walked out?' She clutched his fingers so tight he was stung by a moment's pain. Her nail had accidentally caught on the frayed edge of one sore and swollen knuckle. 'You're so brave, Geoff. Have I ever told you that?'

He pulled his hand away. 'What do you want?'

'I don't want anything.'

'You're being nice to me. You're showing me sympathy. You must want something.'

She laughed as though he was joking. Her smile was broad and bright but there was no trace of humour in her eyes. 'What are you like?' she giggled cheerfully. 'You say the most outrageous things.'

'What do you want?'

She sighed and seemed to put aside the pretence with one long exhalation. 'Where's my money?'

'Your money is safe.'

'I want it now.'

'You can't have it now. We haven't done the job yet.'

'You gave Donny his money last night.'

'Donny was threatening to remove my balls.'

'I could threaten you,' she said. 'I could threaten you with...'

'Don't say it,' he broke in. He held up his hand in a STOP gesture. 'I don't know what you were going to say.' He shook his head and added, 'I don't want to know what you were going to say. But I don't want you to say it.'

She glared at him with obvious menace.

'We have to work together on this job,' he reminded her. 'We have to trust each other. I'm not going to be able to trust you if you're threatening me with repercussions, am I?'

'I suppose not,' she agreed. 'But I just—'

'Let's leave it there,' he said, firmly. He kept his tone hard with an authority that sounded alien to his own ears. 'I'll pay you as soon as I receive the second half of the money from the Church of the Black Angel. You have my word on that.'

'What if someone kills you before then?'

He ignored the question and sipped at his coffee. It felt as though a tooth had been loosened when Don struck him. He could feel the hot liquid of the coffee touching on a raw nerve. He winced from the pain and put the mug unhappily back on the table.

'You're not thinking of backing out, are you?' Nicola asked.

Geoff glared at her.

'Why the hell would I back out?' he demanded. 'I've already put a hundred grand's worth of effort into this project, and I'm getting paid less than seventy after all the expenses I'm paying out. There is no way I'm backing out now.'

She glanced nervously around the canteen and Geoff realised he had raised his voice too loud in protest. He quietly cursed himself for being so careless. He knew the mistake came from tiredness but that excuse didn't make him any less anxious that someone might have overheard what he said.

He rubbed a nervous hand against his brow.

The flesh felt greasy with perspiration. The touch of his fingertips was enough to spark a blister of pain from his throbbing forehead. He winced unhappily.

Nicola placed a hand on his.

She remained silent until his gaze met hers. When she did speak she had lowered her voice to a whisper. 'Didn't the Church of the

Black Angel say you've got to kill someone?' she asked, softly. 'Isn't that what you've just told me?'

Geoff shook his head. 'I won't be killing anyone. I'm not a murderer.'

The words stirred a memory from the night before. He didn't know why they should resound through his thoughts so powerfully but they seemed to be the strongest memory he carried from that night's dream.

'I'm not a murderer,' he said again.

His arms prickled with gooseflesh. The words sounded like a lie.

39

By the following Monday Geoff teetered on the brink of exhaustion.

Every night he had retired to bed drained from a wearisome day at work. Every morning he had awoken as though there had been no sleep whilst his eyes were closed. On two of the nights he had tried to enhance his slumber with alcohol.

It didn't work.

One night he had tried to get himself fully stoned with the remnants of some hash that had been hidden in his kitchen since he first rented the flat. The hash came from a nugget of quality Moroccan Gold. The first hit sent him floating. But, even though it took him higher than he'd been in a long time, Geoff awoke the following morning with the now familiar sense of exhaustion that was quickly becoming the bane of his existence.

On the Saturday night he tried to tire himself out with sex.

He bought a cheap bottle of wine and suggested to Nicola that they should discuss their joint venture back at his place. Half an hour into the 'discussion' she was naked and sucking on his erection. Before midnight had arrived they had wearied their way through a handful of orgasms for her and a final, climactic explosion for him. The whole experience had been exhausting, slightly perverted, and thoroughly enjoyable.

He awoke on the Sunday morning feeling as tired as ever.

Each night, as soon as he closed his eyes, the dream began.

It was always the same dream.

He was sitting at his desk in the Raven and Skull offices. Nicola was standing by his shoulder screaming words into his ear. 'You're a murdering bastard, Geoff Arnold. A lousy murdering bastard.'

'I'm not a murderer,' he told her.

His dream self had been saying the words for a week. Now he was beginning to think that the tone of his voice lacked conviction. If it meant he would be able to get a decent night's sleep, Geoff knew he would happily murder someone.

In the dream, as always happened, he saw the time was close to midday. The second hand of the clock above the office doorway touched noon. In that moment he flinched from the sonorous blast of the explosion. He turned and glanced to where the sound had come from and saw that something horrific had occurred to the wall that housed the lift shaft.

Alarm bells shrieked.

Sprinklers doused everyone and everything with icy water.

'Murdering bastard,' Nicola growled.

He ignored her and stood up. The lights were faltering. They seemed to brighten and dim in rhythm to the wail of the siren. The shifting shadows made the movements of those around him seem staccato and jumpy, like old black and white footage of long-dead actors.

Roger Black stepped coolly from his office.

'What the hell's going on?' Black demanded. 'What was that noise? What's happening?'

'The lift's exploded,' Geoff told him.

Black digested this with a nod.

'The lift's exploded,' Geoff explained, 'and I think Shaun was in there.'

Black took charge. He told everyone in accounts to abandon the building and then he set off to give that same message to everyone else on the fourteenth floor. He headed in the direction of the CNS offices.

Geoff waited and then watched a flood of staff rush to the staircase doors. The sprinklers continued to piss water on him. The siren of the alarm was relentless. It was a punishing noise. The sound hit his ears with a shrill force and he longed to flee from the building and escape its cry.

'You murdering bastard,' Nicola told him. 'How do you sleep at night?'

'Not very well at the moment,' he answered.

Geoff walked over to Roger Black's office and stepped inside.

He grinned at the gold-plated skull on the desk. It was almost as though the artefact was waiting for him. There was a smear of something red on the jawbone of the skull. The stain transformed the glossy yellow gold into something tarnished. He wiped his hand on its sticky redness and knew, without further investigation, it was blood.

Ignoring that detail he lifted the skull and dropped it into his pilot's case.

Is this all I have to do?

'You're a murderer,' Nicola told him. 'You're an evil, murdering bastard.'

He shrugged off the accusations and locked the skull inside his case. Walking calmly and slowly towards the emergency exit, he began to make his way down the stairs. He paused briefly on the way out and glanced at the damage to the lift shaft.

The explosion had clearly been a massive one. The doorway had been blown out and the cables that supported the lift were nothing more than frayed coils hanging limply over an empty shaft. Geoff was curious to know what had happened because he was suddenly struck by the conviction that he would be the one responsible for the explosion.

'I'm not a murderer,' he muttered. 'I'm not a murderer.'

He was awake and, again, he felt as though he hadn't slept.

'What did you say?' Nicola asked him. She yawned the question in his face with sour morning breath.

'You need to get in touch with Don,' Geoff told her. 'Tell him I need an explosive specialist.'

40

The steak in The House of Usher was not particularly good. It was overcooked and tough and the underlying taste was reminiscent of oily sweat. Geoff could understand why Don had been shouting at a junior chef a week earlier.

Admittedly, the dish didn't quite taste like shit.

In Geoff's opinion, Don's crude condemnation of the food with such a description was a tad harsh. But the meal was far from being worthy of the exorbitant price listed on The House of Usher menu.

Geoff chewed it morosely, trying to find some trace of flavour that his mouth was too tired to detect. No matter how hard he chewed, or how much ketchup he added, it still tasted like oily sweat.

He was alone in one of the restaurant's window seats, awaiting the arrival of Don's contact. His seat gave him a view of a concealed courtyard with lush lawns and a decorative fountain. In the summer afternoons he had seen seating around the fountain. The summer seating allowed alfresco diners to enjoy their midday meal in picturesque surroundings.

This evening there was no seating outside. Geoff could only see a solitary couple standing beside the fountain. She was short and dumpy. He was tall and smartly dressed. They were arguing bitterly. Geoff recognised them as Richard and Chloe from the offices of Raven and Skull although he was surprised to see them together. They struck him as a very unlikely couple. He had always thought Richard was happily married to someone attractive and wealthy whilst Chloe's abrasive personality made her too unattractive to date.

As though she was trying to prove Geoff's point, Chloe kept pushing a finger in Richard's face and shaking it in a gesture of obvious angry accusation. Richard seemed to accept her ire with equanimity. There was such an absence of emotion in his features that Geoff wondered if Chloe was safe in his presence.

'Are you the guy looking for explosives?'

'Jesus!' Geoff cried in a shocked whisper. He gestured with his hands for the woman to lower her voice. Richard and Chloe and their argument in the courtyard were immediately forgotten. Panicked, he checked the other diners in the restaurant to see if anyone had overheard the word 'explosives'. He had still been feeling sleepy before she arrived at his table. Now the residues of weariness were tossed aside by the adrenaline rush that coursed through his body. 'Couldn't you use a code word or some clever euphemism?' he asked, hoarsely.

'Bombs?' she suggested.

Geoff rolled his eyes. He supposed the tiredness was making him irritable and nervous. It was likely that his lack of a proper night's sleep was possibly clouding his judgement. Perhaps, he reasoned, the woman wasn't being as loud as he feared. He gestured for her to take a seat and took a moment to appraise her.

She was a tall, leggy blonde with a substantial bosom. Dressed in leather pants and a low-cut top she did not look like the illicit explosives expert he had been expecting. She looked attractive.

'My name's Terri,' she said extending a hand.

'I was expecting a man,' Geoff admitted.

She nodded. 'That's because you're probably a sexist prick.'

He shrugged and decided that was the most likely reason. He also noticed that none of the other diners glanced at them when she used the phrase 'sexist prick'. His worries that anyone was eavesdropping seemed laughably self-involved. Waiting until Terri was settled, and after ordering a glass of wine for her and letting her consider the menu, Geoff asked, 'How much did Don tell you about my needs?'

'He says you need something that will destroy CCTV cables and something that will cause a substantial diversion on the upper floor of an office block.'

Geoff nodded. 'Is that possible?'

She shrugged. 'With enough explosives anything is possible. I suppose the thing that's the main issue is how much do you want to pay. And how much collateral damage can you tolerate?'

He frowned. She was talking about unnecessary deaths. She was asking him how many deaths he could live with on his conscience. He wasn't sure he could live with the burden of any deaths, necessary or otherwise. Worried that such considerations would make him look weak, Geoff said, 'I want deaths kept to a minimum.'

'That's more expensive.'

He grimaced. 'How much will an explosion cost?'

She asked him to explain exactly what he needed.

Carefully, he went over his plans, discussing the layout of the Raven and Skull offices on the fourteenth floor and his need to take something from them during a substantial distraction. Terri was vaguely familiar with the offices. She said her mother, Fiona, used to work for Raven and Skull, although she'd recently been relocated to different offices. As a child Terri had occasionally accompanied her mother to the Raven and Skull building on those rare days when she hadn't been able to organise childcare.

'It's a small world,' Geoff observed.

Terri shook her head. 'It's not that small a world. It's just that we seldom realise how closely all our lives are interconnected.'

The words seemed profound and important but he was too tired to dwell on their meaning. His head throbbed with his desire to sleep.

Terri asked him about building materials and he answered as best as he could. Geoff produced his drawings and explained the illustrations patiently. Terri asked the occasional question and relabelled some of his notes so that doorways and scales were more accurately recorded. When she pointed at the cluster of CCTV cables in the centre of the diagram, and asked him why they were all collected there, Geoff explained that the cables were fed into a conduit that ran into the lift shaft.

'Interesting,' she murmured.

He was struck by the memory of his dreams from the previous week. In each dream he had seen smoke and rubble billowing from the devastation where the lift shaft had once sat.

'I'm not a murderer,' he thought defiantly. 'I'm not a murderer.' Aloud he said, 'That's going to be the best place for an explosion, isn't it?'

She nodded. 'You'll want the destruction of the cables and the distraction of an explosion. A device in that location will satisfy both of those requirements in the same moment.'

Device, he thought. *That was the euphemism she could have used when she approached the table.* He was about to say as much when activity outside the window caught his eye.

Richard and Chloe had been joined by a third figure.

This was an angry looking biker. He snatched hold of Chloe's arm. He held tight and pulled her away from the other man.

'This looks like it's going to get serious,' Terri muttered. 'If the police are going to get called down for this, I'll have to make a quick exit.'

Geoff ignored her. He was watching the action outside the restaurant.

The biker pushed Chloe to the ground and then stormed towards Richard. His hands were balled into big, beefy fists. His features were a scowl of outrage and menace.

'I know these people,' Geoff said, absently.

The biker snatched at Richard's collar and managed to grab hold of his tie. Holding him steady with his left hand he drew his right fist back as though preparing to deliver the sort of punch that would tear a man's head from his shoulders.

Terri pushed back her chair. 'I'm getting out of here,' she said. 'This is going to turn into a reportable incident and I can't afford to be a witness. Can you?'

Geoff didn't answer. He watched Chloe intervene at the last moment. She jumped from the ground and grabbed the biker's arm.

The biker tried to shake her off but the woman was surprisingly tenacious. She kept hold of his wrist and tried pulling him away. Her mouth was open and it was clear that she was screaming at him to stop behaving like a thug. Geoff couldn't hear what was being said but he could read the sentiment in her straining features.

'This double-glazing is very efficient for keeping out the sound,' Geoff marvelled.

'I'm leaving now.' Terri touched him on the arm to get his attention. 'Have we concluded our business here or do you want to make use of my services?'

The argument now seemed to be a feud between Chloe and the biker. Chloe was pointing her finger in his face and waving it with short, sharp staccato gestures. The biker did not appear to take kindly to such attempts at dominance. When he backed away from her there was reluctance in every step and his fist was raised in a warning.

'I want to make use of your services,' Geoff said, absently.

Terri had been on the verge of leaving the table. She sat back down. 'It won't be cheap.'

'How much?'

'For the device you need, I'd want ten grand.'

Ten grand, he mused. *Everyone wanted ten grand from him. Except for those who wanted twenty grand.* He continued to watch the scene outside.

The biker had turned his back on Chloe. Chloe appeared unhappy with that affront. She began to beat her fists against his shoulder blades with a speed and ferocity that, had it not been for the intense expression on her face, would have looked comical.

At some point, Geoff realised, Richard had managed to disappear. The biker scoured the courtyard looking for him and then turned to face a furious Chloe. He roared a question at her and, although the double-glazing was preventing any sound from filtering into the restaurant, Geoff could understand what was being said.

'Where is he?'

Chloe swiped at his face with her hand.

At first Geoff thought she was slapping at him. It was only when the three red lines appeared that Geoff saw she had scratched him with her nails.

The biker wiped away a palm full of blood and reacted furiously. He drew back one meaty fist into a punch and then lowered his hand as though thinking better of the action.

'That was chivalrous,' Geoff muttered.

Terri pressed her mouth close to his ear. 'That was probably for the best. He's a big bloke. If he'd punched her with that right hook he was raising, he would have taken her head off. She's wouldn't have gotten up from that punch.'

Geoff nodded agreement. The warmth of her breath on his ear was enough of a distraction to make him forget about Chloe, Richard and the biker. He turned back to her ample bosom and asked if she could have the device ready for the following morning.

'Of course. Can you have the money by then?'

He nodded.

He was about to add something further, invite her back to his place so she could collect the money herself, when someone in the restaurant shrieked and pointed out towards Chloe and the biker.

Chloe was flat on the lawn beside the fountain.

'What happened?' Geoff asked.

Terri shrugged. A handful of other diners were pointing at the scene. Some of them were pulling out mobile phones and Geoff heard someone talking with the police. Listening to the chatter of excited voices, from the other diners and from Terri, Geoff didn't take his gaze away from Chloe.

She remained motionless on the floor.

'Did that biker hit her?' Geoff asked Terri. 'How did I miss seeing that?'

'It's just struck ten o'clock and it's past my bedtime,' Terri told him. She leant across the table and gave him a peck on the cheek.

Geoff barely noticed the pressure of the attractive woman's lips on his face. He was mesmerised by the sight of Chloe's unmoving body.

She's dead, he thought.

'In twelve hours from now I'll have a device for you with a timed detonator,' Terri said. She was checking her wristwatch. 'I'll meet you in the smoking shelter outside your offices at ten tomorrow morning.' She drained her glass of wine and stood up. 'The device will be large enough to cause a huge distraction. If it's placed in the right location it will certainly blow out the CCTV cables. And, unless you're very unfortunate, it won't take more than six lives at the most.'

41

Nicola didn't appear in the office until ten thirty the following day. Her eyes were swollen from crying. Her cheeks were dull from a poor night's sleep. She looked dishevelled and completely unlike her usual well-groomed fashion-conscious self. For some reason Geoff couldn't quite fathom she even appeared shorter. 'Did you hear about Chloe?' She was struggling to contain tears. The whites of her eyes were red and glistening. 'Did you hear?'

Geoff glanced up from the accounts he was pretending to work on. He tried to look concerned. 'Chloe? What happened to her?'

'Last night she got into a fight with her boyfriend, Kevin. He claims he caught her cheating. Witnesses say he punched her in the face. The blow was so hard it killed her instantaneously.'

'Jesus,' Geoff muttered.

'Donny says it happened near his restaurant. Of course Kevin's denying that he punched her. He says it was her boyfriend. The bloke she was screwing behind his back.'

'That's terrible,' Geoff said.

'I'm worried this is my fault,' Nicola told him. 'Richard wanted to see Chloe last night. I'd organised for them to meet up. I wonder if Kevin misunderstood what was going on between the pair.'

'Terrible,' Geoff repeated.

He tried to sound sympathetic but it was difficult to pretend that he cared. He was still tired. Sleep had been a long time coming as he tried to come to terms with the fact that he had seen a woman's freshly slaughtered corpse the night before. He had watched a life ending and he had not cared.

What sort of inhuman monster had he become?

When sleep did arrive it had not provided any rest. Once again he had been dreaming his way through scenes of damage and destruction in the Raven and Skull offices. There were broken pieces of building, active sprinklers, dirty smoke and incessant alarms.

It worried him that the chaos had given him an erection.

Following his poor night, Geoff had endured a busy morning where he exchanged ten grand in notes for a small metal box that was meant to be a powerful explosive device. He worried that the box might not work and that he'd paid out ten grand for nothing. He worried also because Terri had pressed her lips close to his ear and whispered, 'Be careful. This explosive is an unpredictable commodity.'

What the hell did that mean? Was there a danger of it going off before he had it in place? It was sitting in his jacket pocket and he didn't like the idea that an unpredictable commodity of explosives could suddenly explode and tear out his kidney.

'You're not even listening to me,' Nicola wailed.

Her voice was loud enough to attract the attention of colleagues. Geoff cowered from the intrusive curiosity of their glances.

In his memory he tried to mentally play back whatever words she had been saying. It was a futile exercise. His thoughts had been wholly immersed in his own world. By way of an apology he gave Nicola a sheepish grin.

'You know I've not been sleeping well,' he reminded her. 'I must have been zoning out again.'

She shook her head with dismay. 'I'm not sure I can do this.'

Then she was running off to the bathroom.

A couple of the others in accounts glanced at him. He tried to give a shrug that said, 'Women! What are they like?' He wasn't sure his stilted body language conveyed that exact sentiment. He suspected it looked more like he was either indifferent or had a nervous twitch.

He saw her an hour later talking to some old woman he vaguely remembered seeing in the offices. She had a warty face and looked like she was consoling Nicola and showing her some knitting.

'How many women have you got on the go?'

The voice was murmured in his ear.

Geoff flinched when he realised Roger Black was talking to him. He tried to exercise a politic smile as though he wasn't sure what the question meant.

Black looked as darkly menacing as ever. His head, with its low brow and piggy eyes, did not look as though it belonged to the company's only active senior director. Even wearing a lecherous smile, Black looked thuggish and dangerous.

'How many women?' Black repeated.

'I'm single at the moment.'

Black raised one thick eyebrow. 'You have dinner every day with her,' he said nodding at Nicola. 'Surely you're banging her?'

Geoff opened his mouth and tried to decide how to reply. It was true that he did share a lunch table with Nicola. But that didn't mean they were in a relationship. The fact that they'd ended up in bed twice this past week was more coincidence than relationship and he didn't want it to become public knowledge that he had been 'banging her'.

Nicola was involved with Don.

Don was psychotically jealous.

Geoff had enough problems in his life without trying to incur Don's easily roused wrath. He wondered how closely Roger Black was currently watching him to have noticed that his relationship with Nicola was more than platonic.

'Nicola and I are just friends,' Geoff said, quietly.

'What about the blonde at the smoking shelter? Who was she?'

Black had seen him make his transaction with Terri?

Geoff's heart raced.

It had been the briefest of meetings. Terri had sent him a text message telling him she would be at the smoking shelter at nine-thirty. He was to have her ten grand in a carrier bag. She'd said she would come up to him and they would embrace. Whilst they were embracing she would slip the explosive and the instructions into his pocket. He would then give her the carrier bag as though it contained groceries of inconsequential importance.

Geoff thought the exchange had gone unnoticed. The smokers in the shelter, huddled together from the gloom of a grey morning's sky, had barely acknowledged his presence.

Geoff had been more preoccupied by the money he was handing over.

He was giving her ten thousand pounds. The bundle of notes looked insubstantial in size and seemed to have no weight in the bottom of the Asda carrier bag he held. Yet that sum of money represented a sizable chunk of the payment he had been hoping to pocket in return for this theft.

And now it seemed Roger Black had watched the transaction take place.

Geoff tried to keep his features composed.

'Who was she?' Black repeated.

'An old school friend,' Geoff told him. 'I'd promised to pick up some groceries for her on my way to work. She was just collecting them.'

Black laughed and clapped Geoff on the shoulder. His hand landed heavily. It took all Geoff's willpower not to shriek as though he was being beaten.

'You're a lying fuck,' Black said cheerfully. 'I think you're banging them both and maybe a couple of others besides.' He shook his head when he could see that Geoff was trying to protest. 'I like that you play things discreetly,' Black explained. 'That sort of class should carry you well if you receive a promotion.'

Geoff blinked at this. He was about to ask Black what he meant but the man was already walking away.

Nicola stood where Black had been. She'd finished her discussion with the warty-faced woman and she now glared at him through heavy-lidded eyes.

'I'm not doing this anymore.'

Geoff checked his watch and shook his head. Ignoring her protest he grabbed Nicola by the wrist and dragged her towards the lift. Without letting go of her he pushed his thumb against the UP button.

'I'm serious,' Nicola told him. She was trying to pull herself free. 'I'm out of this now. Chloe was my best friend. I'm too upset to carry on.'

Geoff waited for the lift door to open and then pushed her inside.

She glared at him in disbelief. 'What the hell do you think you're doing?'

'We're going to the top floor of the building,' Geoff said. 'There's no one using the top floor at the moment so we'll have privacy. Whilst we're up there, you're going to keep the lift doors open so I can plant a device.'

'I won't do it,' Nicola told him. 'You can't make me do it.'

Geoff nodded. 'This is true. I can't make you do anything against your will. But I can keep the money that was put aside for you.'

She shot him her angriest glare. 'Stick it up your arse if it makes you happy.'

'Fair enough,' Geoff said, amicably. 'And I can also tell Don how good you were in fucking my brains out the other night.'

She glowered at him. 'You wouldn't dare.'

He held her gaze until she looked away and called him a bastard. The lift arrived at its destination and the doors slipped open. Even though Geoff knew that the floor wasn't being used, he still took the precaution of glancing out into the empty corridor to make sure there was no one there who could see what they were doing.

His bowels clenched tightly as he considered the enormity of the task he was now undertaking. He wanted to swallow but his mouth was suddenly too dry. His tongue was too large.

'Put your foot there and stop the lift doors from closing,' he told Nicola.

Petulantly, she stamped her foot in the lift's doorway. She had her arms folded and her lips were curled into a sneering pout. 'You're using me,' she told him.

Geoff ignored her.

He gingerly lifted the device from his jacket pocket. It was the size of a pack of playing cards. It was a shiny metal box with an LED screen that showed four zeroes. Terri's instructions had told him to fix the device in the top corner of the lift just above the door. Then he would have to press the reset button and a countdown would begin.

Geoff stuck it in position with superglue.

As soon as he felt sure it was adhered to the roof he pressed the button to start the twenty-four-hour countdown. Momentarily mesmerised, he watched the numbers click away:

23:59

23:58

23:57

'Is that it?' Nicola asked.

Her sharp voice dragged him away from his reverie. Geoff drew a deep breath and tried not to shiver. He had just set a countdown on an explosive device that would detonate at noon the following day. It would give him an opportunity to steal from his employer. It would likely kill innocent people. And she was simply asking, '*Is that it?*'

'That's it,' he said, quietly.

She glanced at him and then at the device. Her folded arms tightened over her breasts. 'Can we walk back down to the fourteenth floor?'

He followed her gaze.

The box was only sitting there. It wasn't blinking. It was so small and innocuous it would remain undetected until it exploded. But Geoff could empathise with Nicola's unease. He was suddenly sure he would never again get into the lift.

'Of course,' he said. 'Let's walk down stairs.'

42

'You look cold,' he observed.

The shadow of the Raven and Skull building was behind them. The day's darkening clouds were easing into the blackness of night. A handful of streetlights flickered into life as they walked and the remainder of their journey was illuminated by passing car headlights shining brightly on the slick, wet roads.

'I am cold,' Nicola admitted. She smiled, as though touched by his observation. She began to babble excitedly and Geoff understood she had now moved past her upset at Chloe's death. 'That nice Moira offered to knit me a beret. She's got this lovely lilac cashmere and she thinks a knitted beret might help keep me warm.'

'Who the hell is Moira?'

Nicola shook her head. 'You probably don't know her. She works under Tony.' Her lips were thin and set in a determined line. Her brow was furrowed with wrinkles of concentration.

Geoff had an idea of what she was going to say and he didn't want to hear it. Like the explosive device that Terri had given him, Nicola was also proving to be something of an unpredictable commodity. Because he'd had a lifetime's worth of unpredictable commodities over the past week, Geoff felt sure he knew what she would now demand. In truth, he had been expecting this development since Nicola flashed him her angriest glare in the lift and told him to shove the money up his arse.

She grabbed hold of his sleeve, making him turn to face her.

'I want more money,' Nicola told him.

'No.' He made it a flat refusal and pulled his arm away. There was no opportunity for discussion. No scope for further conversation. Not even meeting her glare he walked past her and headed towards the railway bridge that would lead to his bus route home.

In the distance he could see a train approaching. It was hurtling along at a furious speed. The machine glimmered sleekly in the wet shadows of encroaching night. The windows were aglow with slivers of brightness. The train's headlights were small beady pinpricks of light.

'Geoff!'

He ignored her.

'Geoff!' This time the shriek of her voice was accompanied by the ungainly patter of her footsteps chasing after him. In her grief that morning she had clearly chosen to wear flats instead of heels. Because she was more used to heels the sound of her step was alien and unfamiliar. In a flash of delayed insight he understood that was the reason he had thought she seemed shorter that morning. 'Geoff,' she repeated, grabbing hold of his arm and making him stop. 'You can't walk away from me. You have to listen to me.'

He turned to glare at her.

He had once thought Nicola was attractive but now he could see he'd been wrong on that score. She wasn't wearing make-up today and her face wasn't pretty enough to be seen without some smear of war-paint. Her skin was porous and uneven. Her eyes were piggy without mascara. Without gloss her lips looked thin and uninviting. The wind tousled the lank and tangled tresses of her hair.

'I want more money,' she insisted.

Even though they were alone on the bridge, Geoff instinctively glanced around to see if anyone had overheard their exchange. It was only when he saw there was no one within earshot that the idea crossed his mind.

The train was coming closer. The railing on the bridge was not particularly high. And Nicola was slender and light.

'I want more–'

'No.' He said the word so it cut directly through her forceful demand. Stepping towards her he raised a finger and pointed it at her chest. Before she could interrupt him he said, 'My share of this profit is dwindling by the second. So far I've received fifty grand. Your boyfriend has taken ten of that from me. I've spent another ten buying the explosives. You're already due to get twenty grand for all the help that you've *not* given me so far. I've paid out for meals and gloves and a pilot case and that leaves me with fuck all in the way of a profit so far. Now you're wanting a bigger share of it?'

She rolled her eyes as though she was talking with someone stupid.

'You'll be getting fifty grand tomorrow,' Nicola reminded him. 'I've done as much on this job as you have. If the police were to find out what we've done'

Geoff thought of Roger Black's dour face and realised the police were the least of his worries. It was a chilling thought. He didn't doubt, if he earned Black's wrath, there would be torture, suffering and an unmerciful death. He tried not to shiver. Nicola barely seemed to notice his unease.

'—I'd be considered just as guilty as you are,' she went on. 'I think we should get thirty five grand each.'

Geoff stopped and studied her incredulously. 'You want how much?'

She seemed to back down from his obvious anger. Swallowing, she said, 'I deserve half.'

'For doing what?'

She looked like she was going to respond but he stepped closer and cut her off. 'You've done nothing but moan since we started on this project.'

'That's not fair—'

He pushed his finger against her chest. 'Your dickhead boyfriend had me beaten up in case I tried to stick my dick in you.'

'You can't blame me for—'

He noticed she was wearing a thin coat. He could see there was enough loose fabric at the breast of the coat that would allow him to grab a fistful and lift her off her feet if he chose. The idea was appealing.

'You told him I'd been trying it on with you. That I had a small cock and I smell of chlamydia.'

'I was trying to—'

'This morning I had to drag you into the lift so that you'd actually do something useful on this project.'

'That's not—'

'And now you're demanding a full fifty per cent of the gross profit?'

He was so close now that she cowered beneath him as he spoke over her objections. He could hear a noise rising at the back of his thoughts but didn't know if it was the sound of the approaching train or something symbolic of his mounting anger. 'Fifty per cent?' he repeated. 'Is that what you're demanding?'

'I've fucking earned it,' she hissed.

Geoff shook his head. 'I'll tell you what you have earned.'

She looked at him curiously. There must have been some level of menace in his voice that she hadn't previously noticed because her eyes flickered with uncertainty, as though she knew she had pushed him too far.

'What?' she demanded. He could hear that she was trying to sharpen the edge of her voice with the pretence of defiance. 'What have I earned?'

He grabbed a fistful of her coat and lifted her easily into the air.

Before the panic could properly register on her face he had pushed her over the bridge's railing and into the path of the oncoming train.

Her horrified scream was cut off halfway through.

The clock on the nearby church began to chime six o'clock.

43

Nicola's death didn't trouble him. He suspected it would have been on the news although he didn't bother putting the TV on to watch. Geoff arrived home, snapped open a bottle of scotch and swigged himself swiftly to sleep.

It was the same dream as usual. It began with a loud explosion whilst he worked in the office. The sound was followed by a rush of air pushing past him. Alarm bells shrieked. The hiss of sprinkler water began to patter on monitors, desks and paperwork. Exclamations of 'What the fuck?' and 'What that hell was that?' tried to make themselves heard above the scream of the alarms.

Geoff pulled leather gloves from his desk drawer and slipped them onto his hands. Opening his pilot case he picked the bags of sugar from inside and placed them on his desk. He rose slowly from his desk, took the empty pilot case and walked through the chaos.

Black was out of his office, directing the panicked throng to evacuate using the stairs. Geoff could see Cindy, looking panicked and confused, pushing her way through the doors to the stairs and considering the descent with obvious apprehension.

He glanced at the CCTV units and saw the red eyes of the cameras were no longer lit. The bomb had been effective. He stepped out of the way as Tony and Becky hurried past him. He didn't bother making eye contact with them. He watched Heather rush out of Black's office without locking the door behind herself.

Geoff stepped inside.

The skull was on the table. He expected to see a smear of red on the dome-like frontal bone. The mark had been there during every previous dream. He couldn't understand why this dream would be any different. A voice at his ear whispered, 'That's blood that you're looking for.'

He recognised the voice as belonging to Nicola.

'You won't see blood there, yet,' she told him. 'The blood's not on the skull. The blood's on your hands.'

He looked around, expecting to see her ghostly image at his side.

Instead, he found himself glaring at an old man in a wheelchair. 'Who are you?' he asked.

But the question was redundant. He knew that the man was Charles Raven. He recognised the haggard figure of the man hunched over in his chair. He recognised the unpleasant plastic pipes that dripped from the man's nostrils.

Raven's upper lip trembled in a cruel smile.

'What are you doing in my dream?' Geoff demanded.

Raven considered him, warily. He arched one eyebrow into a question.

In that instant Geoff knew he was no longer dreaming. His heartbeat raced as he realised he was actively involved in the theft of the skull.

44

'Are you working for the Church of the Black Angel?' Raven asked. His voice was surprisingly clear for a man speaking through an oxygen mask. 'Have those devious fuckers decided to try and get some of their power back?'

Geoff didn't bother replying. Picking up the skull was a simple matter. The jawbone had been professionally fused to the upper bone. It was a complete piece that felt light but solid in his hand. Geoff held it awkwardly by the lower jaw. He had his pilot case open but he didn't drop it in there yet.

This wasn't like the dream. Not only did the alarm sound louder and the spray of the sprinkler's water feel colder, he could also now taste the acidic flavour of dust from the explosion. More obviously, in the dream, the skull had been made slippery with blood.

'How much are they paying you?' Raven demanded. He shook his head and seemed to decide that was a ridiculous question. 'Whatever they're paying you, I'll double it. All you have to do is put the skull down and say you'll work for me.'

Geoff considered the old man, sceptically.

Outside the room he could hear the subsiding shriek of voices. The alarm continued to rise and fall. The lights in the room were faltering from shadowy gloom to impenetrable dark. From faraway he could hear the approach of sirens. There seemed to be so many sirens approaching that he suspected the offices had earned a full complement of fire engines, ambulances and police cars.

'Shaun was in there,' someone outside Black's office called. The voice sounded like Tony's familiar baritone. 'I'm not kidding you. Shaun was in that lift when it malfunctioned.'

Geoff smiled when he heard the word 'malfunctioned'. Of all the words that could have been used to describe a chunk of the lift exploding and a downpour of chaos and destruction, the word 'malfunctioned' seemed strangely understated and coy.

'Just put down the skull,' Raven insisted. 'We can make a deal.'

'Like you made a deal with Harry Shaw?'

Raven scowled. 'What do you know about Harry Shaw?'

Geoff could have told him that the rumours about Shaw were common knowledge to all those who worked overtime. He could have said that he had heard people discuss Harry Shaw when he had been drinking with friends on a weekend. But he couldn't see the point in prolonging the conversation.

'You'll excuse me, Mr Raven,' he began politely. He tested the weight of the skull in his hands. Even though it was light he knew it would make a formidable weapon. 'You'll have to excuse me but I don't think I can accept your generous offer.'

'I've seen your face,' Raven told him. His voice spiralled with the threat of panic. He raised an accusatory finger that trembled with age and apprehension as he pointed at Geoff. 'I've seen your face. I know who you are.'

'Yes,' Geoff agreed. 'That's going to be unfortunate for one of us, isn't it?'

He struck the old man with the skull.

The first blow hit him hard across the face. Raven muttered an exclamation of shock and surprise as the respirator was swatted from his nose.

Then Geoff was smacking his face again with the skull.

The second blow squashed the old man's nose.

The third one connected with bone and landed hard enough to make a cracking sound. Raven had been raising a hand in protest. It fell heavily downwards. Geoff guessed he'd killed his employer but, to be certain that was what had happened, he smashed the skull down twice more.

He was panting when he stepped back from the carnage.

Raven's face was a battered mess. Only one eye was visible. The other was lost beneath a flow of blood that had poured from a gash on the old man's forehead. The remaining eye stared at Geoff in blind accusation.

Geoff glanced at the skull and was not surprised to see it was smeared with blood. He didn't bother wiping it off before tossing his treasure into the pilot case. He wanted to get out of the building before anyone found him leering over a violently murdered corpse.

Smiling to himself, Geoff stepped out of the office and into the smoky aftermath of the corridor. The alarm bells sounded louder outside Black's office. The sprinklers were still pouring, pattering his shoulders with a serious dousing of water and washing the blood from his hands. He wondered if it would be bad taste to start humming a few bars of 'Singing in the Rain'.

Even though he had been the one who placed the explosive device in the lift, Geoff still found himself standing before the shattered doorway of the lift and momentarily wondering how he was going to get out of the building. Shaking his head with self-deprecatory admonishment, smiling a little at his foolishness, he walked to the emergency stairway and began to make his way down.

Cindy was still there, clutching onto the rails and struggling to manage the steps. Geoff considered her sympathetically and wondered if he should lend a hand. If he was seen heroically leading a nervous woman from the building it would make people less likely to think he had been responsible for the theft of the skull or the brutal murder of Charles Raven.

But, thinking about Raven, Geoff figured that Black would likely be returning to his office at any moment to discover the old man's corpse. Once he had discovered the body, Geoff could imagine Black hurtling down the stairs, looking for the murderer, and pledging to have vengeance. Although Geoff currently felt confident enough to take on the world, common sense told him that it would be wisest to try and avoid facing Black until absolutely necessary.

Besides, he thought, given the way Cindy was making such a fuss about the coping with stairs, he wouldn't be surprised if the clumsy bitch didn't trip and fall and break her neck before she reached the bottom.

He brushed past her without speaking and hurried onwards and downwards to make his exit from the Raven and Skull building.

Geoff sat in The House of Usher and ordered a plain and hearty steak. He thought of asking if they could make one that didn't taste of oily sweat, and then realised that would likely cause offence in the kitchens. Once this meeting was finished he figured he could start to expand his tastes and explore new flavours and better restaurants. He would be roughly £80,000 up on the deal and able to indulge a range of appetites that had previously been beyond his budget. But for now, for this celebratory meal, it made sense to mark the successful completion of the project with a certain air of tradition. He ordered a bottle of the house Merlot to go with the steak. When it arrived, Geoff thought the wine tasted too dry.

'You heard what happened to Nicola?' Don asked.

He sat, uninvited, at Geoff's table. His eyes were rimmed with red. His jaw was unshaved. He had the dishevelled appearance of a man who had been too distracted to wash and dress properly.

'I heard about Nicola,' Geoff said, softly. 'You have my sympathies.'

It was difficult to tell whether or not Don was properly grieving or merely putting on an act. Geoff had seen the man flirting with other women whilst he was involved with Nicola. Geoff also knew that Nicola had never put a lot of stock in her relationship with the restaurateur. She had always seemed more attached to his wealth than to him. But, he supposed, that did not necessarily mean that Don wasn't grieving. It just meant their relationship was unconventional.

'Do you have any idea how it happened?'

Geoff shook his head. 'I know she got hit by the train.'

Don winced.

'But I haven't heard whether she tripped, got pushed or simply decided to end it all.'

'If she was pushed,' Don whispered. 'I will find the bastard who did it. I will find him and I will make him suffer.'

Geoff said nothing. He wasn't sure there was a way to properly console a psychotic like Don. He put down his knife and fork and tried to grace the man with an expression that combined sympathy, reassurance and condolence.

'Mr Arnold?'

Geoff glanced up to see a vaguely familiar face towering above him. The man wore casual jeans with a hooded fleece beneath a leather jacket. His scalp was hidden beneath a skull-hugging grey beanie. As before, Geoff noted that there was a day's worth of razor stubble dirtying the man's jaw, and a religious scent of incense perfuming the air about him. He was the representative of the Church of the Black Angel Geoff had originally met at Shades.

The man looked conspicuously out of place in The House of Usher. He looked like a merchant sailor on shore leave. Set against the pristine white tablecloths of the restaurant and the polished cleanliness of every surface, the man from the Church of the Black Angel looked grubby and unsanitary.

Nevertheless, Geoff smiled when he saw the man because he could see the man was carrying another large tote bag. He cut himself a slice of steak and chewed on it as he pointed at the bag with his knife.

'Is that my fifty grand?'

'I'll leave you two gentlemen to your business,' Don said.

Neither Geoff nor the representative acknowledged him as he stood up and staggered away from the table in the direction of the kitchens.

'Is that my money?' Geoff prompted.

'Do you have the item?'

Geoff had the pilot's case beneath the table. Without bothering to bend down he kicked it so that it slid towards his contact. He cut himself another piece of the steak and savoured it. The taste was not brilliant. If anything this was a little overcooked. But it didn't have the unpleasant flavour he had come to associate with steaks at The House of Usher.

The representative sat down. He started to fumble with the lock until Geoff told him the combination for both latches. The man nodded a curt thank you and then opened the case.

'*Langet manman*,' he purred.

Geoff didn't understand the man's Creole but he could hear the undercurrent of awe in his tone. He grinned around the steak he was chewing and took a swig at his Merlot.

The contact frowned and pushed his hand inside the case. For one unsettling moment Geoff feared the man was going to bring the skull out of the case and place it on the dining table. He didn't have any genuine qualms about it being seen but he was wary that someone might notice and say something and the talk would eventually get back to Roger Black.

The contact drew his hand out of the case and appeared to be examining his fingers with a mixture of curiosity and disgust.

'There's blood on it.'

Geoff shrugged. 'You never said it had to be clean. It is the correct gold-plated skull that you wanted, isn't it?'

The contact considered him. 'Yes. It's the correct skull.'

'Then I fail to see why you're bitching.' He used his fork to gesture at the contact's holdall. 'Is that my fifty grand?'

The contact pulled the holdall closer to his leg. 'Perhaps I might decide to keep this money,' the stranger suggested. 'You delivered this late. You delivered this dirty. This is not a good way to do business.' He tilted his jaw defiantly and asked, 'What are you going to do if I make the decision to keep this money?'

Geoff shook his head. 'Don't push me.'

Was that a line from Rambo? Or was he quoting Fifty Cents? Geoff wasn't sure and he knew it didn't matter. The sentiment remained the same. He swigged a mouthful of the wine to clear his palate and pointed a wavering finger at his contact.

'Don't push me,' he said again. 'It won't end well for you.'

The contact sneered.

Geoff bristled.

He didn't have to take this shit. After all that he had endured and managed over the past couple of weeks he knew that he didn't need to tolerate the grumbling threats of a miserable go-between. He snatched the pilot's case back.

'What—?'

'No,' Geoff told him. He kept his voice low but it was louder than a whisper. If other diners heard he didn't think it would matter. Two nights earlier he had watched a roomful of diners ignoring Chloe when she got murdered. He figured most of those eating this evening would turn a deaf ear to the transaction he was negotiating with the representative from the Church of the Black Angel.

'I'll give you one chance to retract what you were saying and give me the money I'm owed,' Geoff told him.

The representative considered him with a scornful sneer.

'You've already seen that the skull in there is stained with blood,' Geoff told him. 'That's because I used the damned thing to bludgeon Charles Raven to death.'

The representative blinked but said nothing.

'I take it you've heard about the other death at Raven and Skull today?' Geoff continued. 'The poor fucker who died because of the lift shaft explosion? That's another one you can add to my total. And, if you're trying to calculate my kill-to-death-ratio, you might want to think about what happened to my accomplice yesterday evening. I had no qualms about throwing her into the path of an oncoming train.' He leant across the table and lowered his voice to a menacing whisper. 'I'd have even less qualms about dealing with you in those terms if you try and double-cross me.'

The representative nodded and sat back. Grudgingly, he pushed the tote bag towards Geoff. 'Very good,' he allowed. 'You're the big man who's not scared of killing. You're powerful and you're violent. I won't challenge you. It sounds like you've earned this money.'

Geoff smiled to himself. He was about to thank the representative for finally getting the point when he heard a man's deep voice say, 'I agree.'

Geoff looked up.

It was Don who had spoken. He stood dangerously close to the table. The glint in his eye was manic with rage. He glanced from Geoff to the representative and then back to Geoff. 'I think you've more than earned that money,' he said, stiffly. 'I think you've earned that money and quite a lot more.'

Geoff opened his mouth and tried to think of a way of retracting what he had said. He could tell Don it was a joke. He could tell Don it was merely an off-the-cuff comment to make the representative hand over the outstanding money. But he couldn't say those things in front of the representative.

'Don,' Geoff began. 'Don. I need to talk with you in private once I've finished this meeting here.' He stood up trying to glare at Don and impress him with an expression of silent urgency. 'Don,' he repeated.

The man on the adjacent table stood up and grabbed hold of Don's wrist. He was a squat, dark figure.

Geoff instantly recognised Roger Black.

He stifled a groan.

Black placed a hand on Don's shoulder and tried to calm him. Glaring at Geoff he said, 'I think Mr Arnold here will want to have a private word with both of us once he's finished chatting with his friend,' he said calmly. His smile was bereft of humour as he added, 'And I think, between the pair of us, we can keep him talking for a very long time.'

'You stole from Raven and Skull!' Cindy gasped.

Geoff shrugged. 'I don't like the word 'stole',' he admitted. 'It makes me sound so criminal.'

'You murdered two colleagues in cold blood,' Heather said. 'And you then used a gold-plated skull to bludgeon your employer to death before trying to sell contraband.'

Geoff glared at her.

The silence around the table threatened to become unbearable.

'Do you know the one thing that's more frightening than killing someone?' Richard asked.

They all turned to face him.

It was late in the pub. Late enough to be early. The empties on the table had been cleared a couple of times but now, it seemed, the staff had given up on them and left the office workers to wallow in their own overflowing abundance of glasses and bottles.

Cindy hiccoughed.

Becky giggled.

Tony snored a little and then pulled himself awake with a start.

'Do you want to know?' Richard demanded. 'The one thing that's more frightening than killing someone is the shit that happens after you have killed someone.'

Richard watched Cindy drag Melissa's battered body up the stairs. She hauled with the impressive mechanical industry of a farm labourer. She bent at the knees, grabbed Mel's ankles, and then began to haul his wife's unprotesting carcass up the stairs with relentless determination.

She made no complaint.

She didn't falter from her goal.

She simply lifted and slowly dragged Melissa's battered and broken body up to the top of the stairs.

'I could use a hand here,' she grunted.

He smiled and gave her a thumbs up sign.

Cindy rolled her eyes in exasperation.

Melissa's skull struck one of the marble stairs. She yelled in protest and glared unhappily around. Her gaze fell on his. Her smile was made crimson with bloody teeth. 'Richard?' she called. She sounded confused and not fully coherent. 'Am I upstairs or downstairs?'

'We're working on both,' Cindy said, gruffly. She hauled Melissa up another step and glared down at Richard. 'Can you get up here and give me a hand?' she demanded. 'This bitch might fit into a size eight frock, but that doesn't mean she's lightweight when she's being dragged up a marble staircase. I'm going to give myself a back injury getting her up these stairs.'

Richard nodded and trotted up the stairs to join her. He made sure not to stand in any of the slippery puddles of blood that now made the journey treacherous. He wasn't wholly sure he could do as Cindy expected. He knew that they had to drag her to the top of the stairs and he also knew, if they wanted any hope of staying out of jail, they would have to push her down the stairs again and hope she died this time. But he wasn't sure he could do something so cruel and violent to the woman he had once claimed to love.

'Dicky?' Melissa cried. 'What are you doing?'

He pushed Cindy to one side and took hold of one of his wife's ankles. Working together, and with neither of them bothered about Melissa's discomfort, Cindy and Richard dragged her up to the top of the staircase and then lifted her to a standing position.

She whimpered a little as one shattered ankle was forced to take her weight. She started to fall towards the steps and Richard instinctively reached out a hand to catch her. His fingers clutched tight around her forearm.

Melissa looked at him and smiled.

'You saved me,' she beamed. 'Thank you, Dicky.'

Cindy slapped his hand away and pushed Melissa backwards.

She tumbled away from him, shrieking loudly until she struck the marble with the solid sound of a hammer hitting brick. Richard winced from the noise, although he refused to look away. He watched Melissa's body tumble to the bottom of the staircase where it landed in a broken state of tangled limbs all splayed at impossible angles.

'Dicky!' Melissa called. 'That really fucking hurt.'

'For fuck's sake,' Cindy sighed. She sounded exasperated. 'How many times do we have to throw this bitch down the stairs before it kills her?'

'I don't know,' Richard said, marching down the stairs. 'Let's find out, shall we?' He grabbed Melissa's ankles and again went through the process of dragging her up the stairs. One of the ankles he held felt different. He wasn't sure why at first. It wasn't until his fingers explored the skin and he squeezed a little too hard that he realised he was holding badly broken bone. Melissa remained too drunk to properly understand or decipher her pain.

'Are you taking me to bed, Dicky?'

He ignored her. It was a considerable effort getting her to the top of the stairs and he was grateful when Cindy joined him and took an ankle and helped him haul her to the top. Melissa made a handful of inarticulate mumbles but it seemed the last of her outbursts had now been made. When they let her fall down the stairs for a final time she made no exclamation. They both made their way unhurriedly down the stairs to examine her fallen body and neither of them was able to find a pulse.

'She's dead,' Richard declared.

'About fucking time,' Cindy grunted.

He shook his head. Even though this was the result he had wanted, he could now see that the real work was about to begin. 'I need to call Roger Black.'

48

Black was at the house within twenty minutes. His huge black and silver Jaguar roared up the driveway and parked outside the doorway. Richard explained that he thought Melissa had lost her footing at the top of the stairs. Black looked upset when he saw Melissa's mangled body but he maintained his composure. He bundled Cindy into a car and had her driven home. He promised that her car would be returned to her house by the following morning.

Then he made calls to his solicitors and the police.

There were two representatives from the Raven and Skull legal department in attendance by the time the first of the officers arrived on the scene. They extended their sympathies to the bereaved and told the police that the woman's death had been a tragic accident. Richard explained that he thought Melissa must have lost her footing at the top of the stairs.

The police looked sufficiently intimated to believe the statement without question. It took two hours before the coroner's office had removed Melissa's body and finished taking their photographs. The attendant police officers confirmed they saw nothing to suggest the death was anything other than a tragic accident. By three in the morning Richard was left alone in the house with Roger Black.

Richard allowed the man to walk him into the kitchen where Black poured them each a stiff shot of bourbon from the bottle Melissa had hidden in the fridge.

'My favourite niece is dead,' Black murmured. He sat down at the same breakfast bar where, four hours earlier, Cindy and Melissa had been sitting and chatting and drinking. 'How did it happen?' Black asked.

Richard had an unnerving premonition that Black already knew. He bit back the idea of giggling madly and shook his head. 'She must have lost her footing at the top of the stairs.' It felt as though he had been saying the words repeatedly throughout the evening. 'She must have—'

Black punched him across the jaw. The blow was hard enough to knock Richard off his feet. He fell to the unforgiving hardness of the kitchen's tiled floor, immediately scrabbling to sit upright and assume the appropriate facade of outrage and indignation.

'What the fu–?'

'I don't trust you, Dicky,' Black growled.

Richard fell silent.

'I don't trust you and I'm going to be looking into your history and your habits.'

Richard's bowels turned to water. The pain in his jaw was suddenly forgotten. He glared sourly up at Black, unnerved by the idea of having Roger Black looking into his history and his habits.

'My niece was besotted with you,' Black declared. 'But I always thought you were a slimy piece of shit that was likely to fuck anything with a pulse and an accessible orifice. Some days I'd look at you and wonder if you were even that picky.'

'I don't think–' Richard began.

'Keep your mouth shut.' Black silenced him with a pointed finger. 'Keep your mouth shut and hear me out.'

Grudgingly, Richard fell silent.

'I'll be interviewing my staff at Raven and Skull over the next week,' Black explained. 'I'll be asking everyone if they have any gossip that they'd like to share about you. At first I'll be asking if they know anything about you and Cindy.'

It took an effort of willpower but Richard didn't let his gaze falter. He refused to allow his cheeks to colour with an involuntary blush.

'If that source of enquiry proves fruitless,' Black went on, 'I'll ask for all the dirt I can get on you in general.'

Richard's heart was beating with frantic haste. He wouldn't let himself think about the potential of being found out. He didn't want Black to be able to see any tell-tale details in his expression. He tried to keep his breathing measured and sedate.

'If you're thinking of covering your tracks,' Black snapped. 'I'll warn you now, there will be twenty-four-hour surveillance on you until I've finished my investigation.'

Richard said nothing. He pulled himself slowly from the floor, warily studying Black in case the man decided to hit him again. Considering Black's formidable bulk, and his obvious skill at hitting people, Richard knew he had no way of defending himself against any attack. But he maintained the pretence of being watchful for fear that anything else would further excite the man's anger. Satisfied that Black wasn't going to punch him again, Richard stepped towards the fridge.

'Where are you going?' Black demanded.

'I'm going to get myself a drink,' Richard told him. 'Forgive me if I don't offer you a top up but I'm no longer feeling particularly hospitable.'

He poured a large scotch.

Away from the threatening glare of Black he tried to remember if anyone in the office might possibly know about his relationship with Cindy. Everyone knew that they carpooled, but that wasn't the same as everyone knowing that they were in a relationship. Occasionally they would have lunch with others from the office, Tony and Becky or Geoff and Nicola. But they always made their friendship appear formal and platonic.

They rarely did anything sexual in the office, he reminded himself.

The only time they had done–

The thought left him cold.

The memory came to him in a flash that turned his stomach.

He had visited Cindy in her office at the CNS department. It had been around eleven in the morning. She had made him hard by whispering that she was wearing stockings but no panties.

He had asked if he could see.

When she'd said no, the tone of her voice suggesting he could argue some more and she might relent, Richard had pressed her into a corner with commanding kisses on her lips. She had placed her fingers around the concealed flesh of his arousal. He had slipped a hand on her stocking clad thigh and moved his fingers up beyond the hem of her skirt. He had just been touching the moist lips of her sex when someone burst into her office.

They had broken apart immediately. Cindy had brushed down her skirt and Richard pulled the hem of his jacket over the thrust of his arousal.

He was convinced that the woman had seen nothing. But there was always the danger she might say something to Black if she was questioned.

Her face was easy to remember. She wasn't someone he knew particularly well in the office but she was something of a regular feature in the smoking shelters. He thought she was one of those that usually ended up doing the overtime hours. She was dark haired and busty and a little on the overweight side. He struggled to remember a name and then smiled when it came to him. Cindy had called the woman Chloe.

'Richard,' Black snapped his fingers in front of Richard's face.

Richard flinched, fearing he was about to be punched again.

'I'm sorry I punched you,' Black told him. 'And I'm sorry for threatening you. I'm upset and I spoke without thinking.'

Richard said nothing. He couldn't work out if Black was genuinely apologising or trying to give Richard a sense of false security. Whatever Black's motive for apologising, Richard knew he needed to be cautious.

'Sure,' Richard grunted.

Black considered him for an unnerving moment. 'I can see this has upset you,' he said eventually. 'Do you need a counsellor or a therapist or something?'

'I need something,' Richard said, quietly. He sipped at his drink and swallowed as much scotch as he dared to take.

Black nodded. 'I'll leave you to your grief.' He gave the final word a strange emphasis. 'There's no need to come back into the office until you've got things in order.'

When he said the words, Richard knew that Black would be investigating the possibility of Richard having a motive to see Melissa dead.

49

Richard knew he was being watched from the moment he woke up on the Saturday morning. He wasn't sure how he knew; he had seen nothing out of the ordinary and heard nothing that would suggest surveillance. But he felt confident that Roger Black had acted on his threat of the previous night and put him under constant watch.

'You're being paranoid,' he told himself.

But he knew his paranoia was likely grounded in reality. He had seen enough curious incidents at Raven and Skull to believe that nothing was outside the boundaries of possibility for Roger Black. He had never decided whether the senior management team at Raven and Skull were magical entities or possessed of alien technologies beyond his understanding. In fairness, he supposed the distinction was small and immaterial. If they were choosing to watch him it didn't matter whether they were using wireless web cams or crystal balls. They were still watching his every action and there would be repercussions if they found him wanting in any capacity.

There were a string of text messages from Cindy.

He didn't bother replying to any of them. Instead he began to delete the messages. He needed to act as though he and Cindy were merely work colleagues. He couldn't give Roger Black any evidence to confirm that there was more between them and he didn't want Black gaining access to his phone and reading any incriminating text messages.

After writing down Cindy's mobile number he began to get dressed in trainers, joggers and a sweatshirt. It was early in the day and he found his wallet, checked it for notes, and then put his mobile into his pocket.

Black was waiting outside the door for him.

Richard almost shrieked with surprise.

'Good morning, Richard,' Black said. 'Are you feeling rested?'

It took Richard a few moments to regain his composure.

'I was just going out for a run,' he said.

'I'll join you,' Black said, easily.

'I might run fast,' Richard told him.

'I'll try to keep up.'

'I wanted to be alone,' Richard tried.

'You'll be alone with me.'

Aside from telling the man that he wasn't wanted, Richard knew that he had no other option than to allow him to jog at his side. It wasn't an ideal arrangement, but Richard could see he had no real alternative. Even if he told Black that he didn't want to be accompanied, the man would still join him on the run.

They set off through the morning.

Black was an unsettling presence by Richard's side. He ran with the relentless deliberation of a charging bull. His pace was unwavering and his response to the exertion of the run seemed untroubled, as though he regularly exercised in this fashion. Richard had never thought of Black as the sort of man who was likely to exercise but he maintained a steady pace without any suggestion of protest or complaint.

Ignoring him, Richard tried to think of how best to execute his plan now that he was being personally monitored. Chloe was the only person who knew about his relationship with Cindy. If he could find a way to silence Chloe, to stop her from telling anyone what she had seen, then Black would be unable to prove that Richard had a motive for wanting to see Melissa dead.

Admittedly, it was Saturday, and Richard had no idea how he would be able to get hold of Chloe over the weekend. He couldn't organise a trip to the office with Black by his side. Even if he were able to manage such a thing, Black would be suspicious if he saw Richard trying to gain access to the personnel files.

Not caring where he was going, Richard carried on running.

Black stayed by his side.

Richard remembered that Chloe often hung around with Nicola. She and Nicola were part of the overtime crowd. From what Nicola had said, on those lunchtime dates he and Cindy had shared with her and Geoff, they also spent time together outside the office. Nicola had mentioned a restaurant. It was a restaurant owned by her boyfriend. She seemed to think it made her important that she was the girlfriend of a restaurateur.

The name *House of Usher* came into his mind and he allowed himself a smile.

'Is something making you happy, Richard?' asked Black.

Richard shook his head. 'It will be a long time before I'm happy again,' he managed the words between breaths. The laboured sound of each syllable made his voice crack, as though he was on the brink of breaking with emotion. 'I'm thinking I should go out for a meal this evening,' he added, eventually. 'Would you care to accompany me, Mr Black?'

50

Halfway through the meal Richard stood up.

'Where are you going?'

Richard stopped short of groaning but he couldn't disguise the flash of impatience that glinted in his eyes. After Black had accompanied him on his morning run, the man had continued to loiter outside the doors of Richard's home. From the bedroom where he sat brooding, wondering how to progress now that Melissa was out of the way, he could see Black's shiny Jaguar idling beyond the gates of the driveway.

Later that morning Black had followed Richard to the local undertaker where Richard went through the awkward motions of organising arrangements for Melissa's burial. All the time Richard had been conscious of Black waiting alone in his car outside the undertaker's premises. Each time he glanced at the world outside the undertaker's office, he had found Black's beetling gaze settling on his own.

Black's car had then followed Richard on the return journey giving him no opportunity to surreptitiously stop at a call box or find some other way of discreetly contacting Cindy to let her know that he was still thinking of her.

Black had made his presence known throughout the day with various telephone calls and unexpected experiences and a thousand and one other subtle gestures of determined harassment. Now that they were sharing a meal in The House of Usher, Richard was no longer disguising the fact that he was bored with the man's presence.

'I need to use the facilities,' Richard told Black. His voice was stiff and stripped of all pleasantries. He didn't care if any of the other diners heard him. 'Do you need to follow me in there as well?'

Black studied him solemnly. 'Hurry back.'

Richard turned and followed the sign for the toilets. The route took him past an indoor fountain that poured a constant bubbling torrent of water over a shoal of tangerine goldfish. Richard took his work mobile from his pocket and slipped it into the water. It sank slowly to the bottom. As soon as he turned the first corner towards the toilets, putting himself out of Black's sight, he ducked through a door marked PRIVATE: STAFF ONLY.

The doorway led to the kitchens. He was able to squeeze past a handful of chefs who were ignoring him as they hurried to complete orders for the busy restaurant. The room was rich with heated fragrances and the sharp calls and cries of chefs bantering with each other. Walking swiftly, confident he knew where he was going and what he would find, Richard headed towards a door at the back of the kitchens labelled MANAGER.

He entered without knocking.

The room was a haze of sweet marijuana smoke.

The couple that had been kissing broke apart as though they hadn't been doing anything. Richard figured it was the same pretending-to-be-innocent disengagement that he and Cindy had attempted when Chloe burst in on them at the Raven and Skull offices. He hoped to God that he and Cindy had managed to break apart without looking so obviously guilty. Somehow, he thought, that was unlikely. Richard recognised Geoff and saw, to his relief, that Geoff had been embracing a near-naked Nicola.

Richard almost swooned. This was what he'd been hoping for.

Nicola pulled a flimsy shirt over her bared breasts and tried not to look too uncomfortable with her near-nudity.

'Ric?' Geoff didn't bother hiding his surprise. 'What the hell are you doing here?'

'More importantly,' Nicola complained. 'Why aren't you knocking on doors before barging into rooms marked private?'

Richard glanced at Geoff. 'I need a word with Nicola,' he explained. He glanced back over his shoulder as though he feared Black had already decided to follow him and was about to walk in on this conversation. The idea left a shiver of cold terror crawling along his spine.

Nicola folded her arms across her breasts and stared at him sullenly.

'Your friend Chloe,' he began. 'Where is she?'

Nicola shrugged. 'She's probably in Birmingham.' She looked puzzled. 'Is that what you mean?'

'I need to speak with her.'

'Won't you see her in the office on Monday?' Geoff asked.

Richard shook his head, angry at the interruption. He waved Geoff silent. 'I need to speak with her tonight if possible. Tomorrow at the latest.'

Nicola laughed. 'That's not going to happen. Chloe is trying to do something special for her boyfriend this weekend. It's their anniversary.'

He pulled out his wallet. 'I'll pay her to come down here now.'

She shook her head. 'I just told you, the pair of them are at a concert tonight. That's why I said they're in Birmingham. I think they're at the NEC.'

'Then tomorrow night,' Richard insisted. 'I'll pay for her to see me tomorrow night.'

He could hear the desperation in his voice and wondered why neither Richard nor Nicola was questioning him about his peculiar behaviour. Were they used to seeing him in such desperate straits? Or did he appear so far beyond help that they were humouring him?

'I'm serious,' he insisted. 'This is important.'

'How much are you willing to pay?' Nicola asked.

He relaxed, his paranoia briefly assuaged. If Nicola was trying to negotiate a price then that didn't mean he'd come across as dangerously desperate. 'I'll give her a hundred.'

She seemed to consider this and then shook her head. 'Give me two hundred and I'll guarantee she's here.'

He nodded and reached for his wallet.

Nicola held out a hand and Richard quickly counted the twenty-pound notes into her open palm. A spur of the moment idea came to him and he placed an extra twenty on top of the money. 'Have her bring me a cheap mobile phone.'

51

Throughout the whole of Sunday he could think of nothing except the impending meeting with Chloe. Black's Jaguar was again parked at the bottom of the driveway. Richard could see it lurking there when he peeled back a corner of the curtains from the bedroom window. He didn't bother going for a Sunday morning run. Instead, he hid himself away from the stress of being watched by lounging in front of the TV set.

All the time he tried to imagine what he would say to Chloe.

Black appeared at the front door at noon to tell Richard that his mobile didn't appear to be switched on. Richard explained that his mobile had been misplaced and he was then annoyed when Black barged in offering to help search for it.

There was no logical way he could argue against searching for the phone, not without revealing that he had deliberately tossed it aside the previous night at the restaurant. Grudgingly accepting Black's invitation to help, Roger tried to keep out of the man's way as Black blundered from room to room searching for the missing phone.

Two hours later, after searching through the house, Black claimed to have found it. He handed the phone back to Richard, offering no explanation as to where it had been or why it might be dripping wet.

Richard thanked him stiffly.

'You'll want to be more careful with that,' Black suggested.

'I'm going out for a meal again this evening,' Richard said. 'Will you be accompanying me?'

'What a kind and thoughtful invitation,' Black exclaimed. His eyes sparkled with a glint of wicked pleasure. 'I think I would very much like to join you.'

'I wasn't making an invitation. I just figured you'd still be stalking me.'

Black chuckled as though they were sharing a joke. 'I'll be happy to accept your kind invitation,' he repeated. He paused and asked, 'Are we going to The House of Usher again?'

Richard hoped his shrug looked innocent and casual. 'I guess so.'

Black nodded and then leant forward conspiratorially. 'You want to be careful with your phone whilst we're there,' he confided. 'I heard, last night, some bloke dropped his phone into the bottom of their indoor fish pond.'

Richard was still blushing when he finally managed to close the door on Black. Black, it seemed, knew that he'd been trying to get rid of his mobile. Black had probably guessed that Richard was worried that the text messages on the phone could be perceived as incriminating. With mounting certainty, Richard knew he could not let Black have a chance to talk with Chloe first.

That evening, half an hour before his table reservation at the restaurant, Richard walked to Black's Jaguar and climbed inside. The interior had the smell of a car fresh from the showroom. The seats were redolent of new leather. The dashboard gleamed in the twilight with the polished glossy lustre of professional valet services.

Black considered Richard warily.

'We're going in the same direction, aren't we?' Richard reminded him. 'I figured you could give me a lift.'

Black said nothing. It was obvious that he didn't want to give Richard a lift and the air of animosity between them was set for the remainder of the evening. They sat on opposite sides of an intimate table each working through their meal as though they were dining alone.

Black was devouring a large rack of ribs whilst Richard, unhappy with the taste of the previous evening's steak, had ordered the haddock. The meal was a slight improvement on the previous night's fare, but it still wasn't spectacular. Lost in the introspection of his thoughts he glanced out through the window onto the courtyard.

The fountain looked pretty in the fading evening's twilight. There was no one standing there yet but he wasn't expecting Chloe to arrive early. He picked unhappily at the batter on his haddock and then ordered a bottle of white to accompany the dish.

Black glanced up from his ribs. 'You look like you're coping with your grief.'

'I've been fortunate that I've been allowed the privacy to grieve,' Richard said, coolly. 'I think that's helped.'

It was a comment that managed to kill the conversation.

He sipped at his wine when it arrived and continued to pick disinterestedly at his food. Two tables across he could see Geoff sitting alone in front of an unappetising steak. The previous evening it had surprised Richard to discover that Geoff and Nicola were in a relationship. He had thought they were platonic friends in the same way he had always tried to convince everyone that he and Cindy were platonic friends.

Did that mean that Tony and Becky were also fucking? Was everyone in the offices of Raven and Skull involved with someone else from the offices? If that was the case, why was he even pretending that he hadn't been involved with someone else? Surely Black must have known that all his staff had the lascivious needs of rutting animals? He wondered if he could shape those thoughts into a question for his dinner companion.

Movement near the fountain caught his attention. It was Chloe. She was alone. He tried not to react too hastily, counted to twelve, and then stood up. It was time to talk with her.

'Have you finished?' Black asked.

'I'm going to the toilet.'

'I think I'll come with you,' Black grinned.

Richard tried to keep his features indifferent. 'I had no idea your surveillance was going to be this close.'

He waited for Black to climb from his chair and then followed the squat man to the gents. After they had both visited the urinals Richard washed his hands and waited for Black.

It was as they were making their way back to the restaurant that Richard clutched his stomach and pulled a face. 'Excuse me,' he grimaced. 'I think I need to go back there.'

Black considered him doubtfully.

'Dodgy fish,' Richard explained.

Black continued to hold his gaze for an instant and then nodded.

Richard walked back to the toilets. He glanced back over his shoulder to confirm that Black was no longer watching him. Then he hurried further down the corridor to the doorway that led to the courtyard.

Outside, the evening was clear and cool and liberating after the oppressive mood of spending time in the company of Roger Black. Chloe stood beside the fountain holding a small box.

She looked bored.

She was not particularly attractive, he thought. With her features hidden by too much make-up, and wearing clothes that were intended for someone slimmer, she looked like a fat ugly girl trying too hard to impress.

'Chloe,' he began. His voice dripped with forced good cheer. 'Thank you for coming here on such short notice. It's much appreciated.'

'This better be good,' Chloe said.

She passed him the box and he could see it contained the cheap mobile phone he'd requested. It was nothing special but he reasoned it would do to get a single message through to Cindy. He mumbled heartfelt thanks.

She brushed his gratitude aside. 'This better be good. I had a weekend planned with my bloke. We were going to spend our Sunday night in Birmingham but your message to Nicola fucked that.'

He flashed a grin that he hoped she would interpret as an apology.

'Has Roger Black been in touch with you yet?'

'Black from the office? No. Why would he be in touch with me?'

'Black's trying to find out if I've been screwing anyone in the office,' Richard explained. 'If he asked you I was worried you might have misinterpreted that time you saw me in the office with Cindy.'

'Misinterpreted?' Chloe scoffed. 'She was tugging you off and you had a finger in her. What was there to misinterpret?'

His jaw worked soundlessly for a moment. He could imagine Chloe saying those exact words to Roger Black. An icy finger traced down his spine. He forced himself to take a deep breath, stop trembling and regain his composure. His smile was fixed into a rictus.

'I can see how it might have looked like that,' he admitted. 'But there was nothing sexual in that contact.'

Cindy raised a sceptical eyebrow. Her over-painted lips smirked.

'So,' Richard went on. His cheeks were turning crimson. He could feel the weight of her stare boring into him. 'So, if Roger Black was ever to ask you about my friendships in the office, you'd say that I wasn't romantically involved with anyone, wouldn't you?'

'How much is that answer worth?'

He stared at her in amazement. 'You want money?'

'You're asking me to lie to Roger Black. Of course I want money. He's a scary fucker.'

Before Richard could express his outrage further he was grabbed by the shoulder and thrown to the ground. He closed his eyes and prepared for the beating that he knew Black would inflict. When he opened his eyes, instead of seeing his employer, he saw a burly biker in a leather jacket. The man towered over him.

'Kevin!' shrieked Chloe. The boredom she'd been displaying was now gone. 'This isn't what it looks like,' she said hotly. 'Don't hit him.'

'Who the fuck is he?' Kevin demanded.

'This is just some guy from the office.'

'What the hell are you doing with some guy from the office?' As he asked the question, Kevin slammed one meaty fist into the palm of his hand. The impact made a wet smacking sound.

Richard flinched as though he had been struck.

Kevin's brow was furrowed. His eyes sparkled with a mean and wicked intent as he turned to glare at Chloe. When he flexed his fingers, the knuckles made a sound like the cracking of thick bonfire twigs.

He's going to kill her, Richard thought.

The thought was not distressing. Considering the way Chloe had demanded a bribe and looked ready to sell him out to Black, Richard thought he might be safer if she was dead or seriously injured. The idea came to him immediately.

'There's no need for violence,' he told Kevin.

The biker glared at him.

Richard pulled himself from the floor and spread his hands in a gesture of appeasement. 'I'm done with the bitch,' he admitted. He glanced at Chloe, fixed her with an innocent smile and said, 'I've had my money's worth this evening. If you want to go in there for sloppy seconds I'd say you should go for it before her real boyfriend gets back.'

Kevin drew back his fist and aimed at punch at Richard.

Richard wondered if he would be able to get out of the range of the blow before it inflicted too much damage. It looked like it would cause a formidable amount of pain when it connected. He suspected he was going to have a broken nose, a missing tooth or two, and maybe a fractured jaw. He refused to let his eyes close. He wanted to see the blow when it landed.

Chloe leapt on Kevin's back. She tried to pull his arm downwards.

'Don't listen to him, you stupid bastard,' Chloe insisted.

Richard glanced at the restaurant windows surrounding the courtyard. Their entanglement was already capturing a lot of interest. He saw that Geoff was no longer sitting alone. The smooth bastard had been joined by a very attractive blonde. Roger Black was still methodically attacking his rack of lamb ribs and seemed oblivious to the fact that Richard was in the courtyard with Chloe and her psychotic boyfriend.

'I'll kill the fucking pair of you,' Kevin bellowed.

'He's only saying this shit to wind you up,' Chloe told him. 'You know you're the only person in my life. I thought you'd always known that.'

Kevin hurled her to the floor. She landed heavily with a crunch of bones that sounded uncomfortable. He glowered down at her.

Richard took the opportunity to scoot out of the courtyard and back into the restaurant. He didn't care what happened between Kevin and Chloe now. He had hoped he would be able to politely ask her to lie to Black. But, since she'd tried to blackmail him, he now figured she wouldn't be able to say anything against him without her animosity coming through.

He paused before returning to Black and sent a short text to Cindy.

DONT CALL BK. IM USIN A DSPOSBLE MOB TO SND THIS MSG. DONT FONE OR CALL. ILL B N TOUCH AS SOON AS THE HEATS DIED DOWN. RICH XX

Chloe moaned. He was close enough to the courtyard's doorway to hear her miserable wail. The sound was cut off by what sounded like the impact from a powerful fist.

Richard swallowed. Smiling tightly to himself, he absently dropped the disposable mobile into the fountain where he'd dropped his own phone the previous night. Sitting back down at the table, contemplating the cold and unappetising remnants of his fish, he swigged from the glass of house white and topped his drink up with the last of the bottle.

'Is your stomach any better?' asked Black.

'Better?' Richard had to think about the question for a moment before he remembered he had pretended to need the lavatory. 'Oh! Yeah. Much better.'

He replenished his drink and then downed another swig. It was a light and fruity white with undertones of apples and pears. He could also detect some sort of chemical flavour that he didn't think had been there before.

The room seemed to be swaying. 'This is strong stuff.'

He glanced out of the restaurant window and saw that Kevin was standing over Chloe's motionless body. On the nearby table, Geoff and his blonde dining partner were staring at the scene with frightened wonder.

The woman kissed Geoff and then rushed out of the restaurant.

She reminded Richard of Black's former secretary, Fiona.

He glanced at Black, ready to ask him what had happened to Fiona. Black was glaring at him. He seemed more interested in watching Richard swig wine. It struck Richard as unlikely that he would want to share the excitement of the apparent homicide that had occurred in the courtyard or reminisce about his former secretary. The conversational gambit Richard had been about to make disappeared as he took another swig of wine, licked his lips, and said, 'This really is strong stuff.'

'Strong stuff indeed,' Black agreed. 'Although, I suspect the tranquiliser I put in your wine has added to its potency.'

It was the last thing Richard heard him say before passing out.

52

Richard rubbed fingers against the itch of a beard. How long had it been since he shaved? He remembered using his electric razor on the Sunday evening, prior to going out for a meal with Black. That was the evening, he remembered, when he'd sent Cindy a text message and argued with Chloe. He remembered seeing Chloe's prostrate body with Kevin the biker towering over her. He remembered hearing that final wet punch that had probably ended her life. With a guilty flush he recalled that he had been the cause of their argument. He was the one who exacerbated the situation by intimating that he'd paid Chloe for sex.

That memory of his involvement was enough to make him sit up in bed.

The sudden movement sparked a furious pounding in his temples.

Hangover? Sickness? He couldn't decide. Whatever it was, it was strong enough to make his stomach churn. His bladder was a huge swollen ball that needed emptying. His muscles ached as though he had flu.

He groaned.

'You're awake?' Roger Black observed.

Black sat in an armchair at the foot of the bed. His profile was lit by the lamp from Melissa's bedside cabinet. Black looked composed with a tablet on the arm of his chair and a stylus that he was tapping against the screen. His grin was the predatory leer of a starving vulture.

Richard did not like waking up to find Black in his bedroom. Involuntarily, he clenched his buttocks, hoping that the man hadn't chosen to violate him whilst he was unconscious. Everything felt normal down there and he sighed with gratitude. But he still didn't like waking to find the man so close to him. Warily, he shifted up in the bed.

'Were you watching me sleep?'

'I'm the one who added something to your wine,' Black reminded him. 'I thought it only responsible to come here and check on you each evening.'

Richard digested this statement.

'Each evening?' he asked, doubtfully. 'What do you mean each evening?' He rubbed the growth of beard stubble on his jaw and realised it was no longer Sunday night. A prickle of disquiet spiked his stomach.

'What day is it?'

'Tuesday.'

Richard stared at him in disbelief. 'I slept through all of Monday?'

'You've slept through most of Tuesday too.' Black checked his wristwatch and said, 'It's almost ten o'clock at night.'

There was a creak outside the bedroom door. It was the sound of someone making their way through the house. Richard could hear the sound of someone calling his name. Whatever chemicals Black had placed in his drink were still messing up his system.

He couldn't hear very clearly.

The voice sounded small and faraway.

'Who's that?' he demanded.

Black shrugged. 'Maybe it's a ghost from your past come to haunt you?'

Richard glared at him. 'Is that one of your lackeys?'

'I came here alone this evening. If there's someone out there, it's not someone I invited.'

'Richard?'

It was a woman's voice. He was struck by the idea that it could be Melissa's ghost. Gooseflesh pricked his arms. He had never believed in ghosts. He had always thought the idea of spirits and spooks was so much rubbish for the entertainment of idiots and the easily impressed. But, even if there were such things as ghosts, he fervently hoped there was no such thing as Melissa's ghost.

'Richard?'

'Is this another of your women?' Black asked.

He looked as though he was enjoying Richard's discomfort.

Richard frowned at the question. 'Another of my women?'

'Is this another of the hundreds of women you were screwing behind my niece's back?'

'I wasn't screwing hundreds of women behind Melissa's back.'

'Just the one?'

Richard shook his head. He couldn't meet Black's gaze as he said, 'I wasn't screwing anyone.'

'Richard?' The woman's voice sounded closer. She was climbing up the stairs. He thought that was the sort of thing that Melissa's ghost would be likely to do. She had died going down the stairs. She would be likely to haunt him by climbing up the stairs and calling out his name.

His bladder ached as though it was about to burst.

'See who it is,' Richard told Black.

Black shook his head. He sneered with disdain. 'This is your house. You can go and see who it is.'

Unwilling to show that he was scared, Richard climbed out of the bed. His legs trembled from the lack of exercise he'd suffered over the past forty-eight hours. He trembled as he tried to stand, and warned himself, when he did summon the courage to go out of the bedroom, he should avoid going too close to the top of the stairs until he was properly stable.

'Richard?'

'She sounds like she's getting closer,' Roger Black noted. 'I hope she's not dangerous.'

Richard glared at him. He lurched awkwardly past his unwanted guest and hesitated in the doorway.

'Richard?'

It was Cindy. She had almost reached the top of the stairs. Sighing with relief he suddenly fretted that she might mention something about what had occurred when Melissa suffered her fall. The idea that Black might overhear such a conversation was unthinkable. He rushed towards her, hoping he could get her to stay silent.

Cindy seemed to stiffen as he approached.

Richard didn't know if she was unnerved by his stilted gait or frightened by something else she saw at the top of the stairs. Whatever the reason, she backed away from him with her eyes lighting in terror. He could see that she was going to stumble even before she lost her footing.

One hand went out, trying to catch the banister.

Her foot went down too hard and too fast.

And then she was falling backwards and screaming as she went.

'Cindy,' he called.

His voice could barely be heard beneath the spiralling shriek of her scream. And then her voice cut off to flat, mortal silence.

'Cindy?'

Black clapped a hand on the centre of Richard's back. The blow was almost enough to push him down the stairs. He clutched at the handrail and glared at his unwanted houseguest.

'Dear, dear,' Black grumbled. 'This is a terrible state of affairs, isn't it? It looks like you've killed her.'

'She fell by accident,' Richard protested.

Black nodded agreement. 'Yes. Unlike Melissa's second and third falls down the stairs, this was an accident. Unlike Chloe's unfortunate demise at The House of Usher on Sunday night–'

Richard glared at him, sharply.

'–this clearly was an accident,' Black concluded. He shook his head wearily. 'I expect you'll still go to prison for it. If this country had a death penalty, you'd fry for this accident. Considering the evidence I'll be giving against you, I'd say every juror in this country will want to hang you.'

His smile was smug and accomplished.

Richard squared his shoulders and met Black's gaze. 'This country doesn't have a death penalty,' Richard reminded him. 'So that's not even an issue, is it?'

Black laughed. He was standing too close to Richard. His face filled Richard's world. 'No,' he agreed. 'This country doesn't have a death penalty. The worst that will happen to you is that you'll end up in a nice comfortable cell, suffering a long, long sentence.'

Richard could hear a falseness in Roger Black's voice.

'You're going to try and kill me, aren't you?'

Black shook his head. 'Of course not. There's no need. I'm just going to use all my connections to make sure you spend your short time in prison sharing a cell with Chloe's former boyfriend, Kevin. He was an angry young man to begin with. Now that he's been imprisoned for her murder, he's quite the livid young man. And, when he finds he's sharing a cell with the man who's responsible for him being in jail, I think he might just push himself to new extremes as he tries to show just how angry a young man he can be.'

Richard shook his head. 'You wouldn't. You couldn't.'

Black's expression was an inscrutable mask. 'The wheels are already in motion.'

From faraway, Richard could hear the rise and fall of sirens. And, whilst he suspected one of those sirens might be an ambulance making a too-late dash to assist Cindy, he felt certain that the other siren belonged to the police car that would drive him off to his miserable destiny.

Cindy squeezed his hand. Richard gave a shame-faced smile. They shared a brief but chaste kiss to punctuate his story.

'That's the dumbest one yet,' Heather exclaimed. 'And there've been some pretty dumb stories so far this weekend.'

'You can't tell him his story is dumb,' Tony protested. He was shaking his head and pointing at her with an angry finger. 'We're sharing stories, not passing judgement.'

Geoff nodded agreement as he sipped from his pint.

Heather rolled her eyes. She put down her wine glass.

'That was a story where his girlfriend, who is currently sitting next to him, died. It's a story where he ends up in prison getting beaten and bum raped and probably dying.'

'I don't remember bum rape being mentioned,' Geoff complained. 'Did I drift off to sleep?'

'I would have remembered bum rape,' Becky agreed. She spluttered drunken laughter across the table and everyone joined in with her mirth.

Heather shook her head in disappointment. 'The bum rape was just implied,' she said. Her voice trailed off when she realised no one was listening to her. They were all still laughing at Becky's exclamation that she 'would have remembered bum rape'.

Despite herself, Heather found herself grinning at the words.

'Go on, Heather,' Tony insisted. 'If you've got a story that beats Richard's, you know we want to hear it.'

Heather studied him for a long moment before she began.

'I need this typing up, fast,' Roger Black said. 'Is there someone here who can do it?'

Heather beamed at him. 'I can do it for you.' She reached out and snatched the sheet of paper from his fingers.

He considered her, warily. 'Where's Fiona?'

'Bathroom break. She'll be back in a moment. But if this is urgent I can get this typed up for you in ten minutes. I'll have it printed out and in your office for your signature if it's that important.'

Black sighed. His usual gruff manner seemed to flounder in the face of her enthusiasm. 'Whatever,' he told her. 'Just see that it gets done.'

And then he was gone.

Heather's smile stretched wide. This was proving to be one of those days when everything went right. Her horoscope for that morning had promised this would be a day when luck was on her side, she would meet a handsome stranger, and her career would shift up to the next level. She had managed to find a parking space that was fairly close to the Raven and Skull building. She had even found a twenty-pound note on the floor of the lift. Now she was being given a chance to impress Roger Black and prove she was capable of Fiona's job. Heather was still smiling at the development and didn't notice Fiona Davies standing in the doorway, glowering.

'What's that?'

Heather jumped, startled by the question. 'It's a letter that Mr Black asked me to type.' She glanced at the handwriting on the page and then frowned. She had expected to see letters. She had expected to see something in a squat printed hand that would have suited Mr Black's squat appearance. Instead she found herself staring at a page of alien markings. There were loops, slashes and cruciforms. The symbols looked ancient, archaic and pagan. Her vision began to blur as she stared at the unfamiliar characters.

'Do you really think you can do my job?'

Fiona snatched the sheet of handwritten paper from Heather's fingers.

As soon as the page was gone Heather was struck by a sickening headache. The pain appeared above her right eye, as though she had been stung. She placed a hand there, gasping in surprise, and expecting Fiona to show some measure of sympathy or concern.

'You're a snivelling little wretch,' Fiona declared.

Heather shrank from the woman's abrasive voice.

'You have no discipline,' Fiona went on. 'No sense of what goes on in this building and you're of no fucking use to anyone.'

It wasn't just her scornful tone of voice that made the insults humiliating. For Heather, the most damning part of Fiona's diatribe was the fact that woman didn't bother to look up from the page she was working on. She had rolled a blank sheet of vellum into the typewriter, placed Black's handwritten page on the copyholder beside her desk, and started typing. She had managed to do all of that whilst reminding Heather that she was useless and making her believe that everyone at Raven and Skull held the same disparaging opinion.

'Go and fetch me a coffee,' Fiona sniffed. 'Then, once you've done that, you can get back to that filing I gave you earlier, you can complete your other menial chores, and you can stop trying to do my job.'

Heather knew there were a lot of people in the office who were scared of Roger Black. He had a gruff manner and a physically imposing presence. She had also heard people talk about Charlie Raven in the same whispered tones of terror. He had a reputation for being bossy and cruel. She knew that there were elderly members of staff, those who were getting ready to retire, who said that John Skull had possessed the most dangerous and volatile reputation in the company. But, to Heather's mind, there was no one more formidable than Fiona Davies.

She took Fiona's mug, went out of the office and hurried to the canteen. Her cheeks burnt with embarrassed blushes. Her eyes stung with the threat of tears. It took an effort not to sob as she considered the scathing words that had been fired at her.

No sense of what goes on.
No discipline.
No fucking use to anyone.

As she brooded on the insults, she had to stifle the moan of despair that wanted to tear at her throat. She'd only been trying to be helpful. Was this how her efforts should be repaid?

'Is Fiona being a bitch again?'

The question came from a handsome stranger. She knew she hadn't seen him in the building before but there was something about his features that was uncannily familiar. If she had been pressed to say what it was, Heather would have settled on the fact that he looked like the older man in the portrait that dominated the lobby. The handsome stranger looked like he was closely related to John Skull.

She wiped away a tear from the corner of her eye and smiled weakly.

'Is it Fiona?' he repeated. 'Is she acting like a bitch again?'

'That would be impolite of me to say,' Heather said. She managed the words in a stiff tone that didn't give away her upset. She refused to meet his gaze for fear that he would see the tears brimming on her lower lids.

'You're right,' the handsome stranger agreed. 'It would be very impolite.' He nodded at the coffee she'd ordered. It sat in Fiona's mug emblazoned with the words 'World's No. 1 Mum'. He raised a speculative eyebrow and asked, 'Is that for her?'

As soon as Heather said it was, he dropped two tablets into the drink.

She stared at him in amazement. 'What was that?'

'That's something that will help Fiona to calm down.' His tone was wonderfully reassuring. His smile glinted as though he knew everything was going to work out to everyone's best advantage. His teeth, a solid even line, reminded her of the teeth on the skull in Black's office. He patted Heather's fingers with his cold hand and said, 'You'll thank me for it later.'

Heather shook her head. She put the coffee cup back on the counter.

'I can't give Fiona a drink that you've just drugged.'

He laughed and shook his head. Lifting up the mug and placing it in her hands he said, 'Of course you can give it to her. Not only are you going to give it to her but I believe you're also going to thank me for this favour later.'

55

Heather placed the coffee cup in front of Fiona and then had second thoughts. It was the words 'World's No. 1 Mum' that pricked her conscience. If Fiona was a mother then that suggested she had commitments and family and a life outside her role as the office tyrant. Heather had no idea what was in the tablets. There was a chance it could be something incapacitating or potentially fatal.

She held her breath with that thought.

If Fiona drank something that made her ill, that would give Heather lots of opportunities to prove her worth to Roger Black whilst the office tyrant recovered at home. If Fiona drank something fatal that would mean Raven and Skull would need to find a replacement for her. She brushed those ideas from her mind, unhappy that her thoughts were so uncharitable. Determinedly, she tried to think how she could stop Fiona from drinking the coffee.

'I've just seen a strange man in the canteen,' Heather began.

'How exciting for you,' Fiona said, drily. 'You really do live a thrilling life, don't you?' She picked up her mug, raised it to her lips, and then seemed to decide it was too hot for her palate.

Carefully, she placed the drink back down beside her typewriter.

'I haven't seen him here before,' Heather explained. 'That's why I called him strange. But he looks very much like the picture of the man in the lobby.'

'Which man in the lobby?'

'The Raven and Skull portrait,' Heather said. 'He looked like he could have been related to John Skull.'

Fiona was scowling as she focused on her work. 'Why do you say that?'

Heather shrugged. 'The shape of his head, mostly. And maybe there was something in his eyes that was in the painting. You know how he's got that mischievous smile?'

Fiona nodded. She lifted her drink and placed it close to her lips. 'I remember John Skull's mischievous smile.' She blew on the drink to cool it.

'Could it have been John Skull's son?' Heather asked.

Fiona considered this and then shook her head. 'I don't think he had any sons.' She looked set to sip from her coffee and then paused. 'John Skull didn't like me.'

Heather arched an eyebrow. If she had felt braver she would have said something sarcastic. If she had felt more confident in her position at Raven and Skull, Heather would have said, 'What a surprise! I can't imagine anyone not liking you. You're such a charmer to everyone.' She bit her lip to suppress the volley of nervous giggles that threatened to erupt from her throat as she imagined herself saying something so bold.

'I was responsible for Skull transferring to a different office,' Fiona explained. She laughed. The sound was caustic and unpleasant. 'He's the father of my little girl and I didn't want her growing up around his influence. That's why I organised for his transfer.'

Heather blinked at this.

'But surely, if he just transferred to a different office, he'd still be able to come back here occasionally and visit you and your daughter or—'

'No.' Fiona's voice had a flat calmness to the tone. 'Where I had him sent, there was never any danger of him coming back.' Her smile was bitter but tinged with cruel satisfaction. She looked thoughtful as she said, 'If he ever got the chance, I suspect Skull would try to get even with me for the way I got him out of these offices.'

Heather nodded agreement. She tried to think of something else she could say in response to what Fiona had shared but only one phrase came to mind.

'You should drink that cup of coffee,' she told Fiona. 'You should drink it before it goes cold.'

Fiona thanked her and took a brisk swig from the cup.

Immediately her eyes opened wide. She glared at Heather with panicked horror and understanding. The mug was dropped. It struck the corner of the desk and shattered into a dozen wicked-looking shards. Fiona was no longer 'World's No. 1 Mum'. She slapped at the desk and clutched at her throat. Her eyes bulged. As she began to vomit, spewing bilious volumes of bloody liquid across her desk, Heather turned her back.

'You fucking bitch,' Fiona gasped.

Heather ignored her. She picked up the phone on her desk and rang down to janitorial. 'Is that Harry Shaw?' she asked. 'I think we need a clean-up on the fourteenth floor.'

56

'Where the hell is Fiona?' Black demanded.

'She's been taken poorly,' Heather explained. 'But I'm her assistant. I'm sure I can do whatever it is you need me to do.'

'You'll have to do,' Black grunted. 'Follow me.'

He led her into his main office and she was introduced to Charlie Raven and a shadowy man who sat in an unlit corner of the room. At first Heather hoped the stranger would prove to be the nice man who had looked like John Skull but, the more her eyes got used to the dim light of the room, the more she realised this wasn't the man she had seen in the canteen. This was some shadowy man who was clearly held in high regard by both Black and Raven.

'We're looking at making a few modifications to our current staffing,' Raven explained. He smoked whilst he talked, flicking his cigarette ash into a gorilla's paw ashtray. He was talking to the shadowy man. 'We're looking to streamline our workforce here in the city either by downsizing or relocating.'

Black nodded agreement.

'We've got a few names that head the list of excess staff,' Raven said.

'Such as?' The shadowy man's voice was deep and sonorous. It was a voice that Heather didn't like hearing.

'Chloe in personnel is becoming a waste of space,' Black said. 'As are Nicola and Shaun from marketing. You can write down those three names.'

Heather wrote the names on her pad. She was surprised to see the letters of each name flare in a blaze of bloody orange. It was almost as though the words had seared the page and left behind a smouldering fragrance of incense. The phenomenon did not strike her as being out of the ordinary for Raven and Skull.

'I think we can let Tony go from sales,' Raven decided.

Black nodded.

'And I'm not sure Rebecca Wilson is pulling her weight, even though that's quite a substantial weight she has to pull.'

The shadowy man and Black laughed at Raven's comment. Heather thought they were being mean. She liked Becky even though the woman was a few pounds overweight. Prudently, she kept those thoughts to herself.

'Cindy from CNS can go. We can lose Geoff Arnold from accounts. I think Richard from legal should also go.'

Heather wrote down the names. Each one burnt its way onto the page. She noticed, each time Raven suggested a name, the shadowy man nodded solemnly as though agreeing with the decision.

Black raised a hand. 'Richard is married to my niece. I'd rather we reassigned him instead of getting rid of him completely.'

Raven smiled. 'They're all being reassigned, Roger.' Frowning sympathetically he said, 'Doesn't it trouble you that Richard is balling the brains out of CNS Cindy at every opportunity?'

Black scowled. 'Is that true?'

Raven nodded.

Heather was no expert at reading expressions but she thought it looked like this was the first Black was hearing about Richard's infidelity. He didn't look happy. 'Put Richard on that list,' Roger snapped.

'Is that it?' Charlie asked.

Black shook his head. 'Times are hard. Economic recession. I think it might be prudent to get rid of one more.'

'Such as?' asked the shadowy man.

'Earlier this morning I was beginning to wonder why Fiona needed an assistant,' Black said.

His mood seemed to have darkened since he discovered that Richard was cheating. He now spoke with an authority that Heather suspected could be vindictive or cruel.

'I was wondering why Fiona needed an assistant but now, seeing the way this helpful young lady has stepped into the breach, I'm beginning to wonder why Fiona's assistant needs a Fiona.'

'Eloquently phrased,' Raven smiled. He glanced at Heather and asked, 'Did you get that, sweetheart?'

'I think so,' Heather said. 'You were going to put my name on this list, but now you want Fiona's name on here.'

Raven nodded. He glanced at Black and said, 'It looks like you've got a new assistant.' Turning to Heather he added,

'Congratulations on your promotion, sweetheart. Now, get that list typed up and have a copy forwarded to Moira in accounts.'

'Moira in accounts,' Heather repeated as she added Fiona's name to the list. 'Will she know what to do?'

Raven, Black and the shadowy man laughed. She wasn't sure which of them said it but the words stayed with her for long after the meeting had finished.

'Moira has always known what to do.'

57

'What a depressing story,' Tony mumbled. He yawned.

'And likely as true as anything else I've heard round this table tonight,' Becky grumbled. She checked her wristwatch and groaned. 'It's morning. How the hell did that happen?'

'It's Monday morning,' Geoff pointed out.

'No.'

Cindy pulled herself away from Richard's lap. 'Didn't I tell you that this is what hell is? We spend all week working in that shitty office, then we squander the weekend doing nothing but talking about the damned place. If that's not a definition of hell, I don't know what is.'

She started towards the door, unable to stop herself from ambling in a drunken, tired lurch.

'This can't be hell,' Heather protested. 'Otherwise we'd be doing it for all eternity, wouldn't we?'

'Isn't that what we have been doing?' Richard asked. 'Haven't we been doing this same routine for as long as you can remember?'

As she brooded on the question, Heather began to suspect that Richard might be correct. She began to suspect that they'd been trapped in the same routine for as long as she could remember.